DWARF 'EM ALL

DWARF 'EM ALL

DWARF BOUNTY HUNTER™ BOOK ELEVEN

MARTHA CARR

MICHAEL ANDERLE

THE DWARF 'EM ALL TEAM

Thanks to our JIT Team:

Dorothy Lloyd
Diane L. Smith
Peter Manis
Dave Hicks
Jackey Hankard-Brodie
James P. Dyer
Thomas Ogden
Jeff Goode
Zacc Pelter

If We've missed anyone, please let us know!

Editor
SkyHunter Editing Team

"Quit being so paranoid, 'coz." Charlie Walker clapped a hand on Johnny's shoulder and gave him a little shake. "It's been…what? Almost eighteen hours? If the unkillable blood magic witch hasn't found us by now, we're all good."

The bounty hunter squinted through the crack he'd opened cautiously between the door and its frame. They were staying in yet another crappy motel room along the endless stretch of California highway between Yuba City and Sacramento.

With a scowl, he shut it again firmly, locked it, and turned to his cousin. "No. We ain't."

"Oh, come on. The screaming hero over there hit her with your rental." The dwarf shifter sniggered and pointed at Jake where he was seated on the lumpy mattress in the adjoining room. He shook his head when the man buried his face in his hands. "Fair enough, she's tough, but I'm very sure breaking a brick wall with her back takes a little more recovery time."

"Not to mention the fact that Johnny destroyed her car," Lisa added casually. "She might be insanely, weirdly powerful, but I'm sure she can't fly."

When her partner turned to look at her, she raised her eyebrows and shrugged.

Sure. I imagine that's the first time and last time I'll get the nod of approval for blowin' somethin' up.

Johnny sniffed. "Still. I ain't fixin' to step outta here until I'm damn sure the coast is clear. Then we're hightailin' it to the airport. Shit just got way too complicated out here."

"What?" Galfrey poked his head through the doorway of the adjoining rooms and stared at the dwarf. "We aren't even a little closer to finding Hux and you're simply giving up?"

"Yeah, and do you have a better plan? Do you think either of y'all is in good shape to go huntin' all over the state for your shifter-napped buddy when there's a dark witch on your tails? Literally and figuratively." Johnny pointed through the doorway at Jake, who'd flopped back on the narrow mattress and now lay there unmoving and stared blankly at the ceiling. "Does he look like he has another hit and run in him?"

"So that's it?" Galfrey stepped through the doorway and looked at Lisa for backup. "We had one close call. That's it. And now we're running away like everyone else? Jesus. If you guys can't handle this, we're all screwed—"

"Now hold on a minute." The bounty hunter scowled warningly at his cousin, pointed at Galfrey, and cocked his head. "No one said a damn thing about throwin' in the towel. That ain't what we do."

"But we're getting on a plane to leave California."

"Uh-huh. Which y'all should have done long before your buddy got snatched and shoved into a shifter-huntin' van. We know a hundred percent that Agnes is after you and Jake now. I have no idea how she found y'all, but there ain't no point in keepin' y'all locked up in the same state as a blood witch packing serious magical heat, understand? We'll find a better place to hide y'all once we land on the other side of the country. Then Lisa and I will deal with the rest of it." He met her gaze and she was surprisingly generous with another nod of approval. "We'll find your friend. But I ain't riskin' two more shifter lives outta geographical convenience."

"What about me?" Charlie muttered.

"Well, you sure as hell ain't makin' yourself at home again in my house. And when I said Lisa and I will deal with it, that's exactly what I meant."

"Not that." The shifter dwarf waved him off and shook his head. "We all know you guys need me anyway. I'm talking about the witch."

"Uh-huh. So am I. What's your point?"

"Johnny, she said she was at the motel for me." Charlie scratched the side of his head beside the slightly bent spikes of his thick black mohawk. "That she wanted the dwarf with the orange Harley."

"Huh." Johnny folded his arms and studied him for a long moment. "The way I remember it, she called you the idiot with the orange Harley."

His cousin spread his arms in a "whatever" kind of gesture. "Are you gonna hide me too?"

"Come on. You just said you ain't hunkerin' down 'cause you think we need you. So make your mind up."

Lisa drew a sharp breath and raised a finger. "Hold on. Why would Agnes want you?"

"Yeah, that's the other half of your problem that doesn't make sense," Johnny added.

Charlie's eyes widened and he looked like he was about to either throw up or spin and run out of the motel room. "How should I know? That was the first time I ever saw the lunatic."

"Are you sure?"

"Johnny. Would I lie to you about something like that?"

"Yep."

The shifter dwarf rolled his eyes. "Okay, fine. The old Charlie would have. Not the new Charlie."

"New Charlie?" Lisa inclined her head with a bland expression. "That's a nice way to put it."

"You're a transformed shifter," Galfrey said as he leaned against the conjoining doorframe. "Agnes hunts transformed shifters. It's a fairly simple question to answer given that she's been doing it for months."

"It ain't like you keep an especially low profile either." Johnny shook his head. "Listen, it doesn't matter why the witch wants Charlie or the two of y'all or whoever the hell else she's been draggin' in for Kaiser at the end of a blood-magic rope, all right? The point is, we're gettin' y'all outta here and outta the way so we can get to the bottom of what the hell's been goin' on."

"Fine." The man nodded. "As long as you find Hux."

"It's top of the list, pal."

"Have you had any word from Felix yet?" Lisa asked.

"Nope." Johnny scowled and uttered a growling sigh as he pulled his phone from his back pocket to double-check. "This is the last time I tell the man to take a few days off while we make an indefinite stop in California."

"Wait, you told the guy who pilots your private jet to ignore you for a few days?"

He shrugged.

"How many days, exactly?"

The bounty hunter puffed his cheeks out and headed toward the flimsy armchair in the corner of the room. "The rest of the week."

"Johnny—"

"Don't worry about it, darlin'. I already called him six times this mornin'. He'll get it eventually."

Lisa stared at him. "Did you leave a message?"

"Hell, I ain't talkin' into a phone when the guy's not even there to hear it."

"What about a text?"

"He's on vacation, Lisa."

"Wow. Okay…" She stood and gave him one of the wide-eyed, stern-faced nods usually reserved for parents about to lose their shit with a five-year-old. "Either you leave him a message or text him that this is an emergency, or you give me Felix's number and I'll take care of it."

He stared at her in return and squinted with one eye.

It ain't fair when she's had thirty-some odd years to master that look on her kid.

The dwarf clicked his tongue and flipped his phone open. "All right."

"Great." Charlie clapped and smiled bitterly at all of them. "Well, as fun as it is to keep stewing in all this misery with you guys, I have a few errands to run."

Johnny shook his head as he typed the emergency text to his pilot. "No, you don't."

The other dwarf scoffed. "Yeah, I wasn't asking for permission, 'coz. Let me know when your off-duty pilot shows up."

"I think that'll be in the next few hours—"

The motel door opened and closed again abruptly.

Before he'd even had the chance to press send on his text, Johnny looked up and scowled at the empty space left by his good-for-nothing cousin on his exit from the room. Lisa and Galfrey exchanged a wary glance.

"Dammit, Charlie." He wagged his finger from one to the other. "And y'all didn't even try to stop him."

She pressed her lips together to hold back a smile. "Well, you could always blow his bike up. That might keep him in one place."

"Fat chance." The bounty hunter strode toward the door and looked at the hounds curled together in the corner, completely asleep. "Y'all ain't much more use than he is. Come on."

Luther snorted and struck out blindly with a hind leg. "No. No, no. Not the carrot—"

Johnny rolled his eyes, jerked the door open, and marched

down the hallway of the motel's second story. He reached the bottom of the staircase and turned toward the parking lot when one blindingly orange Harley roared to life.

"Hey! This ain't the time for you to go ridin' off into the sunset. Are you tryin' to get locked up like the other missin' transformed?"

"They'd have to catch me first, Johnny. We both know that won't happen on the road." Charlie grinned and heeled the kickstand into place, revved the engine with two quick twists of the throttle, and walked the bike back. "I promised a few friends I'd stop by while I was in town."

"You ain't in town, man. You were only kind of on a case and now you're on the run. Your friends can sit the hell down and wait."

The shifter dwarf grimaced. "Yeah, but I can't. Call me when we're ready to go. I charged my phone so it'll be on."

"Hold up. What kinda friends are you—"

The crackling, sputtering growl of the engine revving to its maximum drowned Johnny's protest. Charlie swerved the bike in a tight circle and roared out of the parking lot.

"Dammit, Charlie! What friends?"

His cousin raced down the frontage road. The tips of his mohawk fluttered in the wind and the California sun winked on the obnoxiously bright orange paint of his bike. In the next moment, he was gone.

"Uh-huh. I see how it is." With a sniff, the bounty hunter spun and stormed toward the stairs. "You ain't gonna tell me? That's fine. I'll find out anyhow."

When he reached their motel room—only slightly less hellish than the last—he could have opened it with far less banging but he didn't.

Lisa looked at him with wide eyes. "He's gone."

"Do you see a moron steppin' in behind me, darlin'?"

"Excuse me?"

"'Course he's gone. There's nothin' I can do to stop him short of bashin' his face in, and that ain't exactly aligned with what we're fixin' to get done."

She glanced at Galfrey, who tried to sneak into the adjoining room to give the pissed-off bounty hunter more space. The door closed softly, and Johnny stalked to his duffle bag on the other side of the bed.

"You're worried about him. I get it." Lisa shifted on the bed to watch him rummage belligerently through his things. "I thought you two had worked things out, though."

"Maybe." His belt of explosive disks, a kit of small tools, and a few extra gadgets toppled onto the floor as he searched for what he wanted. "I ain't worried."

"Seriously."

She's gotta know by now I can feel her starin' at me.

"Seriously."

"It's okay to be worried about your cousin, especially with a history like Charlie's. He left you here and we both know he won't answer his phone if he doesn't want to. When you can't get hold of him and have no idea where he went or what he's doing, that's a perfectly valid reason to be concerned. It's normal."

"I don't need to know what he's up to. Where he went? I have that covered."

"What?"

With a smirk, Johnny finally found the small black device he was looking for and jerked it out of the bag. He stood, grinned at her as he wiggled it in front of her face, and turned it on.

"Johnny." She frowned at it and tapped her fingers against her lips. "Is that what I think it is?"

"Do you still think I can read your mind?" He tapped a quick sequence into the keypad and raised his eyebrows, waiting for the display to show him exactly what he wanted to know.

"Answering a question with a question means you know

exactly how much someone won't approve of what you're doing. Including me."

"Much as I love ya, darlin', your approval ain't exactly at the top of the list on this one." He widened his eyes and grunted when the screen flared to life to display a slowly moving map with one bright red dot pulsing in the middle. The soft, slightly obnoxious peep of the GPS signal pinging back to the device in his hand was the only sound in the room before Rex interrupted with a three-second snore and licked his muzzle in his sleep. Johnny sneered at the screen. "There you are."

"You put a tracker on your cousin's bike," Lisa muttered.

"It only took me thirty years to learn my lesson."

"Wow. And what will you do if he goes somewhere you don't think he should be?"

Johnny squinted at her and shrugged. "I'll go haul his ass outta there before I kick it to kingdom come."

"Johnny—"

"Hell, darlin'. You said it yourself. It's perfectly normal to wanna know where my dumbass cousin' is off to without explanation."

"Okay, admittedly, I spoke too soon." She pointed at the receiving end of the GPS tracker. "That isn't normal."

"Huh. For who?"

"Everyone." As she held his gaze, a slow realization washed over her features and morphed into a grimace. "Except you."

"Then I assume I have your approval now, huh?"

"Not really, no." Lisa flashed him a bitter smile and leaned toward the device in his hand to get a look at Charlie's location. "But it's not the worst idea you've ever had."

"Trust me, darlin'. There are many more where that came from."

CHAPTER TWO

Ten minutes later, Lisa stepped out of the bathroom and shook her head. Johnny was still hunched over the tracking device, obsessed with following his cousin's unexplained side trip. "Okay, now I'm starting to think this was a bad idea."

"It ain't." He sniffed and slid his finger briefly across the screen. "I aim to see exactly where he's stoppin'."

"Hasn't he stopped yet?"

"Nope."

"Well, where is he?"

"Just past Auburn."

"Hold on." With a frown, she sat beside him on the edge of the bed and stared at the device. "I thought I heard you say he was in Auburn."

"There's nothin' wrong with your hearin', darlin'."

"Johnny, that's almost forty minutes from here. Charlie left fifteen minutes ago."

"Now you're sayin' what I already know." The dwarf looked at her and cleared his throat. "Do you still think it's a bad idea?'

"Oh, man." She rubbed her forehead. "Well, at least we'll be able to see it in real time if he crashes into the back of another vehicle already going twenty over the speed limit."

"He ain't dropped his bike once in damn near seventy years." He shook his head and stared at the remarkably quick-moving red dot on the screen. "And he ain't about to—"

"What?" Lisa opened a bottle of water, took a long drink, and paused when her partner's scowl deepened. "He's not about to what, Johnny?"

"Huh." The bounty hunter squinted at the screen, tapped a few times, and rubbed his mouth. "He stopped."

"Okay. You know, I can normally tell, but this time I feel like I have to ask if that's a good thing or a bad thing."

"I dunno." He showed her the map and the faintly pulsing red light in the center. "What does it look like to you?"

"It…it looks like the middle of nowhere."

"Good. We're on the same page again." He handed her the tracking device and retrieved his phone. "Do you mind lookin' that up on one of your fancy devices, darlin'? Mine's pinned him down like a worm on a hook, but it ain't satellite."

"What?"

"Double-check those coordinates, huh? Make sure my cousin did stop in the damn middle of nowhere and not out at some other unmarked ranch or a pop-up mall off the highway."

"Got it." Lisa began to compare Charlie's coordinates with a more comprehensive display of the area—Google Maps, which he still hadn't learned how to use—and the bounty hunter made his call before he pressed the phone to his ear.

The line rang four times, then five, then six. Finally, the voice-mail service picked up.

"Yo. It's Charlie. Tell me something."

With a snort, he ended the call and tried again. "Did he start movin' again?"

"Not that I can tell." Lisa shook her head. "And I'm certain I'd be able to tell. It seriously is in the middle of nowhere, Johnny. There's nothing out there but open land. That's it."

"All right. Keep an eye on him."

This time when he called Charlie, it went directly to voice-mail and didn't even ring once.

Dammit. None of this feels right.

"Darlin', do you know how to check the cell reception out where he is?"

"Give me a second…" She tapped her tablet a few times and shrugged. "It's in the green zone for almost every carrier, so he should be getting your calls."

"Well, he ain't." Johnny snapped his flip phone shut and grimaced. "My call went through once but now the phone's dead. I swear if that lyin' sonofabitch is yankin' my chain again, I'll—"

"Johnny." She stared at the tracking device and leaned slightly toward him. "Is there any chance the tracker you put on his bike ran out of battery power too?"

"What? I put the damn thing together before we came out here and made the battery myself. There is no way in hell it died in a few weeks."

"Then it's probably safe to say Charlie's phone didn't die either." She extended the tracking device toward him and he scowled at it.

The pulsing red dot was completely gone.

"Dammit, Charlie." He leapt off the bed and snatched his belt of explosive disks from the floor. "I told him to stay put and he goes off thinkin' he's Evel Knievel in black leather and studs."

"Hey, I wouldn't jump to conclusions about this. His phone turned off before the GPS signal cut out. After you'd already called and he didn't answer, right?"

"It happened two minutes ago, darlin'. I remember just fine."

"Right." She stood, grabbed her purse, and dumped the tracking device inside it in her haste to get his attention before he jumped into anything rash. "Is there even a small chance he knew you were tracking his bike?"

"Nope. Knowin' Charlie, he would have come here and chucked the damn thing right in my face and laughed. And he told me he'd just charged his phone."

"So maybe this isn't him trying to pull one over on you."

"Darlin', this ain't—"

"No, hear me out. I know you're still angry with him for…a whole host of things, but I don't think this is Charlie trying to piss you off—"

"Lisa." He spun toward her and spread his arms in a gesture of frustration. "I know. This smells bad to me too so now, I'm goin' in expectin' the worse from someone else instead of my idiot cousin, understand?"

"Oh." He'd surprised her but she recovered quickly and shrugged. "Good. So this was already a rescue mission, then."

The bounty hunter snorted. "Uh-huh. Whatever he got himself into, I reckon it ain't part of his plan. Whatever it was."

"Do you think Agnes got to him?"

"I don't see how. But that witch has more up her sleeve than an amateur magician."

Lisa stopped at the adjoining door and raised her hand to knock. Jake opened it before she even had the chance. "I assume you heard the entire conversation, right?"

"Yeah. Someone got to Charlie?"

"That's what we're gonna find out," Johnny said as he opened the door. "Let's go."

His piercing whistle startled both hounds out of their incredibly deep sleep. Rex whipped his head up, his ears raised and on high alert. Luther snorted, bucked, and flopped onto his back before he scrambled to his feet. "Johnny! What's up?"

"Y'all got too comfortable. Come on."

"Wait, you woke us up 'cause we got a little comfy? What gives?"

"You smell that, bro?"

"What do you… Oh. Oh, yeah. Hey, Johnny. What happened?"

"What are you so worried about?"

Licking their muzzles and yawning, the hounds trotted after their master down to the waiting SUV.

"Pack your things before we go," Lisa told Galfrey and Jake. "We don't know how long we'll be gone or where we'll end up."

The transformed shifters shared a concerned look and hurried to do as she'd said.

It had taken Charlie less than half an hour to barrel down the California highway before he'd stopped on 49 in the middle of nowhere and Eldorado County. Even though Johnny stepped on the gas and ran a little wild with his dangerous-driving habit, they reached the same location an hour later.

"That's it." Lisa pointed straight ahead and shook her finger at the windshield. "It has to be. That's his bike."

"Uh-huh." He didn't slow until he was almost upon the orange Harley on the dusty shoulder. When his foot pressed the brake, Galfrey and Jake grunted and surged forward against their seatbelts. Luther's head thumped against the rear of the back seat, and Rex burst out laughing.

"Oh, no." Lisa's seatbelt was off before the tires crunched to a halt and Johnny was close behind her as they bolted from the vehicle.

"Johnny! Hey, Johnny!"

"Yeah, what about us?" Rex whined. "Let us out!"

"Damn." The dwarf tugged on his wiry beard and scanned the surrounding mountains and scattered California Redwoods that had begun to recede this far south. "This wasn't him."

"And there's no sign that anyone walked off the shoulder in the trees." Scanning the ground, Lisa shrugged. "There are tire marks, sure, but how many people pull onto the shoulder on the highway? There's no way to tell who was here with him."

"You mean who took him." He approached his cousin's bike,

which had been left out in the dirt and now lay on its side, slightly dented and covered in red-brown dust. The engine was off but the keys were still in the ignition. "No way in hell would Charlie up and leave his ride behind like this."

"So someone found him."

"Johnny!" The hounds raced toward them and skidded to a stop behind their master. Rex snorted. "That's Charlie's death-on-two-wheels thing, right?"

He glanced down and pointed at the dirt. "Y'all smell anything?"

"Besides how pissed you are? Nope."

"Nothin', huh?"

Luther sat, sneezed, and pawed at his nose beneath the spray of dust flying around him. "Hey, maybe if you didn't make us climb over two scaredy-cat shifters to get out the front doors, we'd pick up a trail."

Johnny snapped his fingers. "Scent. Now."

"Jeez. Just try better next time."

"He's way too distracted, bro."

"Yeah, I could tell."

The hounds sniffed the area, their tails in the air as they headed systematically across the wide shoulder.

"Only the smell of transformed shifter, Johnny," Rex muttered.

"Yeah, a ton of it. The pirate dwarf." Luther buried his snout in a patch of tall brown grass at the edge of the shoulder and snorted. "Nothing else."

"That doesn't give us anything," Lisa said.

"Well, he didn't disappear into thin air and leave his bike on the side of the road." Johnny turned and fervently scanned the craggy hills that climbed into the mountains. "We didn't pass any emergency vehicles so there was no crash, no debris on the high-way, and a dead dwarf in black leather—"

He stopped when his gaze settled on the motorcycle.

"What?" Lisa stared at him as he walked slowly toward the hunk of orange-painted metal.

The bounty hunter pointed at the underside of the engine and hissed a sharp breath through his teeth. "That ain't mine."

"Wait, Johnny, you ride death traps too?" Luther licked his muzzle.

"I thought it was only four wheels and boats," Rex added.

"And half-Light Elves."

The hounds' sniggering cut off when he snapped his fingers. He crouched beside the bike and stared at the second small black device fixed beside the tracker he'd put there. "That. It ain't mine."

"Do you think it's another tracking device?"

"I dunno what the hell it is."

Lisa patted her pockets. "Okay, well at least let me find gloves or a rag or—Johnny."

He plucked the foreign device off the bike and held it out in front of him to examine it under the sunshine.

"Right. Good idea. Get rid of any possibility of fingerprints."

"And run 'em through what, darlin'? The Johnny Walker Investigations database?"

"No, we could have—" Lisa shook her head. "You're right, it's a good point. No one in the department would touch this with a twenty-foot pole."

"Not even if we asked real nice." He stood and scowled at the new clue in his hand.

It's the only damn clue we have now, ain't it?

Then he saw the small, barely visible blink of an orange light beside his thumb.

"We don't need fingerprints anyhow. The damn thing's still on."

"If it's still sending a signal to whoever put it there, we can't take it with us."

"Sure we can." Whistling again to call the hounds, Johnny stormed toward the SUV.

"Hey, has it occurred to you that the magical who tracked Charlie and took him off his bike might still be watching?"

"Why? They have what they needed. And now I aim to get mine."

She rolled her eyes, opened the back hatch of the SUV, and nodded for the hounds to get in.

"Hey, Lisa. What's wrong with Johnny?"

"Yeah, he's grumpy…er than usual."

"So it's probably a good idea to keep quiet for a while." She gave each of them a warning look before she closed the hatch and slid into the passenger's seat.

"He's gone?" Galfrey asked. "Just like that. Disappeared."

"No, some asshole thought it would be fun to snatch him," The dwarf growled in irritation as he handed the device to Lisa.

"I knew it." Jake closed his eyes and dropped his head back against the headrest. "We're next."

"Will you cut it out with all the doom and gloom already? The only reason Charlie's missin' is 'cause he can't stay in one place, especially with me. Y'all aren't gettin' taken and I don't wanna hear another word about it."

"Yeah, don't make him come back here," Rex muttered.

Luther sniggered. "He will."

Jesus, it's like I picked up a couple more kids on the way. When the hell does it stop?

"Johnny?" Lisa lifted the device between them and widened her eyes. "The light flashed and went out. It won't come on."

"It ain't a dead battery, either. Someone turned it off."

"So they know we found Charlie's bike, then."

"Maybe but it doesn't matter." He jerked the gearshift into drive and didn't bother to let the sedan coming up behind them pass before he accelerated off the shoulder and fishtailed across the righthand lane.

The driver behind them pressed the horn and glared through the window as he passed.

Lisa gritted her teeth and clutched the oh-shit handle above her head as she caught her breath again. "It does matter, though. We can't lock onto a signal if there is no signal."

"Maybe you can't."

"Do you care to share your master plan?"

"Sure. We're goin' shoppin'."

Jake choked on a laugh in the back seat and leaned forward. "For what?"

"Supplies."

CHAPTER THREE

They stopped in Placerville at a rundown, empty-looking Radio Shack. Lisa frowned at the faded marquee above the front door. "I didn't know there were any of these left."

"The best way to go is old-school." Johnny exited the car with a grunt and practically slammed the door shut.

"I don't get it," Galfrey muttered. "His cousin got kidnapped and he wants to buy toys."

"Wait. You'll get it."

With that kind of vague explanation, the shifters didn't let him out of their sight once they stopped at another ridiculously cheap motel. The bounty hunter unpacked all his tools and two boxes' worth of random devices and tech gear he'd purchased in a rage and set to work without a word.

"What is that?" Jake asked.

"Mine." Johnny grunted and pried apart the shell of the tracking device.

"It's not some kinda bomb, is it?" Galfrey scratched his head. "Like those other things you used to blow the witch up —"

The dwarf thumped the tiny-headed screwdriver onto the

table and glared at them. "I can't work with a pair of naggin' idiots breathin' down my neck. Shut up or get out."

"I'm...gonna try to find some coffee or something." Lisa pointed at the door. "Does anyone wanna come?"

"Yeah. Maybe some lunch." Galfrey shook his head and joined her. Jake looked entirely dejected but continued to glance over his shoulder to watch the dwarf's tinkering.

"Hey," Luther whispered as he crawled on his belly beneath the table toward his master's feet. "Hey, Johnny. You didn't mean us, did you?"

"Yeah, we don't even drink coffee," Rex added.

"Y'all say one more word and I'm lockin' y'all in the bathroom," he responded belligerently.

"Yeah, okay. Wait, but you'd still be able to hear us—"

"Luther!" The dwarf pounded a fist onto the table and stared straight ahead at the wall.

The hound panted noisily below the table but he didn't say another word. Rex stalked across the room, sniffed the old, worn carpet, and curled in the corner.

It's finally back to how it oughtta be—quiet. Dammit, if I miss one piece of this, we'll never find Charlie. I can't believe that's suddenly a bad thing.

Two hours later, they were all in the car and headed southeast across California again. The hounds and both shifters in the back seat were completely silent. Lisa stared at the transmission receiver with a dubious frown. "Okay, I hate to say this—"

"Then don't."

She darted him a warning look but he stared at the road, his hands locked on the steering wheel. "This doesn't look very different than the middle-of-nowhere scene where we found Charlie's bike."

"'Cause it ain't. Instead of a dropped motorcycle on the side of the road, that device will lead us directly to the bastards who took him."

"I hope so. Truly. But with how crazy everything's become in the last few weeks… Don't you think we should double-check everything before we burst in with guns blazing?"

"And a GPS signal ain't double-check enough for ya?"

With another glance at the screen to make sure they were on track, Lisa drew a deep breath and prepared her next words. "Hey, I know you're upset. This is your cousin we're talking about. I'm only trying to bring a little more clarity to—"

"Darlin', I ain't nearly as worried about Charlie as I am about the shits who thought they could take him and hold him." The bounty hunter glanced in the rearview mirror before the sharp bend in the road straightened and the asphalt became bumpy, uneven gravel with far too many potholes. "Not more of these damn roads. What kinda state won't keep things easy to drive on?"

"You're—" She braced herself against the door as they went over a giant bump and the hounds yelped in the back. "You're deflecting."

"I'm drivin'."

"What do you mean when you say you're more worried about his kidnappers?"

"Charlie ain't a young dwarf green behind the ears, darlin'. Just 'cause he got snatched doesn't mean he can't make 'em drop him again."

"So…this isn't a rescue mission?"

They went over another huge bump that thrust her shoulders against the door.

"Hey, man," Galfrey said. "Do you wanna slow down a little?"

"Nope."

Jake puffed his cheeks out. "I'm gonna be sick."

"Johnny, if he can get himself out of this, why—"

"That rogue Walker callin' himself family has been steppin' on my toes since I was old enough to use 'em. If we don't get to the kidnappers first, Charlie will. Meanin' we get nothin' but leftover corpses, if that."

"I thought you said he hadn't killed anyone."

"You didn't ask what was covered under self-defense."

"Guys?" Galfrey pressed his hand against the rear window and leaned closer. "Hey. Johnny. You should stop the car."

"We ain't where we need to be yet."

Rex yipped. "He's right! Johnny, stop!"

"What are you—"

"Angry wolf alert!" Luther uttered a bloodcurdling howl, and his master slammed his foot on the brake pedal. The SUV slid forward along the loose gravel and small rocks before it rocked to a halt.

"Wolf?"

"Shifters," Jake muttered. "On the other side of those trees."

"It's him, Johnny." The hounds panted as they paced from one side of the vehicle to the other.

"Yeah, that's him."

"Charlie?"

They each barked once, too excited to use words even with their translating collars.

"You gotta be kiddin' me." Johnny leapt out of the car, slammed the door shut behind him, and loped into the trees that studded the rolling hills stretched ahead of them for miles.

"Great." Lisa opened her door and turned to address Galfrey and Jake. "Stay in the car."

"Seriously?"

She left without a reply and hurried after her partner.

"Charlie!" the bounty hunter bellowed. "What the hell are you tryin' to pull?"

"Maybe we should find out who's out here with him before we try to—"

"Charlie Walker! Furry or otherwise, get your goddamn ass over here. Now!"

A streak of red fur darted through the trees up ahead, followed by a low snarl.

"Johnny," Lisa whispered as she crept up behind him. "Was that him?"

"How the hell should I know? I didn't know he was transformed until he arrived at my door and—"

"Look out!" She barreled into him and knocked him sideways as a blazing streak of red light rocketed toward them. It crashed against the tree where they'd stood and splinters of wood spewed in all directions.

The two partners helped each other to their feet and stared at the destroyed tree until more leaves rustled ahead.

"That looked very much like the kind of attack Agnes would have thrown," Lisa muttered.

"Uh-huh. Do you still think the blood magic witch can't fly?"

"That's ridiculous."

Johnny took an exploding disk from his belt and hovered his thumb over the button on the top. "If it ain't her—"

A furious snarl came from their right, followed by a loud scuffle. Bushes and low-hanging branches rustled and snapped before the red wolf they'd seen sneaking through the trees burst out of the foliage again and headed toward them.

"What the—"

Before it could move any closer, a massive black shifter leapt from the thick underbrush and onto the much smaller but equally fierce shifter.

"Hey!" The dwarf stepped out of the way and tugged Lisa with him. "Y'all give it a rest and tell me which one of y'all is my damn—"

"Johnny! Johnny!" The hounds howled and raced toward them from the car with Galfrey and Jake close on their heels. "It's a trap!"

"Ya think?"

"She's here," Galfrey shouted.

The fighting wolves snapped and snarled and rolled each other across the ground before they raced away again.

In the next moment, the edge of the woods erupted with shouts, the sounds of weapons being drawn, and a voice they all recognized.

"There they are!" Agnes stormed across the open area toward them. "Tyro wants the shifters alive. Get rid of the others."

"Dammit." Johnny thumbed the button trigger of his exploding disk and hurled it at the half-dozen shifters who raced through the trees toward them.

Gunfire peppered the bark before the disk detonated with a deafening bang and the two gun-wielding shifters were catapulted away across the grass.

The others dropped their firearms and shifted, and the witch hurled another crackling, shrieking burst of dark-red magic into the trees. The hounds barked and howled and threw themselves at another wolf who'd broken away from the rest.

Lisa tossed two massive fireballs at the blood witch before she summoned two more. "How are we supposed to know which one is Charlie?"

"Take 'em all down and find the ugly one." Johnny drew his knife, crouched, and sneered at a shaggy gray wolf that bounded toward him.

Before he could use his knife or engage the shifter at all, a brown-and-gray blur appeared from his right and collided with his attacker powerfully enough to knock it off its feet.

"Galfrey!" Jake shouted and paced agitatedly as Lisa launched more fireballs. The hounds snarled and leapt from one of Agnes' hired wolves to the next. "Aw, come on, man. We can't—"

"Either jump in or get back to the car," Johnny snapped before he activated another disk and lobbed it at Agnes.

The witch stepped aside and raised a crimson shield next to her face when the device exploded.

"Then you could make yourself useful and hit her with my car again!"

"Shit." Jake shifted too and joined his friend to fight tooth and claw. Unfortunately, the other wolves darted around the clearing and fought Galfrey and two coonhounds off. They wouldn't let anyone get close to the dark witch who stood in a black trench coat way too hot for the season.

"Get the shifters," Lisa muttered and snuffed out the fire in her hands. "I'll deal with the bitch."

"You mean the one who busted your damn leg like swattin' a fly?"

As if he hadn't spoken, she strode through the trees toward Agnes, her fists clenched at her sides.

"Dammit. Everyone stopped listenin', is that it?"

A low, rumbling growl rose from his left. He turned slowly and stared into the flashing silver eyes of another gray wolf that stalked toward him.

With a snarl, he adjusted his hold on the utility knife and spread his arms invitingly. "Let's dance."

The wolf lunged and snapped his jaws shut less than an inch from his outstretched blade. His first swipe with the knife missed but they continued to test each other as the rest of the fight raged through the trees. They circled slowly and when the wolf darted forward, Johnny slid to the side and dropped to one knee as he slashed up with the tip of his weapon. The blade sliced across fur-covered flesh.

His adversary yelped and limped as he turned to face him again, panting heavily. A moment later, his eyelids fluttered, his head sagged to the side, and he fell as a naked man with a three-inch gash in his shoulder.

"What the fuck?" The bounty hunter kicked a rock at the unconscious shifter and rolled his eyes. "Who the hell hires muscle that passes out after a papercut—"

The sharp crack of gunfire echoed from the edge of the tree line, followed instantly by a snarling cry of pain.

The dwarf sprinted through the trees, hurdled rocks and fallen branches, and barely avoided being knocked off his feet when another of the wolves raced past him with Galfrey's brown-gray muzzle snapping at his heels.

"Lisa!" She stood over the blood witch with her service pistol —no longer technically in service—held in both hands.

Agnes sat on the brown grass, clutched her thigh with both hands, and snarled at the thick bloodstain that bloomed on her black jeans. The woman was effectively trapped inside a cage of shimmering golden light.

"I didn't know you could hold prisoners with elf energy," Johnny muttered.

"If it works as a shield and a bomb, why not?" His partner holstered her gun and looked around the open field. Naked and concussed shifters lay scattered among the trees. "I count six."

"Uh-huh." He pointed at the tight knot of four snarling wolves and two barking, growling coonhounds. "And one of them's my idiot cousin. Keep an eye on her, darlin'."

"She won't go anywhere." Lisa tilted her head and fixed her hard gaze on Agnes. "It hurts, doesn't it?"

The witch sneered at her. "Not as much as I'm gonna hurt you."

"We'll see."

The dwarf uttered a piercing whistle and only the hounds responded. They backed away from the three wolves who pinned the massive black beast between them and stared at their master.

"This is him, Johnny," Luther barked.

"We know it's him. Same smell by the bike."

"Then who's the other shifter?"

"No clue, Johnny, but he fights like a real asshole."

He strode forward and shoved Galfrey aside—or maybe it was Jake. It was honestly hard to tell when he'd seen enough shifted wolves for one day. Whoever it was snarled but stopped instantly when the bounty hunter stepped forward brazenly and pointed at the black wolf. "Last straw."

The beast snorted, then lunged forward to snap at him. The second his jaws opened, Johnny swung his fist into the side of the shifter's massive head and he reeled sideways. With a yelp, he toppled, tried to rise, and slumped in defeat.

"Well shit, 'coz." It was Charlie's voice, for sure, but it didn't come from the black wolf that now panted at his feet but from the red-furred shifter instead. "If I'd known it was that easy to take the bastard down, I would've clocked him myself."

"What the—" He stared as his cousin shifted and forced himself to not drop his gaze below the other dwarf's chest. "The hounds said you were the black wolf."

"Um…no, we didn't." Luther trotted forward to sniff the wolf's heaving flanks as Galfrey and Jake shifted to human form and crouched in the grass.

"Yeah, Johnny. Pay attention." Rex darted away from the black wolf's menacing growl and snarled in retaliation. "It's not Charlie but we've smelled this guy before."

"Aw, hell." Johnny pointed at his cousin. "Who's this guy?"

Charlie responded with a crooked smile. "Tyro, apparently."

"No shit."

"Is everything okay over there?" Lisa called, her gaze fixed firmly on the snarling witch in her energy cage.

"I just punched one of the sneakiest goddamn shifter-killers in his wolf face, darlin'. I think that counts."

And he's hangin' onto consciousness like a real champ, ain't he?

"That's Tyro?" Galfrey scowled at the wolf. "That's the asshole killing us off like we're a plague?"

"Now hold on a second—"

"You sonofabitch!" The angry shifter sprang toward the bleary-eyed wolf and Charlie moved hastily to intercept him. The wolf seemed to have gathered enough strength to whip his head up and try to bite Galfrey's hands off.

"Whoa, whoa." Jake went to restrain his furious friend as well and the bounty hunter reacted on instinct.

He punched the black wolf in the face again and this time, knocked him completely unconscious.

When the shifter lost his fur, fangs, and claws, the commotion ceased immediately.

Everyone stared at the naked man sprawled on the grass.

"Would you look at that," Charlie muttered. His hold on Galfrey's arm went slack and he lowered his hands at his sides.

Johnny widened his eyes and peered at the last face he'd expected to see. "I ain't been this surprised since my fourth-grade teacher told me I should run for president."

His cousin snorted a laugh.

Jake stared at him in horror. "What?"

"Johnny." Lisa sounded more than a little perturbed now. "I'd come take a look but this cage won't hold itself. And it won't hold forever either."

He straightened, stepped away from Tyro, and met his partner's gaze. "It's Bronson Harford."

CHAPTER FOUR

"What?" Lisa started to head toward the four naked shifters, two coonhounds, and one uncharacteristically surprised Johnny Walker. "Did you say—"

Agnes sniggered. She still clutched her leg and her hands were coated with her blood. "And you call yourselves professionals."

"Shut up."

The witch laughed now. "You have no idea what's going on here, do you—"

"I said shut up!" Lisa didn't exactly know what she was trying to do when she thrust her hand toward her wounded prisoner. If she hadn't holstered her weapon, she might have shot the woman again. Instead, a bolt of bright silver light streaked from her outstretched hand and struck the witch in the throat.

Agnes choked, her expression one of shock, then tried to smile before her eyes rolled back in her head and she dropped back into the grass.

"Darlin', don't tell me you killed our quickest ticket to finding out the rest of this."

"What? Of course not." Lisa peered closer to double-check. "No, she's still breathing. Are you sure that's Bronson?"

"I'm sure." Johnny nudged the unconscious Harford heir with the toe of his boot and sniffed. "I'll eat my own damn sock if he ain't."

Luther sat and licked his muzzle. "You could share if you want."

Ignoring the commentary, he turned his confusion onto his cousin. "What the hell happened?"

"Whew. Lemme tell ya, 'coz, I'm a little fuzzy about the details myself. Especially now."

"We found your bike."

"Hey, thanks. Did you get a trailer for it and everything?"

"No. But you tell me how the hell you ended up all the way out here and I'll let you pick it up off the side of the road."

"Aw, you left it there? Man, what's wrong with you—"

"Focus!"

Jake shifted into his wolf form and loped across the dry grass toward the next rising hill. Galfrey finally pulled his glare away from Bronson and shifted as well before he hurried after his friend.

"Okay. Look." Charlie shrugged. "I went to go see a couple of friends like I said. Then some asshole tried to drive up my ass or run me off the highway or something. He was insane, this guy. Who drives that fast?"

"You, for one."

"No, I mean in a cage. A car—"

"Stick to the play-by-play, how about that?" Johnny glanced at Bronson's unconscious form and folded his arms.

The guy's gonna wake up before Charlie gets his mouth to work.

"Yeah. Sure. I pulled over, the dude behind the wheel stayed on me the whole time, and then he got out. I thought he was some lunatic who wanted to pick a fight with a biker. I was still focused on him when a red light zapped out of the car and I blacked out."

"Agnes.'"

"Well…maybe. I don't know. I was seeing red anyway, Johnny—furious. You don't hog the road like that, know what I'm saying?"

"Was Bronson driving the car?"

"Again. I don't exactly see faces when I'm ready to start beating them."

The bounty hunter rubbed his mouth and turned toward where Galfrey and Jake had disappeared. "Then what happened here?"

"I woke up. Well, not *here* here." His cousin turned and scanned the landscape, gave his cousin a full-moon view, and rested his hands on his hips. Johnny turned away and shook his head. "Somewhere over that hill, probably. I came to in front of a rundown shed. A shed with nothing else there. A couple of these other idiots were trying to haul me inside. It looked like they were about to tie me up." He turned toward his cousin and shrugged. "And hey, I'm all for a little bondage from time to time but not by those hairy beasts. Certainly not by a horde of dudes—"

"Man, I don't need to hear about all that." Closing his eyes, Johnny drew a deep breath. "Stop. Please."

"You asked."

"Not for that information."

"Johnny!" Rex bayed wildly but was nowhere in sight. "Johnny, he's here! We found the other one."

"We can smell him," Luther added. "Right here in this—whoa. Hey. Come on, guy. Put some clothes on."

The bang of wood on wood came from the other side of the hill, and Johnny pointed at his cousin. "Stay right here. If he moves, knock his lights out again."

"Who, Tyro?"

"Yeah. Bronson."

The bounty hunter sprinted up the hill and when he crested

it, the hounds were sniffing around the outside of what must be the same dilapidated shed Charlie had mentioned. "Smell who?"

"The other guy, Johnny."

"The shifter-napped shifter."

"The what now?"

"The guy we were trying to find 'cause his friends couldn't stop— Ooh, hey. Mushrooms."

Rex snarled and herded his brother away from the shed.

With a grunt, Johnny strode down the hill. "Are y'all talkin' about Hux?"

"Yeah, yeah. Duh." Luther looked at his master and licked his muzzle. "Who's that again?"

A grating rumble and squeal rose from inside the shed, followed by a boom that made the walls quiver and thick layers of dust fall from the roof and the thin, decaying wooden slats. The frail door burst open, and Galfrey and Jake emerged with a beaten and bloodied Hux supported between them.

"Aw, hell."

"Yeah, we need to get him to a healer or something," Galfrey muttered. "He's in bad shape."

"So are my goddamn eyes." Johnny turned and shook his head as the three transformed shifters hurried up the hill. "Doesn't anyone give a shit about clothes anymore?"

Jake scoffed. A low wheeze came from Hux and the hounds burst out laughing.

"What's so funny?"

"Hux is right," Galfrey said and darted Johnny a quick look over his shoulder. "It's very liberating. You should try it sometime."

"It ain't gonna happen, fellas. Get your buddy to the car. Then we have a whole lotta mess to keep cleanin' up."

"He's right, Johnny." Rex howled through his laughter. "It's so liberating."

"Yeah, take it from us." Luther trotted past his master up the hill. "We're naked all day every day."

Lisa looked relieved to see Hux being led toward the car, although she looked quickly away from his friends who hadn't bothered to pick their clothes up from between the trees.

"That was a lucky coincidence," she said as Johnny approached her and scowled at the unconscious witch still imprisoned within the golden light.

"There ain't nothin' about this I'd write off as coincidence, darlin'. We got Hux out and now, I aim to squeeze the truth outta Bronson until we know exactly what we stepped into."

"What about Agnes?"

He shrugged. "We can't cart her around in the back of the SUV with the hounds, can we? But we can't let her go either."

"Well, I'm not staying here while you question the Harford kid."

"Naw. I suppose we oughtta haul everyone into the city. I have a favor to call in with someone down there. They are something of a pro at keepin' magicals in magical cages."

Lisa raised an eyebrow. "So we freed one prisoner only to take two more of our own. Is that it?"

"Exactly." He gestured toward the scattered bodies of Agnes' shifters. One of them groaned and stirred. "It's a bad idea to start all the questionin' here with these fellas comin' to."

"You need transport," Charlie said as he walked up behind them.

"Hey. I told you to keep an eye on Bronson."

"I did. I'm very sure he'll have a black eye in the morning. But back to business, 'coz. If you need a way to get the blood witch and Tyro into custody somewhere, I'm your guy."

Johnny snorted. "You left your bike on the highway. That's not real convincin'."

"But I have friends with cages—"

Lisa frowned. "Cages?"

"Cars."

"Oh…"

"What do you say, Johnny? I'll make a few calls and they'll be out here in no time."

The bounty hunter glared at his cousin.

We have no other options. And I'll never hear the end of it.

"Fine. Call 'em."

"That's what I'm talkin' about!" Charlie fired imaginary pistols with both hands and grinned before he broke into an excited dance that would have been funny to see in any dwarf under different circumstances. "I told you so. You guys need me."

"Oh, boy." Shaking her head, Lisa looked at the sky.

"Jesus Christ, Charlie." Johnny sighed and rubbed his forehead. "Put some damn clothes on, huh? If Bronson gets one look at you like that, you'll kill him before we can even have us a talk."

His partner snorted.

"Done and done, 'coz. Now I gotta find my… Right. Yeah. I shifted at the torture shed. Two minutes, Johnny. Then you'll have your transport on the way."

"Uh-huh. I'm real glad I skipped lunch."

<hr>

As obnoxious and infuriating as Charlie Walker was, he was a transformed dwarf of his word—at least with this. His friends arrived at the out-of-the-way location half an hour later in a painter's van, the inside of which had been refitted to look more like a prison transport vehicle for inmates.

Lisa scanned the back, then stepped away and grimaced. "What exactly did you guys say you do? Professionally, I mean."

A Kilomea with huge burn scars along the side of his neck where the hair had stopped growing lowered his head. "What did Charlie tell you?"

"Transport."

The gnome who wore cut-off jean shorts and with a pile of dreadlocks coiled on his head chuckled and spread his arms. "Then that's what we do, lady. Transport."

"Right. You know what? I don't even want to know more than that."

"Good. 'Cause unless you have a warrant, we're not talking." Both of Charlie's friends burst out laughing and she left them to their fun and games as the hounds raced through the trees.

"They're coming, Lisa," Rex panted.

"Yeah, they might need a little help, though. Who knew that crazy witch would give them so much trouble?"

"She's awake?"

"Nope." Luther sat and scratched vigorously behind one ear. "Just very heavy."

"That's your cue, big guy." The gnome smacked a hand against the Kilomea's arm. "Heavy witch is your thing—wait." His eyes grew comically wide as he turned his head slowly toward Lisa. "Were you talking to us or those dogs right there?"

"Um…" She wrinkled her nose. "The dogs."

"You can hear them?"

"It's a long story." She studied the odd pair for a moment and plastered a grim smile onto her lips. "And judging by the fact that you can hear them too, I'm gonna take a wild guess and say you're more of Charlie's transformed friends."

"Well, yeah." The gnome snorted. "Gnomes don't talk to dogs. That's ridiculous."

"Light Elves don't either," his friend added with a grunt.

"You know what, Chuckles? Leave the lady out of it and go help them with the cargo, huh?"

The Kilomea heaved a sigh and strode through the trees.

Luther giggled shrilly. "Chuckles? His name is Chuckles?"

"It's a nickname. Don't worry about it." The gnome scowled at the hounds. "This is weird."

"Only a little." Lisa shoved a few loose hairs away from

her face and looked at the SUV, where Hux sat in the back beneath the open hatch, his legs dangling over the side. Galfrey and Jake caught him up on what was happening and handed him bottled water after bottled water. "Out of curiosity, exactly how magic-proof is your…uh, transport van?"

"Oh, we have the best." The gnome slapped the side of it. "You can't get in or out of this baby unless you got the key—which is in the ignition right now. But I keep it on me all the time. You know, you'd be surprised how many people like to steal things out of other people's cars."

"Hmm. Probably not."

"I play it safe, though." He puffed his chest out and nodded. "I'm always on high alert. Nothing catches me off guard and Chuckles? Well, he's the muscle—"

"Are you fucking kidding me?" the Kilomea bellowed. "No way are we doing this!"

"Uh-oh." The gnome smiled warily at Lisa and pointed through the trees. "I'll handle this. Don't worry."

"You're insane, Charlie. No. You said it was a quick and easy cleanup."

"Come on, Chuck. It is quick and easy. We schlep these jerks into the back of the van, you guys drive them to Johnny's friend's place, and you pack up and leave. Quick and easy."

Chuckles roared. "Or I could rip his head off right now and finish the whole damn thing."

"Crap." Lisa darted after the gnome to where Charlie and the Kilomea squared off.

Bronson had been dressed in clothes way too baggy for him and bound by the wrists, and he now lay face-down on the ground. He glared at the arguing transformed shifters who to anyone else would look like a mohawked dwarf and a burned Kilomea.

Johnny watched the entire confrontation with his foot

propped on Bronson's back and his thumbs hooked through his belt loops.

"Listen." Charlie pointed at his hairy friend. "We need your help. I vouched for you. Don't turn me into the asshole here."

"You are the asshole. He doesn't deserve to be carted to some magical cage somewhere. Someone needs to end that motherfucker before he wipes us off the map!"

"Whoa, whoa, whoa. Hey, buddy." The gnome raced toward Chuckles' side and patted his hairy arm. "What's gotten into you, huh? It's only a job."

"Only a job my ass, Pat." The Kilomea thrust a finger at Bronson. "They want us to move fucking Tyro."

"Ha. Good one. Funny. But seriously, we got—" Pat cleared his throat and looked slowly at Bronson, who fixed an icy glare on him. "That? That's Tyro?"

"It's not his real name," Charlie muttered.

"You piece of shit! See how you like it when I kill you." Pat darted forward with a snarl. His eyes flashed silver before the beginning of what would have been a shift if Johnny hadn't leapt over Bronson's prone form and drawn his utility knife.

"It's time to step back now," he warned, the tip of his blade a hair's breadth away from the underside of the gnome's chin.

"Do you know who that is?" Pat snarled.

"Yep."

"And you're saving him?"

"I'm on a case, pal. For now, I'm the only one who lays a finger on him. Understand?"

Pat stepped back slowly. His lips twitched into a sneer and his eyes burned with hatred. "You're working with the goddamn enemy, Charlie."

"What? No. Come on. He's my cousin."

"What?"

"Okay, yeah, I'm working with him and Lisa right now, but he's not my boss or anything. Jesus. That would be sad."

Chuckles growled and stepped away too. "You're in way too deep this time. We're out."

"Hey, guys. Hold on."

"Charlie." The bounty hunter pointed at his cousin with the tip of his knife. "Fix it."

"Yeah, yeah. Of course. That's what I do. Pat! Chuck! Hold on a sec." The mohawked dwarf hurried after his transport buddies and Johnny strapped the knife onto his belt before he turned to look at Bronson. "You have some serious explainin' to do. You know that, right?"

The Harford heir merely returned his stare and remained silent.

"Yeah. But I guess there's much more weighin' on your conscience right about now too."

"Johnny." Lisa glanced at the still-unconscious Agnes whom they'd hog-tied like Bronson and somehow managed to drag into the trees before they gave up. "What's going on with her?"

"Charlie doesn't wanna touch her."

"What?"

"It's some kinda superstitious somethin' or other. I have no clue."

"Well, if she wakes up anytime soon, I'm very sure a few ropes around her wrists aren't gonna stop her. We need to get them both somewhere seriously secure as soon as possible."

"Yup. Secure, untraceable, unbreakable, and with as many goddamn wards as we can get. I know."

"So if Charlie can't get his friends off the revenge train and willing to help us…" She shrugged. "What's our Plan B?"

"Give it a minute, darlin'." Johnny rubbed his mouth and turned toward the tree line, where Charlie's low, imploring voice carried wordlessly toward them. "That dwarf's spent a lifetime perfectin' the art of talkin' the horns off a goat. They'll come around."

His cousin's negotiating skills must have been incredibly

honed because he returned with his friends only five minutes later, grinning like he'd won some grand prize. "All good, 'coz."

"Uh-huh."

Chuckles and Pat moved to Agnes without looking at the bounty hunter or his partner. They took extra care to not look at Bronson on the ground behind Johnny as they hefted the dark witch between them and carried her through the trees.

"Shit," Pat muttered through his teeth. "A tiny witch like this feels like she weighs three hundred pounds. What the hell?"

"All right." Johnny stooped beside Bronson, grasped the shifter's arms that were tied behind his back, and hauled him to his feet. "You can walk. So walk."

When he passed Charlie and his cousin's suspiciously unwavering grin, he paused. "How did you convince 'em?"

"Come on, 'coz. How does a Walker convince anyone of anything?"

"A punch in the face. Excellent weapons. A couple of coonhounds, if the situation calls for it. Threats to skin a smartass alive…"

Charlie sniggered. "Money. That's how."

"Oh, sure. 'Cause you have loads of extra cash stored somewhere, huh? I hope it wasn't in your bike."

"You truly think I'm stupid, don't you?"

Johnny shrugged.

The mohawked dwarf clapped a hand on his cousin's shoulder and laughed. "I don't promise anyone something I can't deliver, Johnny. Which is why I told them you'd double their fee."

"I'd double their—are you shittin' me?" He lurched toward his cousin and dragged Bronson with him. The other dwarf leapt away and raised his arms placatingly.

"All for the greater good, 'coz. We're stopping a war and helping two hard-working entrepreneurs like Pat and Chuckles. Win-win."

"You little—"

Lisa cleared her throat as she stepped closer. "He's not wrong."

"It ain't his money to throw around."

"Well, it can't be more than you were willing to pay for fifty pounds of marijuana we're not gonna buy."

He grunted and shook his head. "It's Charlie, darlin'. He could've told 'em anythin'."

And he ain't nowhere near in his right mind to tell 'em the most important part.

Bronson remained perfectly silent and cooperative when Johnny slung him into the back of the transport van. Agnes sneered at all of them, her leg tied off with a rag Pat had used as a tourniquet.

Before Chuckles shut the double back doors, a flicker of green light raced around the interior walls like a flash of static electricity and a low hum rose from inside. When the doors slammed shut, all trace of magi-tech security vanished behind the completely blacked-out rear windows.

"Now what exactly was all that?" Johnny asked.

Pat rounded the van from the front, holding a square device with a giant red button in the middle. "This is a magic-dampening frequency," he said and wiggled the device. "It packs a hell of a punch if magic's used inside the perimeter."

"Huh." The bounty hunter glanced at Lisa and raised an eyebrow. "And why don't we have one of those?"

"Well, we've never had to transport our bounties before."

"Do the feds have this kinda tech?"

"Probably not."

He pointed at Pat. "You and me are gonna have us a chat about what you did to rig the van."

Charlie's friends shared an unamused glance. The Kilomea snorted and the gnome folded his arms and regarded Johnny with disapproval. "You're paying us to drive these two assholes who've slaughtered transformed shifters when what we should do is kill them ourselves while we have the chance. The job doesn't include giving trade secrets away."

Huh. A Californian gnome givin' me what for on my own damn case. Shit, this whole thing's gonna bleed me dry.

After a few seconds of staring at the mouthy gnome, he pulled his wallet from his back pocket. One eye twitched with his effort to not lash out instead like he wanted to. He pulled out all the cash he had—almost a thousand dollars in large bills—and slapped it into Chuckles' furry hand. "That's what y'all get for now."

"This isn't anywhere near the price of the job." Chuckles growled disapprovingly.

"Naw, you have to send an invoice for that."

"We don't send invoices." Pat sniggered. "But we take credit cards."

"Fine," Lisa replied. "Johnny, we need to get going."

"Uh-huh." He pointed at the wad of bills. "That ain't job payment. Y'all keep your mouths shut about who you picked up today and who paid you to do it, understand?"

"A thousand bucks in hush money?" The Kilomea snorted. "Man, Charlie said you were cheap."

Johnny fixed his cousin with a scathing glare as the mohawked dwarf snuck to the SUV where Galfrey, Jake, and Hux waited for the others. Charlie seemed completely oblivious and didn't say a word.

"That's only the start." The bounty hunter pointed at the transport team. "You get the rest when Lisa and I finish this job and get everythin' squared away—without word gettin' out about us cartin' Tyro all over California. If I hear one whiff of y'all runnin' your mouths off about this to anyone else, we all know how easy it'll be for me to find you."

Chuckles ran his tongue along one of his long, sharp eyeteeth, then grunted and shoved the wad of bills into his pocket. "Deal."

"What?" Pat glared at his partner, but the Kilomea turned and stalked toward the front passenger door. The gnome sighed and shook the red-buttoned device at Johnny. "Fine. But this is a one-time thing, man. And if you wanna know how I rigged the van to keep magicals in it from getting out, that'll cost you extra."

Rolling his eyes, Johnny moved to the SUV with a piercing whistle. "Boys!"

"Right here, Johnny." Rex barked and pawed at the inside of the rear window from the rental's back seat.

"Yeah, we've been ready to go since forever," Luther added. "Hey, the bloody shifter's gonna take the back, right?"

"He probably needs to lay down and spread out."

"Y'all get in the back."

"Aw, man."

"Oh, sure, Johnny. We see where your loyalties lie."

The hounds scrambled over the back seat as the trio of transformed shifters specifically hunted by Tyro over the last six months opened the rear doors to squash together in the back seat.

Johnny slammed the rear hatch shut, then headed around the side of the SUV and almost knocked Charlie over. "What the hell are you doin' just standin' there?"

His cousin shrugged. "I need my bike."

"Dammit, Charlie. I ain't a damn tow service—"

"Tow service? Is it that banged up?"

"It might be. And it also might not even be where your dumb ass left it when you roared off and got yourself kidnapped."

"Come on." Charlie raised his eyebrows. "Do you honestly want me to sit in the back of your car the whole time? I don't do cages, 'coz. They make me nervous."

The bounty hunter gritted his teeth, stepped back to open the hatch again, and pointed at the hounds. "Then get in. And I ain't waitin' around for you to make sure your ride starts. If it doesn't, you get your own ride to LA."

"Deal." With a broad grin, the shifter dwarf climbed into the back with the hounds, who sniffed him and scampered out of the way of his thick riding boots.

When Johnny slipped behind the wheel, he took a moment to rub his temples and pretend he didn't hear three shifters whispering in the back seat and two coonhounds panting heavily.

I gotta get these fellas off my hands and somewhere safe.

Lisa buckled up and waited for him to remove his hands from his face before she spoke. "Where exactly is this magical-caging friend of yours?"

"LA." He glanced in the rearview mirror and started the engine. "Y'all buckle up. We have a long drive ahead of us and I'm fixin' to hit two magical birds with one goddamn city."

CHAPTER FIVE

Charlie's orange Harley remained untouched on the side of the road, and Johnny continued south before his cousin had lifted the bike out of the dirt. It wasn't much of a head start. The shifter dwarf rocketed past them five minutes later and disappeared around a sharp turn in the highway, his engine's roar a faint echo behind him.

Lisa watched him race ahead of them and paled but didn't say a word.

The bounty hunter refused to make any stops until they reached LA, but no one complained. Hux was still completely shell-shocked, although he muttered more than a few times about how long it took his friends to find him and pull him out of the torture bunker under Tyro's shed in the middle of nowhere.

For the first two hours, Galfrey and Jake filled their friend in on the rest of what had happened since Agnes snatched him from the bar and shoved him into one of Kaiser's getaway cars. After that, the transformed shifters could only speculate about what was happening now and Johnny lost patience.

"Y'all ain't got all the pieces to this situation, so zip it. The last thing we need is more rumors spreadin'.'"

"Okay." Galfrey glared at the rearview mirror. "So fill us in on the rest."

"Active case." He sniffed and shook his head. "Classified."

Lisa pressed her lips together and stared through the windshield.

Oh, sure. The first time I use that line and it's funny, huh?

They arrived in peak LA rush-hour traffic. Johnny almost lost his temper a few times when cars swerved in front of him to squeeze into his lane. The hounds bayed wildly when he thumped the horn in his frustration.

Somehow, Pat managed to keep the transport van behind them the whole time. He thrust his hand occasionally out of the driver's window to flip off anyone who tried to cut in front of him too.

"I hate LA," Johnny grumbled. "Nothin's changed except maybe gettin' worse."

"What do you mean?" Lisa asked and fought back a laugh.

"The last time I was here, kids were livin' under the streets. Now, they're gone and the city ain't any better for it."

"The Everglades are, though."

He surprised everyone when he pulled the SUV up alongside a church.

"What's this?" Jake asked. "I thought you said we were taking the murderers somewhere safe."

"It ain't for them. Stay in the car." The dwarf leapt out with a low growl and the driver's window of the transport van parked behind the SUV rolled down.

"The power of Christ won't compel the cargo in the back of this van," Pat shouted. "We're not letting anyone out here."

The bounty hunter pointed at him. "Don't make me compel you. Stay put."

"Johnny!" Luther howled and pawed at the rear window. "Johnny, don't go in there."

"Yeah, what about us?" Rex added.

"Everyone just wait!" He stormed through the front doors of the church and toward the curved stairwell at the back that would take him to the same crowded, disorganized, stale office he'd visited only a year before.

The hallways beneath the church were empty for the most part. A man in red, yellow, and blue-striped parachute pants paced at the end of the hall and muttered in agitation before he thrust a finger in the air and declared, "In the name of pepperoni pizza."

"Yeah, I'm a fan of pineapple," Johnny muttered.

The man whirled with wild eyes and pointed at the bounty hunter instead. "Blasphemy!"

"Don't knock it until you try it." He stopped at the closed door on his right and knocked three times. The stranger returned to his mumbling and pacing and darted wary glances at the dwarf every time he turned.

"It's open."

Johnny opened the door and poked his head inside. "Hey, Doc."

Doc Leahy looked up from the stack of papers on his desk, his eyes red-rimmed and bleary and his gray hair disheveled. His frown deepened before his eyes widened, and he stood with a smile. "Johnny. I didn't know you were in LA."

"I'm passin' through."

"Well, come in. Come in." With a chuckle, Doc stepped around his desk and gestured vaguely at the perpetual disarray of his office. "I'd tell you I would have cleaned up a little if I'd known you were coming but that's a lie. How are things in Florida, huh? It's been a beautiful summer, I hear. I wish I could have another vacation out there. Miami was something else. How's the academy—"

"I merely built the school, Doc. Beyond that, I have nothin' to do with it. And this ain't a social call."

"Oh?" The man lifted a mug from the desk, took a sip, then grimaced and spat the old coffee into the cup before he set it down again. "Then to what do I owe the pleasure?"

"I'm callin' in a favor." He raised three fingers. "Do y'all have room for three shifters to lay low for a while? This is the safest place I can think of in the state."

"Three shifters." The reformed wizard shrugged. "We have room, sure. I wonder if they wouldn't be safer with the Coalition, though."

"Three transformed shifters." The bounty hunter sniffed. "I thought you had some experience with 'em the first time around. Now things are gettin'—"

"Dicey." Doc nodded. "Yes, I've heard a few things through the grapevine. How long is a while?"

"Until I wrap this case up."

"Ah. I see. Well, of course I won't turn them away, Johnny. Give me a day or two to prepare some space—"

"They're sittin' outside ready to go and I need 'em off my hands and with someone I can trust."

Doc stared at him in bemusement, then conceded with a chuckle and shrugged. "The perks of service work, right? I hope they're not expecting the Ritz-Carlton."

"Trust me, Doc. After the last few weeks, that's what this will feel like."

Galfrey, Jake, and Hux didn't complain about being hidden under the church. After a promise to call Doc when the coast was clear to let the hunted transformed return to their lives, Johnny returned to the SUV that now felt blissfully empty and silent with no extra cargo but his partner and his hounds.

Rex and Luther had, of course, already taken their usual places in the back seat.

"That went well," Lisa said cheerfully.

Johnny cranked the engine and gave her a sidelong glance. "Are you the prayin' type, darlin'?"

"Well…I'm not opposed to it. Why?"

"The Doc's puttin' himself on the line with this one. Someone oughtta pray Kaiser doesn't find those shifters there." Pat pressed the van's horn behind them and made them both jump. Johnny growled and shifted the vehicle violently into drive. "And that I don't toss that damn gnome around by his stupid hippie hair."

It took another hour of crawling through traffic to reach their next stop in south Los Angeles. When they approached the wide, squat building on a property overrun with tall grass and brown weeds, his partner grimaced. "Are you sure this is the right place?"

"Charlie found it. The address ain't changed, darlin'."

The orange Harley was parked in the corner of the cracked parking lot that was almost overrun with weeds. Charlie leaned against the wall and stared at his phone until both vehicles pulled into the lot. He looked at his cousin, grinned, and shoved his phone into his pocket.

"Well, at least he didn't crash and burn on the road." Lisa pointed out the window at the faded marquee on a tall vertical sign. The backlight behind the silhouette of two parted lips biting down on a knife flickered in the evening glow, and the crackling buzz of the neon light on the fritz filled the air. "But The Devil's Playground? Seriously?"

"Trust me. This is exactly where we wanna be." Johnny slid out and was immediately bombarded by questions as his cousin approached.

"Please tell me this isn't only a rendezvous, 'coz." The mohawked dwarf laughed. "Or wait. Are you and Lisa trying to spice things up?"

He ignored him completely and headed to the transport van. "Y'all hang tight for a while. I might need you to drive the van around back."

Pat scowled through the open driver's window. "We're not a taxi service, man."

"Well, maybe you should start. You know, keep the meter runnin' and bill me once the cargo's been delivered."

Chuckles gazed at the shop's sign and sniggered. "I thought this was a pitstop."

"It's the last stop for y'all. Then we go our separate ways." His teeth gritted, Johnny strode across the lot toward the building's entrance.

Lisa stood with her hands on her hips and frowned at the faded, peeling paper notice taped to the front door. "Guests are required to sign a liability waiver upon entry?"

"It doesn't apply to us, darlin'."

"Johnny, what kinda place *is* this?"

"The best kind," Charlie interjected. "Man, I should hang out with you more often, 'coz."

"Nope." The bounty hunter snapped his fingers and the hounds raced away from a pile of discarded and crumpled cardboard boxes they'd been sniffing. "Let's go."

"Smells weird over here, Johnny," Rex muttered.

"Yeah, like…" Luther licked his muzzle and sniffed the bottom edge of the door. He leapt away when his master jerked it open. "Like a torture chamber."

Lisa snorted. "How many torture chambers has he taken you to?"

Johnny held the door open and nodded for everyone to get inside. "My whole damn life at this point."

She forced back a laugh and nodded in thanks before she entered the dark interior. The dwarf started to head after her but Charlie thumped a hand on his shoulder before he slipped past him. "Thanks, 'coz."

He scowled as his cousin raced inside with a renewed pep in his step, then glanced at the hounds as they skirted past his feet. "Don't touch anythin'."

"Come on, Johnny. You can trust us."

"Yeah, since when do we touch anything?"

"No thumbs, Johnny."

"No hands!"

He rolled his eyes and let the door swing shut with a bang behind him.

The last thing I need is to buy merchandise I ain't usin' 'cause my hounds couldn't keep their paws to themselves. Or Charlie.

The interior of the shop was lit mostly by red light and the occasional musty yellow glow from a flickering bulb in the ceiling. The shelves lining the walls were filled to the brim with brightly colored boxes and displays on chipped mannequins that of course hadn't been graced with clothing beneath the straps of leather, silver buckles, and studded accessories.

"Johnny," Lisa whispered. "If you thought we needed a little extra something in our private life, you could have simply said something."

"What? This ain't about us." He jerked his head away from the tickling weight of something that brushed across his head and shoulder and scowled at the leather whips in every color and size hanging from the ceiling. "And I ain't buyin' a damn thing."

"So your friend hangs out in a sex-toy store?" she whispered.

"Naw. Kennedy owns the place."

"Oh, even better."

"Johnny. Hey, check it out." With a snigger, Charlie turned to hold his newest find out in front of him. "Assless chaps. I have a pair, of course, but these are pretty sweet."

The bounty hunter averted his gaze and grumbled, "Sure, if you want folks thinkin' you're compensatin' for somethin' with the front end."

His cousin glanced at the front of the chaps and the attached rubber toy dangling there and quickly tossed the whole ensemble onto the adjacent shelf. "Speak for yourself."

The righthand wall of the shop was decorated with every

imaginable toy including a display of wooden paddles, all surrounded by strings of red Christmas lights. When he reached the desk there, Johnny reached for the bell, then decided to press it with his forearm instead.

It dinged and both hounds barked, and he spun to glare at them.

"What?" Rex snorted. "We're not playing a game?"

"Hit it again, Johnny!" Luther pranced enthusiastically and his tail wagged wildly to send several boxed devices tumbling to the floor. "Hit it again!"

He snapped his fingers. "Y'all settle down. This place ain't hound-friendly."

"That's a new one." The low, sultry voice from behind the curtain of beads over the doorway behind the desk made everyone turn. "But I have to stop you right there and say no dog is too..." The witch who drew aside the curtain of plastic beads stopped when she poked her head through and saw her eclectic group of newest customers. "Johnny."

Rex sniggered. "He's a dog all right."

Luther cackled until Johnny snapped his fingers.

"Kennedy."

The witch slipped fully out from behind the curtains and smirked as she studied him with a raised eyebrow. "It's been way too long." Her smile widened when she looked at Lisa. "And you brought a friend this time."

Johnny's partner stared at him and folded her arms. "You've gotta be kidding me."

"It was a long time ago, darlin'."

Yeah, I knew this was gonna backfire in my face.

"We ain't here to play."

"You aren't?" Kennedy tossed her shoulder-length black hair over her shoulders and leaned forward on the counter so the low cut of her shirt looked even lower. "That's disappointing."

"Again." Charlie shoved his cousin out of the way and rested his hands on the counter to grin at the witch. "Speak for yourself."

Kennedy turned her gaze slowly to the mohawked dwarf and her thick, dark eye makeup gave her even more of a smoldering look in the light. "Who are you?"

"I'm his—"

"He's no one," Johnny interrupted. "And I need a favor."

"Hmm. A personal one, I hope."

"With a job, darlin'." He hooked his thumbs through his belt loops, cast Lisa another sidelong glance, then nodded toward the front door. "I have a couple of bounties in a van out front and need to use a couple of your special cages."

"I see." She leaned forward toward Charlie and narrowed her eyes, still smirking. "What do you need?"

He bit his lower lip. "That's a very, very long list—"

I should have given him the wrong address.

The bounty hunter cleared his throat. "We're on a time crunch here, Kennedy."

"I bet you are." With a low, humming laugh, the witch straightened and gestured toward the doorway behind her. "You're lucky it's slow today, Johnny. I'll meet you out back. A promise is a promise."

She studied Lisa curiously again with the same level of shameless approval she'd given the Walker dwarves, then turned and vanished behind the curtain of beads again.

Charlie practically vaulted over the counter after her. "Hold on a sec—"

"You're stayin' with me." Johnny caught hold of the back of his cousin's leather jacket and hauled him away. "Or I'll kick your ass off the case. Understand?"

Rex snorted. "Bet he'd rather have the witch kick his ass."

"Just to start," Luther added, and they both laughed until it turned to snarls and scuffles on the other side of the room.

Something metallic jangled and clacked against the floor. "Back off, bro. I saw it first."

"And I'm gonna take it." Rex growled.

"Dammit." Johnny spun and only found the hounds when a tray of individually wrapped somethings he didn't want to investigate clattered off the shelves. "Boys!"

When he stalked around the display, Rex and Luther were playing tug of war with straps of black leather, silver loops, and buckles that looked suspiciously like a harness.

The kind not generally used on hounds.

"Y'all cut that shit out."

"It's mine, Johnny. And I'm gonna use it—"

"You wish."

"Hey! Get your own toy."

"Enough." Johnny snapped his fingers, and Rex dropped the unsavory accessory instantly.

With a victorious cackle, Luther spun and tried to run. His master grasped him by the scruff of the neck. "Drop it."

"Aw, come on, Johnny." Brown puppy-dog eyes stared at him as Luther's tail thwacked against his leg and the silver hoops winked in the light. "I won it fair and square."

"I ain't never used one of these before," the bounty hunter grumbled, "but I'm this close to testin' it."

"Why? The whips are over there—"

"Drop it."

Luther whined and barely opened his jaws. The leather slipped from between his teeth and clunked on the floor. "You're no fun anymore, Johnny."

"Git on." He gave the hound a little nudge toward the door and picked up the strange harness before he draped it over the closest hook.

Rex and his brother trotted toward the front door, sniffed everything in their path, and hurried outside when Charlie shoved the door open and stepped into the parking lot.

"So you used to be more fun, huh?" Lisa muttered as she joined the bounty hunter.

He snorted. "This ain't my kinda fun, darlin'."

"But it used to be." It took everything she had to look serious and not burst out laughing. "That's how you know Kennedy, isn't it?"

"It was a long time ago. And she owes me a favor or two."

"Yeah, I bet."

He stopped beside the front door and scowled at her. "Lisa, if you're thinkin' about pickin' up a few things here and takin' them home with us, I'm puttin' my foot down. It ain't gonna happen."

She finally did laugh and raised both hands in surrender. "Trust me, all this is way out of my league."

Johnny cleared his throat and took a final sweeping glance of The Devil's Playground's wares. "Yeah. Mine too."

"So you didn't like it?"

He threw the door open and stormed outside with her laughter trailing after him.

One drunken night over thirty years ago and it's still comin' to bite me in the ass.

CHAPTER SIX

After more than a little scuffling, cursing, shouting, and nonstop barking in the back lot of The Devil's Playground, Kennedy finally stormed out of the rear entrance with a long metal rod in her hand. She jabbed the crackling device into Agnes' shoulder blades and the dark witch dropped to the asphalt with a grunt.

After that, hauling Agnes and Bronson inside and down the long flight of stairs into Kennedy's underground club was far easier. Charlie followed the shop owner like a starving stray, asked about all the props and gear stored downstairs, and sounded—at least to Johnny—like he hadn't cleaned his act up at all.

He sounds like a damn addict switchin' one thing for the other. At least it's right where I can see it.

Pat and Chuckles looked way too terrified to enter the empty club decorated with handcuffs, swings, what looked like torture implements, and real cages and instead, made it a point to haggle with Johnny for numerous extra made-up fees simply for getting them involved in this in the first place.

"Pick a goddamn number," he grumbled as the metallic clang

of steel-barred doors against the steel frames of cages echoed from the next room. "And she'll give you the card number."

Lisa stared at him but the bounty hunter turned away toward the private room Kennedy had specifically set aside for Bronson's interrogation. With a sigh, she turned toward Pat and pulled her phone out. "Do you guys take PayPal?"

The gnome sniggered. "Yeah. Send it to friends and family, though. We're not paying fees for this crap."

She glanced warningly at him as Chuckles nudged his friend so hard, the gnome stumbled sideways into the kind of swing that didn't belong on a playground. Pat yelped and swatted the straps before he skittered away. "Does he always take you on his cases with him?"

"I'm sorry?" Lisa raised an eyebrow.

"Look, Charlie's cousin might be a hotshot bounty hunter, but he can't multitask. It makes sense that he takes his secretary with him to handle the rest of it."

After five seconds of brewing silence, she cleared her throat. "You saw the bullet hole in the dark witch's leg, right?"

"So?"

"Secretaries don't usually carry guns, either."

Pat's eyes widened and he glanced briefly at the shoulder holster peeking out from beneath her light windbreaker before he clamped his mouth shut.

"Hey, guys!" Charlie careened toward them, grinning like an insane dwarf as he rubbed his hands vigorously together. "This place is insane, right? You should stick around. I saw a sign for happy hour starting at midnight and I'm very sure it wasn't talking about drinks, know what I'm saying?"

"You're insane," Chuckles muttered. "We're out, Charlie."

"Are you sure?" Another cage door slammed shut and made the mohawked dwarf jump a little before he uttered a growling laugh. "'Cause I could stay here forever."

Lisa rolled her eyes. "Go see if Johnny needs any help."

"Nah, he's fine." The sharp clack of Kennedy's heels across the dancefloor at the back of the club's main room made him turn. "But she might need a little extra Walker to help her with—"

"Charlie."

"Yeah, yeah. Thanks for the help, guys." He gave Pat and Chuckles eager fist-bumps, which they reluctantly returned, then spun and headed toward The Devil's Playground's owner. "Catch ya later."

Shaking her head, Lisa opened the PayPal app on her phone and fixed Charlie's friends with a tight grimace. "I need an email address."

They quickly got the particulars out of the way and settled on a number—including the transport fee, the rest of their hush money for not saying a word about Johnny's two infamous bounties, the spiked cost of sitting around and waiting for him to do his business at multiple stops, and an added thousand dollars for what Pat called "pain and suffering."

Lisa sent the money straight from the Johnny Walker Investigations account and flashed the confirmation briefly at Charlie's friends. Neither one of them looked close enough to see she hadn't sent payment to friends and family but a "trusted business."

"It was a pleasure doing business with you."

"Not even a little, lady." Pat folded his arms. "If you're not gonna kill that asshole who's been killing our kind, the least you could do is rough him up."

"Yeah." Chuckles growled. "His face could use a makeover."

"We'll take it into consideration." There was more sarcasm in her voice than she'd intended but the transport team either didn't pick up on it or didn't care. They turned and hurried toward the staircase. "And if anyone working for Kaiser approaches you—"

"We'll run like hell." Pat tossed a hand in the air without bothering to turn around. "Got it."

"I intended to say give us a call. We might be able to—" The door at the top of the stairs shut abruptly and she sighed. "Or not. Fine."

Lisa shoved the phone into her pocket and turned to gaze at the darkly lit club that she assumed would fill with the darker side of LA's nightlife after midnight. With a grimace, she stepped around a table displaying handcuffs and moved to the room where Johnny had gone to start questioning Bronson.

You couldn't pay me to hang out in here after midnight.

The door to the private room was open and her partner leaned against the wall just inside, his arms folded as he stared at Bronson inside a physical cage. "It looks like we finally get to question Tyro."

"Uh-huh." He sniffed. "There ain't a ballroom full of high-society yuppies to cut our little chat short this time."

Although the shifter's wrists were bound behind his back and he sat against the far wall of the cage with his legs crossed beneath him, he still raised his chin and stared at his captors with all the courteous etiquette that had been bred into him. "Someone will eventually notice I'm gone."

"You bet." Johnny pushed away from the wall and grasped the back of a low chair upholstered in black velvet to pull it front and center. A ball-gag and something like a feather duster clattered onto the floor but he ignored them and turned the chair to face his most confusing bounty yet. "I think it's best for both of us if you start talkin' and fast. 'Cause we have a long list of questions and you're gonna answer 'em."

"Johnny, I probably wouldn't sit on that," Lisa muttered.

He froze and glared at the cushioned seat. "Aw, hell. Kennedy!"

"I'd forgotten how much I like hearing you shout my name," the witch crooned as she appeared in the open doorway. "but I imagine you want something a little different this time."

Lisa folded her arms and raised her eyebrows at her partner.

Johnny cleared his throat. "It ain't what it sounds like."

The witch chuckled. "Do you know another Kennedy?"

"Naw, that ain't—" He clenched his fists, turned toward her, and added, "Do you have any chairs that ain't been…uh, used in these rooms?"

"What kind of place do you think I run here?"

Lisa snorted. "It's a little hard to get the wrong impression."

"Don't knock it until you try it, Light Elf." Kennedy scrutinized her with a challenging look. "I didn't get your name."

"Kennedy, Lisa. Lisa, Kennedy." Johnny gestured abruptly from one to the other. "That's outta the way. Now back to how about—"

"There's nothing wrong with the chair, Johnny." The witch slid her hand along the doorframe. "Every room gets washable covers. But if you want me to grab that big stick again, I'm happy to help you."

Lisa closed her eyes. "Oh, my God."

Out in the main room, Rex sniggered. "This two-legs is nuts."

"Tell me about it, bro. All this leather here and no one to chew on it. Not even us."

"Yeah, what does Johnny think we are, huh? Cats?"

Oblivious to the hounds' conversation, Kennedy smirked at the bounty-hunting duo and shrugged. "It worked well enough on the blood witch. It might help loosen this shifter up a little."

"*That* stick." Johnny sighed. "We're fixin' to question him, darlin'. Not put him down. Do you have anythin' with a little less punch?"

"How about a pair of jumper cables?"

Lisa spun toward her. "Please tell me you keep them in your car."

"No, that's my extra set. But I do have a special pair in the back."

"Did someone say jumper cables?" Charlie skidded to a stop behind the open doorway, his eyes wide and his mouth practically hanging open in excitement. "'Cause let me tell you, I've always wanted to—"

"Dammit, Charlie. No." Johnny pointed at him. "This ain't a vacation. You do that shit on your own time."

Bronson snorted in the cage and shook his head. "I'm starting to think you've lost your touch, Johnny."

The bounty hunter scowled at him and rubbed his mouth before he extended an open hand toward Kennedy. "On second thought, the giant cattle prod ain't that bad an idea."

"Or..." The witch slipped past him and opened a panel in the wall above an array of "instruments" dangling on hooks and stepped aside. "We could turn the voltage up a little. He is a shifter."

"Voltage." Lisa inclined her head in confusion. "Okay, let me get this straight. You run a...store by day and a club by night where people arrive to be electrocuted by you?"

"Oh, that's not the half of it." Kennedy wiggled her eyebrows. "Nothing's off-limits down here and I'm rarely the one who pushes the buttons." Her gaze flicked toward Johnny. "With a few exceptions."

"Do you hear that, Bronson?" Johnny nodded at the shifter in the cage. "Unless you like gettin' shocked, you might wanna cut out the smartass remarks and start tellin' us why you're runnin' around callin' yourself Tyro and—"

A light click rose from the panel beneath Kennedy's hand and a quick blaze of silver light sparked across the metal cage. Bronson snarled and jerked away from the bars he was leaning against. His poor attempt to leap to his feet ended when his head thunked against the ceiling bars.

"Hey!" The bounty hunter rushed toward the witch. "No one told you to start flippin' switches."

She pursed her lips at Bronson. "Too much?"

"Okay, everyone out!" Lisa clapped and pointed toward the main room. "Now."

Johnny jerked Kennedy's hand away from the wall panel of cheap tricks and ushered her toward the doorway with a scowl. She chuckled and swept out of the room but almost collided with Charlie when he stepped in front of her and grinned. "What else can you do?"

"That caught your interest, huh?"

Lisa took Johnny roughly by the arm to pull him aside. "This was a bad idea."

"I know." He scratched the side of his face through his wiry red beard and wrinkled his nose as Charlie muttered something and Kennedy responded with an unrestrained laugh. "I should have known to keep him away from a place like this."

"Well, yeah. Everyone should stay away from a place like this. But I'm talking about Bronson."

"He'll talk."

"It has to be without frying him, Johnny. Do I want to, knowing that he's Tyro and that he tried to kill your cousin? A little. But we have to do this by the book. He has way too many connections and Jasper Harford will be devastated enough when he hears what his son's been up to. Sending Bronson home scarred from electro-shock torture won't help."

The dwarf frowned and turned slowly to meet her gaze. "I was bluffin'. You should know that."

"Oh, sure. Maybe you were." She raised her hands in exasperation before they slapped against her thighs. "Your BDSM friend wasn't, however. She has to stay out of this."

"No shit. I'll take care of it."

"Uh-huh."

"All right, cut it out." He headed toward his cousin, who looked like he'd died and gone to heaven now that Kennedy was seated on his lap on one of the black velvet couches arranged around the small dancefloor.

Charlie grinned. "I didn't do anything, 'coz. I swear."

"I ain't talkin' to you."

"I haven't done anything either," Kennedy added. "Yet."

"Do I need to make you go check and can you tell me right now whatever security you have on the blood witch in that other room is squared away?"

"She's unconscious, Johnny."

"Uh-huh. It's only the dead ones who don't wake up."

Kennedy slung her arm around Charlie's shoulders and gave the bounty hunter a deadpan stare. "If I told you I put more wards and seriously high-powered repellents around that witch than anyone else I've had to tie up down here before, would that satisfy you?"

"You're killin' me," the shifter dwarf muttered.

Johnny pressed his lips together and his nostrils flared, but his cousin was an even worse multi-tasker. "I'll take you at your word. But until Lisa and I get what we need out of the shifter, y'all gotta stay out of our case. Hands off the electricity. Understand?"

"Perfectly." Kennedy inclined her head with a playful smile. "We'll stay busy."

"Yeah, keep it to yourself." With a grunt, he returned to Lisa. "Agnes is still out and locked up tight. She's in for a rough surprise when she comes to but for now, she's outta the way."

"Yeah, so is Charlie." She nodded at the odd pair on the couch. "So many things could go wrong here."

"Far more things will go wrong if we set him loose and let him ride all over the state flyin' his new freedom in everyone's face. I aim to get Bronson talkin' before anyone sets foot in or outta here."

"I hope Kennedy thought to close up shop until we're done."

The bounty hunter shook his head when his cousin's laughter filled the club as the proprietor led him into another private room. "I'd say we have a few hours but he won't last that long."

"Okay, that was too much information."

"Hell, I ain't talkin' about—"

"It doesn't matter." Lisa paused in the doorway of their makeshift interrogation room. "If he's occupied, that's a good thing. It means we can focus on Bronson."

"I am focused."

"Johnny. Hey, Johnny." Luther pranced across one of the couches before he turned in a tight circle and curled in the corner. "We should get one of these at home."

"Yeah." Rex sat on an adjacent couch and sniffed an unknown garment of clothing before his tongue flopped out of his open, panting mouth. "They're super comfy. Dog couches."

He pointed at his hounds. "Don't touch anythin'. And the next time we stop at a hotel, y'all are gettin' a damn shower."

CHAPTER SEVEN

Johnny pulled the private room's door shut behind him but before he could start the questioning, Bronson began to speak.

"It's not like you discovered some giant secret."

"Oh, yeah?" He stalked toward the chair and sat.

Lisa jumped on his bluff and went to the panel in the wall, which was the only real leverage they had if he decided to not keep talking. The shifter's eyes widened when she pointed at the controls, and he tried to scoot his back away from the cage bars.

"Then how come you were tryin' so hard to not get unshifted when we caught you?"

Bronson swallowed. "Because I wasn't supposed to be there."

"No shit. No one's supposed to be tied up, dragged away, and locked in a room with some other asshole callin' the shots. Includin' the transformed dwarf you snatched today."

"You realize that's exactly what you did to me, right?"

"Sure." Johnny shrugged. "The difference here is I ain't fixin' to kill you after we're done. As long as you don't make me change my mind."

"You can't kill me."

"Wanna bet?"

"Do you want my dad pulling all his strings to take you down?" Bronson leaned back against the cage bars when he realized Lisa wasn't quite ready to pull the electric trigger. "You guys looked very friendly at the gala the other night but Jasper Harford puts his family above everything else, even when he has no idea what's going on."

"Tough guy pullin' the daddy card. That's a first."

"We know you're the one responsible for killing dozens of transformed shifters in the last six weeks," Lisa added. "We know you're working with Kaiser on the side. Your uncle Langley."

The prisoner grimaced.

"And we know you're usin' your old man's name and connections to cover it all up and play the good Harford heir at the same time," Johnny countered. "So now's the part where you tell us why."

The young shifter didn't need much more prompting than that and it only took him ten seconds to start spilling his guts. "I only wanted to get the bastards who killed Addison."

"Your anger's understandable," Lisa said with a nod. "But not your targets. The transformed you had a run-in with that night didn't kill your fiancé, Bronson. Kaiser's posse did."

Johnny sniffed. "It's kinda strange for a shifter mournin' the love of his life to go after innocent magicals when he saw the guys firin' the guns with his own eyes."

"They're not innocent," Bronson all but snarled. "The natural-borns on the docks that night might've pulled the trigger, but we would never have been caught in that mess if that bastard Galfrey hadn't taken her away from me."

"Galfrey told us he let her go."

"Yeah, so one of his thugs could hold her back while the shots were fired." The young shifter uncrossed his legs and leaned forward. "What Addison and I were doing there—what we were to each other—was none of his goddamn business. And because he saw a transformed and a natural-born together, he assumed I was one of Kaiser's idiots. It's his fault she's dead."

Lisa and Johnny exchanged a glance. "Does your uncle know about this?"

"Of course he knows. I went to him first."

"Because you were already workin' for him—"

"No. I stayed out of his stupid war games my whole life because I thought he was insane. He was the only one who could help me track the bastards who still need to pay for killing her but he refused."

"He wouldn't help you?" Lisa regarded him with open disbelief.

"No, he's useless." Bronson grimaced, tried to roll his shoulders back, and failed when his awkwardly bound wrists made it impossible.

"And you decided you had enough knowledge of what he was doin' to play shifter-god all on your own." The bounty hunter folded his arms and crossed one leg over the other. "Plus all your old man's money. You had more than enough resources but none of that did much good when tryin' to hunt three transformed shifters already on the run. Especially when transformed are prone to wanderin' around."

The shifter rolled his eyes.

"You know." Lisa tapped her fingers against her lips and feigned intense concentration. "I wonder how upset Langley will be when he hears you poached his dark witch to do the hunting for you."

Bronson scoffed. "He'll care about it as much as he did to hear his guys killed Addison. My uncle didn't lift a finger to help me."

"Now that's interestin'." Johnny twirled his hand in a keep-going gesture. "Why wouldn't he jump to correct a misunderstandin' like that?"

"It wasn't a misunderstanding! Those fucking transformed murdered her and Kaiser did nothing to make them pay."

"He knows you're Tyro, doesn't he?" Lisa asked. "It makes sense. Until a few weeks ago, Tyro was targeting all the transformed shifters who refused his offer and took care of all the dirty work for him."

"Then you started gettin' greedy," Johnny added. "You and Agnes flushed out transformed on your own and killed whoever you wanted simply because your daddy didn't know and your uncle didn't care."

"They got away," Bronson snapped. "And if my uncle—my own family—wouldn't help me, I had to do it myself."

"Listen, I get wantin' revenge." Johnny leaned forward in the chair. "I let it eat me up too once."

"Johnny—" Lisa said warningly.

"Naw, I reckon he ain't ever heard this side of the story from someone who's been there, darlin'. It might put things into perspective a little."

"What? You wanna tell me getting revenge won't make Addison come back? I'm not an idiot."

"Maybe not but you're actin' like one."

"Right." The shifter hissed angrily. "Because you're sitting there in a chair and I'm in a cage. And you think you can tell me that making those bastards pay for what they did to Addison won't make me feel any better. You can't change my mind."

"Now, see, that's where you're wrong." Johnny propped his forearms on his thighs and clasped his hands together. "I got my revenge, son, and it felt every bit as good as I knew it would. Not nearly as good as not havin' to settle the score in the first place, but I can live with that. What I'm tellin' you is how goddamn stupid it is to take all that rage out on an entire faction of shifters who ain't the ones you're blamin' for Addison's death."

"No." Bronson leaned back against the bars and shook his head. "You're wrong. They're all to blame."

"Is that what your uncle told you?" Lisa asked.

"I can think for myself!" The young shifter snarled again and his eyes blazed with silver light. Fortunately, he didn't try to shift but Lisa raised her hand toward the panel on the wall anyway. "It's everyone else who can't see it. Kaiser's stupid offer worked for a while but now, he's completely lost control."

"Over what?" Johnny grumbled.

"All of it. The few transformed who are smart enough and decent enough to take his offer are the outliers. But the rest?" Spit flew from Bronson's lips as his voice rose to a shout. "The rest are exactly like Galfrey. They can't stand the thought of shifters being able to choose who they want to spend the rest of their lives with. They've judged natural-borns from the beginning. And they hate us because we've been like this forever and they have to deal with the fallout from thirty years ago. That was forever."

Johnny snorted. "Only the blink of an eye, really."

"They think they know who we are and what families like mine stand for. But they ruined it all and they won't stop trying to keep us apart."

"You mean couples like you and Addison," Lisa added.

"I mean anyone." Bronson's chest heaved. "Galfrey couldn't stand to see us together. He couldn't believe Addison wanted to be there on the docks with me. They'll never change their minds about us so it's us or them."

"It sounds like you're lumpin' all transformed into the same boat. If that was Galfrey's crime, man, you're committin' the same one."

"No, I'm settling the score. And you're a dwarf who thinks he's way smarter than he is."

Johnny sniffed and shrugged. "You're still the one in the cage."

Lisa stepped forward. "Everyone who knew you and Addison together knew her background, right? That her mother is a transformed shifter."

Bronson's jaw muscles clenched and unclenched. "Yeah."

"She was from Sacramento. We've met her parents. They're

nice people and they're far outside the social circles you and your family have run in for a long time."

"That didn't matter."

"Not to you and Addison. But you two had many differences to overcome—more than merely being from different shifter factions." She glanced at her partner, who fixed her with a curious look. *Yeah, he's usually the one to push all the hot buttons right off the bat but I'm running with this.* "Bronson, are you even sure it would have worked out between you two?"

"What kind of a question is that?" The shifter swallowed and seemed to deflate against the bars of the cage. "We were happy. Nothing else would change that."

"But y'all were way too different to make it work, right?" Johnny leaned back in his chair again. "Unless the whole point was to show other transformed that you, Kaiser, and the natural-borns could be trusted so everyone else would take his offer to join the shifter club."

Bronson glared at him but said nothing.

All right. So marryin' Addison Taylor wasn't merely a ploy.

"We weren't as different as you might think," the shifter muttered, then quickly lowered his gaze to the floor of the cage. He looked surprised by his words and considerably less full of fiery revenge now.

"And I imagine you still have loads of secrets runnin' through your family," Johnny pressed. "Langley bein' Kaiser and you bein' Tyro are merely the tip of the iceberg. What else are you hidin' behind that Harford name, huh?"

"What?" Now, the guy looked genuinely confused. "My father doesn't know about any of this if that's what you're asking."

"No family secrets, then?"

Bronson laughed bitterly. "You're walking down a dead-end if you think Jasper Harford has any secrets. He's an open book for the entire magical world to read whenever they want. And he's as clean as they come."

The dwarf shrugged and shifted in the chair. "I ain't talkin' about your old man. I mean the other side of your family."

The young prisoner blanched instantly and uttered a low growl. "I have no idea what you're talking about."

"Your poker face says somethin' different." Johnny stood and took two steps closer to the cage. "So go ahead and tell me about your mama."

Bronson clearly struggled against trying to lunge toward the cage—he most likely wanted to rip his throat out—and swallowed thickly.

Now we're gettin' somewhere.

"My mother's dead."

"Yeah, we know. It must've been rough for you as the only son of *the* Harford without his mama around. Tryin' to find time to spend with as much family as you have and the only other option is your uncle. And that's only legally, though, right? It ain't by blood."

"What?" A little color returned to Bronson's cheeks and he looked downright confused.

"Helice Harford was adopted by the Applemans," Lisa added. "Did you know that?"

The young man responded with a bitter, strained laugh. "Of course I know that."

Johnny raised an eyebrow.

Well, damn. I thought that might have put a wrench in his gears but he didn't even blink.

"Everyone knows," Bronson continued. "My parents made it public knowledge when they founded The Appleman House. Trust me, I'm well aware of the kind of legacy I have to live up to."

"So far, it looks like you're doin' a piss-poor job of it," the dwarf added. "The way I see it, your uncle's bitterness toward transformed shifters is somethin' he passed on to you simply by bein' around. It ain't a genetic thing. What do you reckon your folks would think if they knew who Tyro was?"

"My father would never believe it," the shifter all but spat. "He's too naïve. So good luck trying to convince him of anything without proof."

"The proof's sittin' in a cage right in front of us, son."

"What about your mother, then?" Lisa asked. "What would she think?"

Bronson swallowed and glanced briefly at the floor of the cage before he muttered, "She's gone so that doesn't even matter."

"But if she were still here." She stepped toward the cage and folded her arms as she regarded him unflinchingly. "She'd tell you that you have to stop waging this war between shifter factions, wouldn't she? And she'd tell you that everything your family has built is completely at odds with what you're doing. You have to see that—"

"They killed Addison." He snarled with suppressed fury. "And they won't stop until they've brought everything my family built to its knees. The only thing transformed shifters want is to level the playing field and if they won't play nice, why the fuck should I?"

Johnny scowled at the young, disillusioned magical and shook his head. "You ain't had a sit-down with a single one of these transformed since Addison, have you?"

Bronson's eyes flashed silver again. "There's no point."

"Well, what if I told you—"

The door to the private room opened and Charlie cleared his throat. "Johnny."

"Dammit, Charlie. Not now. I told y'all to keep clear while we had our talk here."

"There's something you need to see, 'coz. And it's…uh, big."

Johnny turned and met his cousin's wide eyes as the mohawked dwarf poked his head through the doorway. "Go show the witch out there waitin' for ya."

"She's the one who brought it up. I'm serious. You wanna come see this."

The two partners exchanged a doubtful glance before Lisa nodded and walked to the door. "Okay. We'll take a quick break."

"Are you shittin' me?"

She looked warningly at him and nodded at the door.

With a grunt, Johnny pushed out of the chair and pointed at Bronson. "I know there's somethin' you ain't tellin' us. Otherwise, you wouldn't be spoutin' all this bullshit that makes you sound like you lost your damn mind. 'Cause I also know you're smarter than all this. Use this time to decide how you wanna keep goin'. I have nowhere else to be tonight."

He stepped out of the room and pulled the door shut behind him.

Lisa, Charlie, and Kennedy were huddled together in the main room of the empty underground nightclub and he strode toward them with a scowl. "What the hell's so damn important I gotta put crackin' Bronson on hold?"

His cousin smiled tentatively, looked more confused than excited, and held his phone up. "You're not gonna believe this."

CHAPTER EIGHT

"So we were talking," Charlie continued. "Me and Kennedy. I was telling her about this whole thing with Tyro and Bronson and why we're out here doing this instead of…well, you know. Anything else—"

"Hold up." Johnny pointed to his cousin and the owner of The Devil's Playground in turn. "Y'all are tellin' me you spent all that time talkin'?"

"Well, it didn't start that way," Kennedy responded and trailed her fingers down the side of Charlie's neck. "I guess I'm a sucker for pillow talk."

"That ain't what I need to hear." The bounty hunter shook his head.

Lisa had a hard time hiding her amusement when Charlie grinned at the dark-haired witch who was slightly taller than him and wiggled his eyebrows.

"Are y'all gonna get to the damn point?"

"Yeah. Yeah, here." The shifter dwarf held his phone again out, which displayed a photo of a smiling Addison Taylor. "I took this picture the last time I saw her at a little get-together with some friends, right? I was trying to show Kennedy how all this started and then… Well…" He looked at the witch and nodded toward his cousin. "Go ahead. Tell them who that is."

"Dammit, we already know who that is—"

"Johnny." Lisa placed a hand on his arm but her gaze was fixed on Kennedy. "Please, wait."

The witch pursed her lips and shrugged. "I've seen her before too. Not in person, of course, but a picture much like this one has been passed around a few times in various circles. I see all kinds of things down here when the nights get wild—"

"Darlin', if you don't cut to the chase, I'm headin' through that door."

"This shifter right here?" Kennedy pointed at Charlie's phone. "That's Azure."

"A what, now?"

The witch rested a hand on her hip and nodded. "At least, that's what she calls herself. Second-generation transformed, whatever that means."

"That she was born to an original transformed shifter," Lisa clarified.

"Sure. That might be it." Kennedy lifted one shoulder in a half-hearted shrug. "It seems she's a badass and from what I've heard, Azure is building an army of transformed shifters—underground, of course, and defensive with the plan to bring everyone together so they can stand against whoever's been picking them off like Whack-A-Mole."

"You mean an army to stop Tyro?" Johnny muttered.

"That good-looking guy you had me put in a cage? Sure. Mostly, the word is Azure's army is getting ready to end this shifter war for good and finally give Kaiser what's coming to him. Again, whatever that means."

For a moment, the club was completely silent. The sound of Luther licking under his raised foreleg snapped the bounty hunter out of his surprise and he snapped his fingers. "Cut it out."

"What?" The hound jerked his head up. "Oh, come on, Johnny.

Your pirate cousin can do whatever he wants with the crazy two-legs, but I can't even lick my—"

"That's Addison Taylor," Johnny grumbled and nodded at Charlie's phone. "Bronson Harford's soon-to-be fiancée before she was gunned down in one of the skirmishes. She's dead."

Kennedy tossed her hair out of her face and continued to trail her fingers up and down Charlie's neck. "I don't know who you guys think is dead but I can tell you right now, that's the same magical shifters have been talking about for the last few months, at least. That's Azure."

"It doesn't make any of this less complicated," Lisa muttered.

"It sure doesn't." After a glance at the door with the captured Bronson Harford behind it, Johnny frowned and pointed at the proprietor. "How the hell do you even know any of this?"

"I've always been into dwarves, Johnny. You know that. I didn't realize I had a thing for shifters too until all the trans-formed started popping out of the woodwork." The witch's coy smile widened as she gave Charlie a smoldering glance. "I guess today's my lucky day. I got the best of both worlds."

"Oh…" The biker dwarf chuckled and pulled her closer. "That was only a taste—"

"Y'all knock it off or go get another room." Johnny rolled his eyes and turned away as the unlikely couple giggled and whispered to each other.

Lisa tapped her fingers against her lips. "This most certainly poses a new problem."

"No kiddin'." He tugged his beard. "Too many goddamn lookalikes are makin' my head spin."

"But what if she's not a lookalike?"

He snorted. "Do you buy into this conspiracy theory? Come on, darlin'. Addison Taylor's been dead for almost four months. It's why Bronson went off his rocker and why the shit brewin' between shifter factions finally hit the fan."

"It's not impossible—"

"Hell, if you know someone who can bring magicals back from the dead, that's somethin' you should have shared with me a long time ago, don't you think?"

"Johnny, we thought—"

"Whoa, whoa, hey!" Rex scrambled out of his cozy, curled-up ball in the corner of the couch to avoid being squashed by Charlie and Kennedy who threw themselves down on it, wrapped in each other's arms. The hound trotted across the floor and growled. "Find your own couch."

Luther burst out laughing. "I had no idea you were into ménage à hound, bro—hey!" He snorted and leapt to his feet when one of Kennedy's heels careened over his head and clattered on the floor behind the couch. "Didn't you just put those back on?"

"Y'all take it somewhere else!" Johnny roared.

"Okay, okay. Jeez." Laughing, Charlie hauled Kennedy off the couch in his arms and hurried toward another empty private room. "Someone has a stick up his ass, huh?"

"Is that something you're into?" The witch simpered.

"Jesus Christ." With a furious scowl, Johnny turned to Lisa. "You were sayin'?"

She waited for the door to slam shut on the other side of the club and cleared her throat. "We thought Bronson and Carp were two completely different people at first. That there was no way Jasper Harford's son could possibly be one of Kaiser's employed shifters at that farm. But we were wrong about that. Not to mention the fact Bronson's been living three different lives this whole time."

"And you think that gives us a good leg to stand on in believin' this malarkey about Addison Taylor bein' this Azure shifter?" Johnny snorted. "I ain't puttin' stock in half the crap that comes outta Kennedy's mouth. The witch knows how to find a soft spot and play it to her advantage, and I think her brain's as scrambled as Charlie's after all the wild nights she hosts down here."

Lisa grimaced. "I don't need any more visuals, thanks. But I still think we should look into this."

"Darlin', we saw Bronson and his two other secret lives with our own eyes. In action. We saw Kaiser bein' Kaiser and recognized him as Langley the first time we laid eyes on his—"

"Picture?" She spread her arms impatiently. "That's as much proof as we have about Addison Taylor being dead. Plus, we've heard it from every single source, Johnny. No one found a body. She didn't wash up somewhere else on the bay and wasn't pulled from the water with fatal bullet wounds in her chest. And the transformed community is much more aware of what's happening than the natural-born shifters are. If they knew about Addison and Bronson, they'd also know bringing Addison Taylor back from the dead would only stoke the flames even more. Right?"

"Huh." Johnny sniffed and smacked his lips. "So they're puttin' a new name to a face most don't even know and givin' their cause somethin' to rally behind."

"Right. Except that so far, it sounds like Langley and Bronson have no idea. That might be the point. And if Azure, whoever she is, is uniting all the transformed to end the skirmishes and put Kaiser in his place—"

"Then this will end up turnin' into an all-out bloodbath. Shit." He paced across the club's main room and glowered at the bar in the back. "And it'll give Kaiser even more of a reason to build his army. He'll get all the natural shifters involved until the rest of the world can't keep ignorin' this and shovin' it all under the rug."

Lisa swallowed. "If this is true, we have to find Azure."

"It's a hell of a stretch, darlin'."

"Like every other aspect of this case, right?"

They stared at each other and finally capitulated with a rumbling sigh. "Fine. We get a few names and details from Kennedy, then we—"

A massive explosion rocked the club. Huge chunks of wall

blasted into the main room and flared with blinding red light. Johnny lunged toward Lisa and knocked her prone before the door spun off its hinges and would have done the same thing with far more disastrous results. A blaring alarm cut out everything but the wild barking of the hounds.

"Johnny! Don't worry, Johnny. We'll get her."

"Holy shit, what is that—Johnny, look out!"

He raised his head from where he hunkered over Lisa's body in time to see a blazing red streak of light before it struck him in the face. Every muscle in his body seized and before Lisa could call his name, he blacked out.

<h1 style="text-align:center">CHAPTER NINE</h1>

Jesus, this shit's worse than a hangover I ain't had in decades.

Johnny stirred on the floor of Kennedy's underground club and felt chunks of rubble, dust, and frayed wiring beneath his hands. The fire alarm still blared obnoxiously and echoed around the room.

He gritted his teeth, pushed to a seated position and leaned back on his hands, and opened his eyes.

The establishment was completely destroyed.

Multiple doors to private rooms had been blown off their hinges. The overhead lights had all been shattered, which left the space dimly lit by the red bulbs mounted around the mirror behind the bar. One of the couches had been overturned and now boasted huge, slashing claw marks through the velvet upholstery.

The click of claws across the floor preceded a giant hot, slobbery lick across the dwarf's face.

"Nope. He doesn't taste dead."

"Johnny, you're not dead!"

Johnny pushed his hounds' heads aside and grunted as he maneuvered one foot under him. "Where's Lisa?"

Right on cue, she groaned and pushed slowly off the floor six feet away from him. Dust, plaster, and chunks of rubble coated her hair. "I'm here."

"Christ, darlin'. Are you okay?"

"I think so." Lisa brushed debris off her windbreaker and gazed around in disbelief. "What happened?"

"Agnes happened." A bare-chested Charlie stalked toward them and he zipped the fly of his jeans as he walked carelessly across the wreckage with bare feet. "I tried to stop her but I swear she's got some kinda crazy extra power I've never seen before."

"Johnny." Lisa hauled herself to her feet and pointed at the room in which they'd held Bronson.

That door had also been ripped completely off its hinges and the frame splintered, and the cage inside had a massive hole ripped through the bars.

"Dammit." The bounty hunter grasped the back of the couch beside him and pulled himself up. "We're right back where we started."

"After one hell of an escape." Lisa's eyes widened when she saw the massive cut on Charlie's bicep, which he now tried to tie off with a bar rag. "You fought her by yourself?"

"Hell no, not by myself." He nodded toward Kennedy, whose neat black hair was now in disarray. Her short black skirt rested crookedly around her hips but she had, however, managed to put her heels on either during or after the debacle. "Kennedy gave her a run for her money."

Hearing her name, the club owner pointed at the long metal electric rod she'd used to subdue Agnes the first time. "I turned that baby all the way up and dared the blood witch to test her luck. If it works on the magicals who get a little too aggressive with their fun and games down here, I thought it would work with a blood witch."

Johnny dusted his black shirt and jeans off. "And how the hell did—"

A puff of smoke burst from one of the open private rooms, followed by tongues of flame that licked around the doorframe. Kennedy stalked toward it in her heels, hefted the fire extinguisher she'd abandoned on one of the couches, and released a hissing spray of white foam and mist. The fire snuffed out instantly and she spun with the extinguisher dangling from one hand. "That had better be the last one."

"And you had better tell me how the hell a lunatic witch locked up in one of your unbreakable cages broke through two of 'em and escaped."

The witch stormed toward him and swung the fire extinguisher onto the couch again. Rex yelped and skittered out of the way to avoid the heavy metal canister thunking him on the side of the head.

"Come on, lady! Do you seriously not see me standing here?"

Luther uttered a low whine and trotted toward his brother. "Dude, you're the same color as the couch now. And the floor. And all the other two-legs—"

"Whose side are you on?"

Johnny snapped his fingers and glared at Kennedy as the previously crisp clack of her heels on the floor was now dampened by the littered wreckage underfoot. Her eyes blazed with indignant fury as she stopped mere inches away from the bounty hunter and thrust a finger in his face. "My club was blown to smithereens and you're trying to blame me for it?"

"The only reason we're here is 'cause you have better security than anyone else in the state," he retorted and waved both hands at the wreckage in a gesture of irritation. "So if the witch broke out, you're the only one to blame."

"You have some nerve, Johnny Walker—"

"And I'm ridin' on the very last one. You forgot to set a ward the right way or didn't lock up as tightly as you thought. Say it now. I ain't nearly as pissed-off by mistakes as I am about lyin' to cover 'em up!"

"Ha!" Kennedy stepped back and positioned both hands on her hips as she raked him with her gaze. "You're one to talk. If we're all being so honest, I'm still waiting for you to clear up your lies."

Lisa folded her arms and stared at the argument brewing in the center of the room. The hounds snuck up beside her, their heads lowered warily.

"Hey, Lisa. You want us to break it up?"

"Yeah, this is weird. We don't even know that two-legs."

She shrugged and muttered, "We'll let them duke it out, boys. This is interesting."

"Uh…okay." Luther sat with a low whine. "You feeling okay?"

"Yeah, are you pissed at Johnny too?"

"Nope."

"I ain't got nothin' to clear," Johnny snapped. "I'm doin' my job."

"Um…guys?" Charlie headed tentatively toward them. "I think it's—"

"Admit it, Johnny." Kennedy tilted her head in a challenge. "You couldn't handle me. I scared the crap out of you thirty years ago and you can't stand the fact that you don't belong in a place like this with a witch like me."

"Damn right I don't. I should be this much closer to stoppin' a damn shifter war ragin' across the entire country. Instead, I'm standin' here yellin' at you. Come on. Do you know how many contacts I have who do what they say they're gonna do when I call in a favor?"

"How dare you? I've handled every single lockup you and your contacts sent my way over the years, and this is not my fault!"

"Guys!" Charlie shouted.

They both spun toward him and shouted, "What?"

The mohawked dwarf cleared his throat and pointed at the

narrow door set in the far wall of the club beside the dancefloor. "We were both in the control room."

"Dammit, Charlie. What does that have to do with anythin'?"

"Oh." Kennedy smoothed her hair away from her face and chuckled. "Right."

"No, it ain't."

"Hold on." She stormed across the room and flipped the light switch on in the control room. A sharp laugh escaped her, followed by the groan and snap of something metal before she emerged with a charred strip of leather in one hand. The dented belt buckle dangled from the end of it. "I guess I got a little carried away giving Charlie the grand tour."

"You're shittin' me." Johnny whirled on his cousin. "So it's your fault the damn blood witch who won't die got outta that cage and took our murderin', grief-crazed proof with her?"

His cousin shrugged. "Trust me, Johnny. If you were there instead of me, you would have done the same."

"It was an honest oversight." Kennedy dropped the destroyed belt onto a pile of rubble and dusted her hands off. "We got caught up in the moment."

"I don't believe this. Charlie, you're out."

"I'm what?"

"Get out!"

"Okay, hold on." Lisa placed a hand on Johnny's shoulder and wouldn't let him shrug her off. "Johnny, let's take a break."

"I don't need a break," he grumbled through clenched teeth. "I need my good-for-nothin' cousin to get his useless ass outta my business and quit screwin' everythin' up simply by bein' here."

"It was an honest mistake, 'coz."

"Yeah, on top of a lifetime of dishonest mistakes."

"Johnny." She tugged her partner away by the hand and led him toward the stairs. "Come upstairs with me. We'll get some fresh air and talk about the next steps."

"Next steps?" He whirled halfway around and pointed at

Charlie. "The next step is to get this useless piece callin' himself family outta my life. I mean it. We're done, Charlie. You ain't nothin' but a goddamn headache everywhere you go and it ain't my job to pick up your goddamn pieces."

"Jesus, Johnny. I don't even know—"

"Say somethin' else and I'll make sure it's the last thing you—"

"Johnny!" Lisa shouted and jerked him after her.

They hurried toward the staircase leading to the shop and he whipped his arms out of her grasp before he stormed up in a fury. The hounds scrambled after them and looked over their shoulders at a very silent Charlie and an apathetic Kennedy who tried to clean up what she could of her destroyed club.

When they reached the top of the stairs, Rex and Luther barely slipped through before the door banged shut.

"What is going on with you?" Lisa asked as her partner strode between the rows of The Devil's Playground's merchandise.

"I've had it up to here." The bounty hunter reached the front door, shoved it open, and banged it with a fist before he stepped into the summer twilight outside.

"Johnny, this can't only be about Charlie—"

"It's always about Charlie!" He continued toward the driver's door of the rental and almost jerked it open but paused.

Sure. She ain't gonna argue with me about that part of it, huh?

He turned to look at her where she stood in front of the shop's entrance, her arms folded and her eyebrows raised. "What?"

"It's always about Charlie?"

"When he's weaselin' his way into everyone else's damn business that ain't none of his own? Damn straight it is." He side-stepped toward the rear door and jerked that open instead with a short whistle. "Boys."

After waiting there and glaring at the upholstery for what felt like forever without any sign that the hounds were responding to his command, he turned stiffly. Rex and Luther sat like perfectly well-trained, obedient coonhounds—except they sat on either side of Lisa instead of at their master's feet where they belonged.

"What is this? Some kinda fake-ethics mutiny?"

Luther licked his chops and his tail whisked across the cement. "I have no idea what that means."

"Bro, I think he meant to say mutton."

"Hey, I love mutton! Where is it, Johnny?"

Rex snorted. "We don't have any."

"And that's why he's pissed?"

"Well, it makes sense. Now I want mutton too."

Johnny and Lisa stared at each other before she looked at them. "He's asking if you two are staying with me or going with him."

"Oh, right… Yeah, we're staying with Lisa, Johnny."

Rex looked up at the half-Light Elf and his tongue flopped out over his jowls for a light pant. "Sorry, not sorry."

"Y'all are tryin' to drive me into an early grave, ain'tcha? She promised you treats, is that it?"

"Well, no… But that would be seriously cool." Now both hounds looked pleadingly at Lisa but she ignored them both.

"You can't pin everything that goes wrong on your cousin, Johnny."

"The hell I can't. That damn dwarf can't keep it in his pants long enough to not screw everythin' up."

"Huh." A tight, sarcastic smile lifted her lips slightly. "You know, I wonder if there was ever a time someone said the same thing about you."

His scowl deepened before he slammed the door shut and stalked toward her. "Do you think I can't keep my head in the game?"

"Well, I thought you could. Until you decided it was fair game to keep blaming your own family for whatever might go wrong with this case."

"He is what might go wrong." The dwarf thrust a finger

toward the door. "We had two insane murderers locked up tightly there, right under our noses, and now they're out runnin' round to pick up where they started. It wouldn't even be a possibility if Charlie had more sense than one of these hounds smellin' a bitch in heat."

"Ouch." Rex stood and backed away a few steps. "Way to go for the gut, Johnny."

"Yeah, we can't help ourselves."

"It looks like my cousin can't either."

Lisa shook her head slowly. "We wouldn't have this case if it weren't for Charlie and you know it."

"Yeah, and it's been one massive pain in my ass since the beginnin'."

"And we've come closer to solving this than anyone else who's tried." She stepped toward him and leaned forward to hold him with her wide-eyed gaze. "Because no one's tried before. No one else cares about shifters killing each other except us."

"That ain't—"

"Do you know what I think?"

"Christ, say it already."

"I think you're terrified of finally seeing your cousin starting to clean his act up only to find him dead in the street like every other transformed shifter who wasn't lucky enough to have you there to help them."

Johnny snorted. "That's the dumbest—"

"He's family, Johnny. I know how much that means to you—to both of us. And I know how far you'll go to make sure your family stays safe. Look at everything you've already done for Amanda and she's not even flesh and blood. Charlie is."

"He'd be more useful as a pile of flesh and blood. You know what? Good idea." He started to stride toward the door again, but she stopped him with a surprisingly strong hand on his shoulder and stepped into his path to cut him off.

"Johnny. The closer we keep him, the less danger he's in." She lowered her head to catch his gaze and he finally ripped his glare away from the front door to fix it on her. "He needs us. Honestly, the entire community of transformed shifters needs us, but Charlie's the one who needs us right now. If you want to give him a chance to prove himself, how is he supposed to do that when every little mistake brings you down on him like this? He's trying."

The bounty hunter clenched his teeth and his fists and his legs refused to move.

Goddammit. How the hell is she always right?

He drew a deep breath and shook his head. "He's like a damn kid."

"So treat him like a kid." She raised her eyebrows again. "If it were Amanda here instead of Charlie, would you treat her like this?"

"That ain't—"

"It is the same thing, especially for someone struggling like your cousin has with all his…problems, okay?" Lisa squeezed his shoulder gently. "I get it. You're going with tough love. That's what you do and I don't disagree with it. But tough love doesn't mean you have to be a raging asshole."

"Oh, shit." Luther sniggered. "You hear that, Johnny?"

"Yeah, if anyone else had told you that, they'd be knocked out cold."

Her slow smile was contagious and Johnny responded with a reluctant sigh before he patted the back of her hand on his shoulder. "Accordin' to the hounds, darlin', you got some nerve."

"Please. You've known that from the minute we met."

He snorted. "Sure. But I didn't reckon that it would come back to bite me in the ass over a year later."

"I'll always be here to whip you into shape. That's what partners do."

"Uh-huh."

"And right now, we have a case to work. Maybe one of the

most important ones yet that could save more lives than we real-ized. Charlie's a part of it. Right?"

"Aw, hell." He rolled his eyes and shrugged out from under her hand to turn toward the door. "You already gave your speech, darlin'. Ain't that enough?"

"Nope."

He stared at her for a moment longer, then sniffed. "Well, if it ain't my idiot cousin runnin' me into the ground, it'll be you."

"With pleasure." She patted his shoulder again and gestured toward the door. "So now let's get both our heads back in the game and decide where to go from here. Without making Charlie feel like the scum of the Earth while we're at it, okay?"

"Yeah, you're lovin' this."

"Only when you realize I'm right."

He scoffed, walked to the entrance, and reached for the handle.

The door burst open and Charlie stood there with wide eyes, surprised to see the partners standing in front of him.

"Listen, Charlie—"

"Yeah, we're done. I heard you the first time." The shifter dwarf brushed past his cousin and knocked his shoulder brutally to get him out of the way before he stormed along the outside of the building.

"Now hold up a minute—"

"Make up your fucking mind, Johnny. Either you want me here or you don't."

Johnny stopped walking after his cousin and grunted. "Well, it ain't like I gave you an open invitation."

"That's what I thought." Charlie straddled his bike, kicked the stand up, and shoved the keys into the ignition.

Lisa stopped beside her partner and muttered, "That's not what I meant when I said he's a part of this. Go tell him."

"Shit." He hurried forward and spread his arms in a placating gesture. "Listen, Charlie—"

The roar of the Harley's engine drowned out everything else, and the mohawked dwarf focused intently on the exit of the parking lot.

"Dammit, I have somethin' to say and you're gonna stick around to hear me say it. Charlie!"

With a screech of tires, the orange Harley jerked forward and raced across the lot, and Johnny turned to watch him.

"I ain't huntin' you down simply to talk!"

His cousin raised a hand and gave him the middle finger before he raced down the street with a loud pop from the tailpipe and another angry rev of the engine. The street lamps that illuminated the dark back streets of South LA flickered across his leather jacket and in the next moment, he was gone.

"See?" Johnny spun toward Lisa and gestured in frustration. "He ain't even tryin'."

She folded her arms. "That's probably because you told him you're done trying too."

"Now you're makin' this my fault?"

"It's not always about whose fault it is, Johnny." She shook her head, opened the door to the shop, and let the hounds race inside first. "Things will get easier once you learn that."

The door shut on its own with a bang and he was left in the empty lot to think it all over on his own.

Damn. I'm left alone in front of a sex-toy store with my crazy-ass cousin on the loose and my partner hittin' below the belt. I couldn't make this shit up.

CHAPTER TEN

Johnny reached the bottom of the staircase into Kennedy's club as he sent the text to Charlie that had taken him another ten minutes outside to write.

Don't expect me to haul your ass out of another kidnapping. You're still on the case. Let me know if you want it.

"Well." The witch folded her arms, pursed her lips, and stared at him as he slipped the phone into his pocket and kicked aside a small pile of rubble. "At least I had a little fun before the whole place went to shit."

He ignored the jab and nodded at the wreckage strewn across the club. "Do you have someone to help you clean all this?"

"Johnny, my regular cleanup crew doesn't exactly specialize in explosion control."

"All right." He glanced at his watch, scowled, and sighed. "At least tell me you have a broom and a couple of trash cans."

"Sure. But a broom and trash cans won't magically put the doors back on the hinges and replace the very expensive cages my clientele pays top dollar to rent for a few hours."

Lisa fought back a grimace at the unwanted mental image,

placed a hand on the witch's shoulder, and nodded. "We'll cover the cost of the damages, Kennedy."

"We will?"

"Yes, Johnny. We brought two ridiculously dangerous criminals into her club. We owe her that much."

"Oh." The proprietor batted her eyelashes and studied her with a coy smile. "If you feel like sweetening the deal…"

She removed her hand immediately and stepped away. "I think covering the repairs is enough."

With a chuckle, the witch shrugged and turned toward the back of the club. "You can't blame me for trying. There's another large trash can upstairs and I have a few push brooms here. It'll take a while to clean this mess, so if you change your mind—"

"I won't." Lisa tried to smile and immediately gave up when Kennedy disappeared into the supply closet. She spun toward Johnny with wide eyes. "Is she like that with everyone?"

"She runs a kink club in LA, darlin'. You tell me."

"Uh-huh. And you used to be one of her customers."

Johnny hauled the largest pieces of exploded wall and blasted sheetrock into a pile beside him and grunted. "It was a long time ago. When I was younger and a helluva lot stupider."

"Before you found out what you really want, right?"

He glanced sharply at her and snorted. "It's more like I realized exactly what I don't want. Do you have any other damn important questions you wanna grill me with?"

Lisa laughed and began to remove debris from the couch. "If I think of anything else, I'll let you know."

"Great."

Two hours later, they'd moved the rubble upstairs and into the dumpster at the rear of the building, swept the floors, and turned the couches and chairs upright again. Kennedy gave them a figure for the cost of damages Lisa had been so willing to cover.

"Are you sure that'll do it?" she asked, poised to send the money through her phone.

The witch laughed and waved the question off. "Trust me, even these remodeling costs aren't anywhere close to what I spend on a weekly basis to keep my regulars happy. You wouldn't believe how many—"

"I don't need to know." Lisa sent the money, pushed her phone into her pocket, and nodded. "I'm sorry you have to close for a while."

"Are you kidding?" The witch put a hand on her hip and gazed around the club. "I can turn this into an attraction. People love a good danger zone. You know, I might even keep it like this and test how well it goes over with the regular crowd."

"What?" Johnny shoved his push broom against the edge of the bar in the back. "Then what the hell did we pay you for?"

The woman shrugged. "My time, at the very least."

"Oh, come on—"

"Speaking of which." She looked at her watch and grinned. "I'm about to open down here. Feel free to stick around for the party. Drinks are half-off for the rest of the night."

He pointed at her. "No."

"It's your loss."

"Yeah, my loss was sent to your bank account." He turned toward the stairs and snapped his fingers. "Time to go, boys."

Rex and Luther jumped off the dusted but still damaged velvet couch and padded after their master. "Why aren't we staying, Johnny?"

"Yeah, you never turn cheap drinks down."

"I do here."

They hurried up the stairs but Lisa lingered for a last conversation with the club's owner. "There is something else you can do for us."

"Oh, yeah?" Kennedy bit her lip. "You might want to tell Johnny you plan to stay—"

"No, Kennedy. With the case."

"Of course." The witch brushed her dark hair out of her eyes and smirked. "Like what?"

"We'll follow up with this Azure lead. Do you have any idea where we might be able to find her?"

"I'm merely a club owner. And a witch, of course." Kennedy gestured vaguely. "I provide all kinds of things here but that kind of information is beyond me. You'd have to get in with one of the LA transformed groups for that."

"What kind of group?"

"Well, based on what they're going through right now, I'd probably call it a support group. Maybe even a rally now that they're all talking about Azure." Kennedy drew her phone out and scrolled through her contacts. "There was one insanely hot shifter who came through here a few weeks ago. Boy, was he freaky. He wanted to—"

"Again, I don't need to know those details."

"Suit yourself. Before he left, he gave me this number and said if I came across any other transformed who looked a little more lost than usual, I should give it to them."

"Hmm. And it's that easy to identify a shifter who looks lost?"

The witch grinned. "Everyone who comes here knows exactly what they want, so yeah. Anyone who doesn't know sticks out like a sore thumb."

"Fair enough." Lisa copied the number displayed on the device and nodded. "Thank you."

"Sure. You didn't get it from me, though. The transformed are extremely secretive about…everything, I guess."

"Yeah, and with good reason. If Agnes and Bronson come here to give you any trouble—"

"I'll hit 'em first." Kennedy picked the electric rod up from where she'd propped it against the couch and grinned. "And then I'll look up the phone number for Johnny Walker Investigations and let you know."

"Okay. Have a good—"

Raucous laughter in at least a dozen different voices came from the staircase. The proprietor hurried toward the bar to retrieve the remote from against the wall and the club instantly filled with the loud, fast-paced, heavy beat of hardcore house music.

Lisa grimaced and turned as the first customers staggered drunkenly down the stairs.

"You're welcome to stay," the witch called over the music. "These degenerates are early. The real party doesn't start for another hour or so."

"The third time's not a charm for me on this one." The Light Elf smiled as graciously as she could manage before she scooted around the boisterous group of magicals hell-bent on a wild night she didn't even want to try to imagine. "Thanks for your help."

"Hey, tell Charlie to call the store next time he has a few hours on his hands."

Lisa waved the comment off and hurried up the stairs.

I'm not sure hooking Charlie up with a sex club owner is the best move for either of them. Mostly him.

Johnny and the hounds were already in the car with the engine running when she slipped into the passenger seat. He closed his phone and tossed it into the cupholder. "I talked to Doc Leahy. Our hunted transformed are still on the down-low for now. There's been no sign of Agnes and Bronson at the church either."

"Well, that's good news."

"Uh-huh. I can't believe I didn't think to call earlier."

"There was so much happening 'em in the moment." She strapped her seatbelt on and shrugged. "The good news is they're still safe and hopefully, Agnes doesn't have a way to track them if she doesn't know where we left them. If they stay inside with Doc, they should be fine."

"For how long, though?" He rubbed his mouth and glared at

the steering wheel. "Dammit, what we need is a witch-tracker to play her game back at her."

"Trust me, if I knew someone who had that kind of skill, that would be the first number we call."

"Well, keep thinkin' about it. And don't quit talkin' about next steps now, darlin'. You've been tryin' to get me to move on since we got here. Now would be the time to make a few suggestions."

"You know what I think we should do."

Johnny looked at her with wide eyes. "I still can't read your mind."

Lisa gave him a small conceding smile and rolled her eyes playfully. "Well, we have three options. Maybe the most ethically sound would be to go to Jasper Harford and tell him everything we discovered about his son."

"Beyond breakin' the guy's heart, what good is that gonna do us?"

"At least he'd know. But I agree with you. That would only upset him and I'm very sure the head of the Harford empire doesn't exactly have the kind of resources or connections to go after his son and get involved in a shifter war. Even if he wanted to."

"Which he won't." He cleared his throat. "We could go for the dumbest choice of all and turn it to our advantage."

"Let me guess. That option includes loading up on insane amounts of firepower, taking them to Kaiser's hideout farm, and blasting the place to pieces until he gives us everything he knows about where Bronson might be or how to find him."

"We'd get our drug money back too."

"Johnny, that's a terrible idea and has no advantages whatsoever. Kaiser's smarter than the average criminal mastermind."

"Well, don't give him too much credit. His head's already as big as the state." The dwarf scratched the side of his face and considered what other avenues they could take. "There's no way to know whether or not Bronson and Agnes have already gone crawlin' back to their war boss by now anyhow. So either Kaiser knows we're onto him and his nephew, or Tyro decided to turn it up a notch on his killin' sprees."

"He wouldn't do that." Lisa shook her head but her attention was drawn by the large group of scantily dressed magicals converging on The Devil's Playground's front door. "Bronson knows we'd find a way to pin it onto him if he attacked someone else as Tyro. Especially now that he knows we know it's him."

In the back seat, Luther snorted and shook his head. "You're making my head spin with all that."

"Yeah, can't you two-legs talk about something that isn't a puzzle."

Johnny scowled at the next wave of Kennedy's customers who filtered through the front door. "Did you have a nice little chat with the owner down there?"

"What?"

"You took a while to come up, darlin'. Listen, I ain't one to judge—"

Lisa laughed. "Do you hear yourself right now?"

"I wouldn't give two shits if it wasn't my partner havin' secret talks with the witch who likes to make fellas scream. Professionally."

With a smirk, she slid her phone out of her pocket and pulled up the number Kennedy had given her. "Well, once you get over her strong...uh, forwardness, she's very helpful. And it turns out the transformed shifters are scouting for recruits."

"Is that right?"

"According to Kennedy. This is the number she's supposed to give to any transformed who look a little too lost."

The dwarf glanced at her phone and tried not to look too curious. "Did she give you a name?"

"Nope. But it might give us a good lead."

"Are you waitin' for my permission? Make the call, darlin'."

"I didn't know if you'd rather do it yourself."

"Well, if you're offerin'—"

"I'm not." She leaned away from him with a soft laugh and put the call on speaker.

The line rang three times before an answering machine picked up.

"Do you feel lost, misunderstood, and judged for being who you are?"

"What the hell is this?" Johnny grumbled.

"Shh."

"Do you spend hours out of your day waiting for the news to cover the stories that keep you up at night, only to go to bed feeling like you're next? Are you tired of hiding in your home, sticking to the shadows, watching those you care about disappear without a trace? So are we. It's time to do something about it. You're not alone. There are way more of us than you know.

"Every Monday night at eight o'clock at Reggie's in DTLA, we'll be waiting for you. Change is coming. It's time for all of us to stand together and make the change work for us."

"Well, damn." Johnny frowned at the phone and drummed his fingers on the steering wheel for a moment. "If that ain't a call to arms, I don't know what is."

"That's certainly what it sounds like. Lucky for us we only have to wait until tomorrow." Lisa wrinkled her nose when she saw the time on her phone. "Or I guess it's technically later tonight. We can grab a—"

A giant outburst of drunken laughter and excited shrieks filled the parking lot as another wave of excited magicals surged toward the front door of The Devil's Playground.

Luther bumped his nose against the window and whined. "What's that? Johnny, what did they bring?"

"Whoa, whoa, whoa. Wait." Rex uttered a low growl that ended in a warning chuff. "Johnny, what kinda two-legs puts their friends on a leash? Their two-legs friend?"

The bounty hunter cleared his throat. "The kind I ain't fixin' to stick around and watch."

He shifted into reverse to back slowly through the crowd that couldn't have been dressed for anything but what Kennedy enabled and provided in her underground club. Lisa widened her eyes and stared directly ahead.

"You'll at least let Charlie know where we're staying tonight, right?"

"Sure. But I ain't waitin' for him to pull his head outta his ass again to find us. We're goin' to that shifter meetin' with or without him."

"I have a feeling that might not be entirely true."

He glanced sharply at her and scoffed. "After all this time, you still think I can't get into any place I want?"

"This one might be a little more exclusive than the others. You clean up nice and you can put on one hell of an act when you have to. But I don't think either one of us has any idea how to make our transformed shifter disguises."

"You leave that to me, darlin'."

"Oh, yeah? Do you already have a plan?"

"I have all day to work on it."

CHAPTER ELEVEN

They made a late-night check-in at a Residence Inn in downtown Los Angeles and were both more than a little relieved to finally get a room without suspicious stains, frayed linens, paper-thin walls, or free-loading rodents. More importantly, they had a coffee maker that worked like a charm after the first decent night's sleep they'd had in California since meeting Galfrey.

They were small comforts that felt luxurious, even as they mulled over how exactly they could approach a transformed shifter support group when everyone there would already be highly suspicious.

There was no word from Charlie, but Johnny sent his cousin another text just the same.

Reggie's at 8. More info about Azure.

But even that cryptic attempt to lure his cousin's insatiable curiosity wasn't enough to get a response and it had begun to wear on his nerves.

Lisa watched her partner check his phone for the tenth time in the past hour and leaned back in the chair at the small dining table. "If you're that worried about him, you could track his bike again."

"I ain't worried."

"Hey, if you upgraded your phone, you could track him that way too."

"I ain't gettin' one of those stupid fancy computers everyone calls a phone and I ain't trackin' Charlie."

"Oh." Her smile widened. "So I take it you're starting to trust that he's a grown dwarf and can handle himself when he rides off into the sunset to throw a fit."

Johnny glared scathingly at her and sniffed. "That had better be all this is. If he gets himself snatched a second time by Bronson and his uncle's pet witch, I ain't steppin' in."

"You would and we both know it. But I don't think you'll have to." Lisa pulled up the address for the anonymous shifter group's secret meeting in under half an hour and nodded. "He'll come around."

"How can you be so sure, huh? You only met the guy a few weeks ago."

"He cared enough about this case to bring it to us in the first place so he cares enough to come back. Again." Her attempt to hold back her amusement failed miserably when she snorted a choked laugh. "And I'm very sure by now that Charlie can't stand keeping his hands out of whatever you're interested in."

"Yeah, that ain't changed in eighty years." The dwarf stopped pacing and pointed at her. "Makin' himself at home in ours is one thing. Playin' fetch with my hounds? Fine. He wants to jump on this case with us and prove he's turnin' things around, sure. But if you're tryin' to say you think my cousin's comin' for you next, y'all both got another thing comin'."

"Oh, please." Lisa stood and threw away the takeout boxes from their dinner of to-go burgers before she picked her purse up. "I'm not his type."

"He ain't got a type, darlin'. Woman on two legs. That's about it."

She rested a hand on his shoulder and leaned close to give him a quick peck on the cheek. "You two truly are related."

"Say what, now?"

"Come on. Let's go pretend to be tourists in LA for a while. It's probably not a good look for us if we're early to this meeting we weren't invited to, but I don't want to miss the important information."

"Uh-huh." Johnny turned toward the hounds, who sniffed the floor where they'd demolished their undressed burger patties at least thirty minutes earlier. "All right, boys. Listen up. Y'all are—"

"Yeah, yeah. We get it, Johnny." Rex sat to scratch behind his ear with a rear paw. "We have to stay here alone while you and Lisa go undercover and pretend it wasn't a stupid mistake to leave the hounds behind."

"It's fine. We're used to it." Luther licked the carpet, then turned his head toward the wall beside him and began to lick that instead. "But don't forget to leave the bathroom door open. We can't take ourselves out but at least the shower in this room doesn't smell like something died in it."

Lisa laughed reflexively and immediately covered her mouth when Johnny glanced at her in exasperation.

"Everyone thinks they have me all worked out, huh?" He snapped his fingers and waited for both hounds to look at him. "I was fixin' to say—"

"We totally have you figured out, Johnny."

"Yeah, you're easier than telling the difference between a squirrel and a fox."

Luther sniggered. "Ha. Yep. Wait, Rex, what's the difference?"

"Y'all are comin' with us," Johnny snapped and pointed at the door. "A few extra pairs of eyes and ears on this place will do more good than harm. As long as y'all can keep your mouths shut in a bar full of shifters."

"Are you kidding?" Luther perked up and trotted toward his master. "When do we ever keep our mouths shut—"

"Shut up, dummy." Rex snapped at his brother's flank and herded him toward the door. "You got it, Johnny. You want muzzled hounds, we'll be your muzzled hounds."

"Bro, he doesn't even give us leashes. Why would he use—"

"Hey, do you wanna leave this hotel room or not?"

"Oh… Yeah, yeah, Johnny. Muzzles. All the way."

With a smirk, Lisa opened the door for all of them and they stepped into the hall to head to the elevators. "You haven't come up with the rest of the plan yet, huh?"

The bounty hunter cleared his throat and shook his head. "I'm still workin' on it. I think we'll know more about what we need when we get there."

"Before terrified and suspicious transformed shifters trying to build an army realize that Johnny Walker and Company want to infiltrate their meeting? Yeah, I hope so."

They spent the next fifteen minutes canvassing the two square blocks around Reggie's before the first of the transformed shifters pulled into the parking lot in small groups of two or three. It looked like merely another rush of bar patrons heading into a dingy, dimly lit bar with Bacardi posters and live-music fliers tacked to the windows, but the tension was already quite thick in the air—and especially because very few of the magicals who slipped through the front doors as close to 8:00 pm as they could manage said anything at all.

"Oh, sure. That ain't shady at all," Johnny grumbled as they circled the block toward the bar for the fifth time.

"Right. Because everyone knows the only people or magicals who enter bars are the chipper, overly talkative ones who smile at everyone and are trying to make friends."

He glared at Lisa, then cocked his head. "Okay, that's a fair point."

"Those are definitely shifters, Johnny," Rex whispered as he sniffed the air.

"Yeah." Luther stopped to pick a rock up between his jaws,

carried it for a few feet, then dropped it again. "Not the normal kind either."

Lisa cleared her throat. "Okay, that falls under the list of things to not say when trying to get into a secret meeting."

"Uh-huh." Johnny snapped his fingers and nodded at the two giant bouncers who stood outside the bar before he muttered, "Y'all keep quiet for now. And for Chrissakes, don't say nothin' about natural-borns. Understand?"

"Zipped up tight, Johnny."

"Yeah, natural-born whats? All shifters are created equal, right? Except for that super weird smell they have like burning—"

"Hush." They reached the front of Reggie's and the dwarf jerked his chin up at the shifters who stared without any expression at all. "How's it goin', fellas?"

"The bar's closed for a private function." The shifter on the right with gigantic muttonchops that didn't quite go with his yellow Bermuda shorts or the patterned Polo shirt of white lobsters on a navy background stepped in front of them and folded his arms. "Sorry."

"Private function?" Johnny scoffed. "Since when does a bar like this close to the general public in LA?"

The bouncers shared a perturbed look before the second shifter, his hair pulled back into one long blonde braid down his back, pointed at the bar's business hours posted against the inside of the glass door. "We're closed on Monday after eight."

"Clearly not." He scowled at a transformed wizard in a business suit who looked as confused by the two partners standing outside the bar as the bounty hunter was to realize they might be turned away. "Look at that. You let that guy in."

"He's on the list."

"What list?"

"The private function list, man. You and your girl need to keep walking." The first man gestured down the street and fixed them with an unyielding expression. "You can find other bars down that way."

"Hey, cool." Rex pulled away from sniffing the potted flowers and trotted toward the bouncers. "Looks like we're in, Luther. Just you and me. The two-legs are out."

"Hell yes!" Luther skittered around his brother before he was distracted by a dark stain on the sidewalk. "Sorry, Johnny. You heard the shifter guy."

"Better luck next time."

"Dude, this is great. We never get to go somewhere Johnny can't—whoa. Hey." The smaller hound looked at the first bouncer and wagged his tail despite the muscular shifter staring at him with a raised eyebrow. "You didn't see me, huh? That's cool. It's easy to miss someone down here on four legs instead of up there on two. Hey, Rex? You think this guy gets overlooked when he's wolfin' it?"

"Doesn't smell like it, bro. He's probably the same size on four legs and covered in fur."

"Yeah, you're right. Hey, Johnny, don't wait up for us, huh? Just come back in a few hours when we're done having fun in the—"

"Your dogs need to be on a leash," the first man interjected. "And all four of you need to find somewhere else to get your drinks."

"Aw, man..." Luther sat on his haunches and stared at the shifter. "Are you serious? I thought we were cool, shifter guy. Come on. This is discrimination. You hear that, Johnny? This guy has a thing against hounds."

Johnny snapped his fingers, and both hounds retreated reluctantly toward their master's side. "All right. I'm gonna be straight with you." He raised a hand to stop the man's response. "The truth is we know about your private function. We called the number, heard the message, the whole kit and kaboodle, and we want a seat at the table."

The man with the braid threw his head back and released a thunderous laugh. "I told you leaving that number all over town was a bad idea, Jim. It dragged in a dwarf and his pets."

"Excuse me?" Lisa unfolded her arms and glared at the laughing bouncer.

The shifter immediately recognized his slip of the tongue and cleared his throat. "I was talking about the dogs."

"And I'm standing here too, thanks." She shook her head, looked at the mutton-chopped Jim, and narrowed her eyes. "Are you the only shifter in LA who has given that number out 'all over town?'"

With a deep chuckle, the shifter with the braid answered for his buddy. "It was his idea in the first place. It looks like it's not as foolproof a plan as you thought, huh, Jimbo?"

Jim turned toward the other bouncer and hunched his bulky shoulders. "Do you mind? We're on the clock."

"Hey, I'm just saying."

"I have a question for you, Jim." Lisa pointed at him and tried to muster a coy smile when he met her gaze. "Does The Devil's Playground ring any bells for you?"

For the first time, the shifter widened his eyes and looked thoroughly surprised although he tried to cover it with a grunt. "Nope."

"It doesn't? How about a witch named Kennedy?"

"Listen, lady. I don't know what you think you're trying to do here, but you both need to—"

"Because now that I think about it," she continued and studied him from head to toe. "She most certainly mentioned you."

"Dammit." The other bouncer hissed a breath out in annoyance. "Are you serious?"

"Ford." Jim growled warningly. "Can it."

"It must be you if you're the only shifter who has handed that number out." Lisa stepped toward him. "But it sounds like it's not exactly preapproved, though. And The Devil's Playground is unquestionably one of those places—"

"One of those places?" Rex whispered. "Are you kidding? I didn't know places like that existed."

"Yeah, and we almost died in there," Luther added.

Ford frowned at the hounds and Lisa shrugged. "So if you let us inside, I won't have to bring it up again to anyone else."

He cleared his throat. "Again, I have no idea what you're talking about and this is a private function. Move along."

"Aw, hell." Johnny stalked forward and pointed at the hounds. "We were sent by friends of transformed shifters to learn about more transformed shifter business so we can help y'all. That's the honest truth, pal. Let us inside the damn bar."

Both bouncers sniggered. "You're crazy, man."

"Oh, crazy, huh? Are you sure you wanna go there?"

Lisa shook her head. "You seriously don't want to go there."

"How's this for crazy, huh? I've been around enough transformed shifters to know y'all smell like burned rubber." The bounty hunter folded his arms and stared from one bouncer to the other with a hard light in his eyes. "My cousin's one of y'all, all right? He's a biker dwarf who now has shifter added to his belt. We're on your side. If we get a little more info about Azure, maybe we can help y'all—"

"That's it. I've heard enough." Ford strode forward and reached for Johnny's arm, but the dwarf smacked his hand away. "Hands off, pal."

"Then start walking."

"Johnny, maybe you should drop Charlie's name," Luther suggested and spun in a circle as he sniffed the concrete. "They might know him."

"Hey, good idea." Rex trotted up to Jim and craned his neck to look at the shifter. "Hey, you know a Charlie Walker? Two-legs on an orange metal thingy that growls and goes real fast. The death-cycle."

"It's worth a try," Lisa muttered.

"No. No, I can talk my way into a goddamn bar, darlin'. What are the odds Charlie's name means anythin' but trouble around here anyhow, huh?"

Jim pointed at Rex and frowned at the investigative duo. "Your dog was just talking about that."

"No shit, genius." Johnny turned toward him and tossed his hands in the air in exasperation. "We can both hear these two hounds like they had damn voices and could speak English. That's gotta count for somethin'. Come on. Ask 'em. They can't lie."

"Pshh." Luther looked over his shoulder at his master. "Johnny, who told you something as stupid as that?"

"It's a common misconception, Johnny," Rex added and continued to stare at Jim.

"Common—" The bounty hunter snorted. "Listen to you and your big words."

"We lie all the time."

"Yeah, like when you ask us if we ate the leftovers you set out on the counter."

"Bro. Feel free to keep lying."

"Oh, yeah. Whoops. But seriously, shifters. We're trying to help." Luther sat to scratch behind his ear. "I think."

Lisa watched the bouncers with growing trepidation.

Now we look like a couple of magicals who've completely lost their minds, talking hounds or not.

"We truly can help," she added. "We're trying, anyway. And we have information on Tyro—"

"Yeah, that's where I draw the line." Ford surged forward. "Out. Now. And try to not get yourselves killed when you toss that name around. Go!"

"All right, all right." Johnny raised both hands and took two slow steps back. "How about I give y'all a little piece of advice, huh?"

"We're not interested."

"Ford, they talk to their dogs."

"It's good stuff," he added. "You're gonna wanna hear it."

"Whatever, man."

The bounty hunter stepped toward the bouncer again, waved Ford even closer, and opened his mouth like he was about to drop all his knowledge at once. Instead, he darted around the shifter, who was too slow to catch him, and barreled toward the door.

"Johnny." Lisa rolled her eyes when her partner was instantly intercepted by Jim.

"I don't think so, dwarf. Nice try."

"Y'all are makin' fools of yourselves. Gatekeepin' information like this." The dwarf snorted. "Ain't y'all interested in what we already know about Kaiser and Tyro and how the hell to keep all the transformed from gettin'—"

"I'm interested in ripping your head off." Ford's eyes flashed with silver light as he snarled and grasped him by the back collar of his shirt. He thrust the dwarf off the sidewalk and into the row of parking spaces in front of the bar.

Johnny staggered between two cars and turned instantly as he reached for his utility knife. "All right, I tried playin' nice."

"You can try playing dead." Ford pointed down the street. "Get lost or we won't be playing at all."

"Seriously, how stupid can you be—"

"Johnny." Lisa pulled his hand subtly away from the hilt of his blade and tugged him with her down the sidewalk. "It's time for us to take no for an answer and leave, okay?"

"Like hell it is. We gotta get—"

"We'll find another way," she muttered through clenched teeth. "But doing it your way will only make this worse."

With a snarl of defeat, he shrugged away from her and uttered a piercing whistle. "Boys!"

"You sure you don't wanna let us in?" Luther asked and

pranced in front of the bouncers. "Can't say much for Johnny, but we're fun?"

One of Ford's eyes twitched as he glared at the hound and growled a warning.

"Well, jeez. You don't have to be a complete douchewolf."

"Ha. Good one, bro."

"Yeah, I can do better."

The hounds trotted after the two partners and left severely confused and even more suspicious transformed bouncers guarding the entrance to Reggie's. They frowned after the entire team like they couldn't believe what they'd seen with their own eyes.

The bounty hunter gritted his teeth and pounded one fist into his opposite palm when he and Lisa rounded the corner of the building. "I don't believe this. For the first time in my entire damn career, I walk up to a fella at the door and tell him the whole truth from stem to stern and they turned us the hell away!"

Lisa rubbed the back of her neck. "Yeah, I was a little surprised that was your last-minute plan."

"Well, we can't go in there firin' weapons and expectin' the whole damn meetin' to let us sit in after that. Shit. It's always somethin' with these shifters."

"Okay, so the more traditional Johnny Walker route of breaking in to bust a few bad-guy heads doesn't exactly apply here." She turned in a tight circle and bit her lip in concentration. "We could try to distract them."

"With what, darlin'? We stood there for five minutes havin' us a friendly chat. If they don't recognize our faces, they'll recognize our smell."

"True. Well, what about your little spy spider thingies?"

"Thingies?" He darted her a crooked grin. "Is that the best you can do?"

"You know what I mean. Did you bring one?"

"Nope." He patted his pockets and looked up the street in the direction of their hotel. "I stashed the high-frequency shifter-headache gun, though."

"Johnny, we're trying to get in the bar, not make everyone come running out clutching their heads."

"Well, damn." With a scowl, he turned and trailed his gaze slowly up the drainpipe leading toward the roof. "How you feel about climbin'?"

"Johnny, it's a one-story building. Being on the roof won't get us inside either."

"That's it." He yanked an explosive disk from his belt and stalked toward the back of the bar. "If I ain't gettin' in by bein' honest and playin' nice, I'm blowin' somethin' up."

"That's the complete opposite of what we're trying to do! You can't get into a private meeting by detonating a bomb on the back door—"

"Watch me."

CHAPTER TWELVE

"Do I need to sic your hounds after you?" Lisa demanded in a hissed tone as she hurried after her partner.

Johnny paused briefly to frown at her and glanced at the hounds trotting at her sides. "It's the first time I heard you make an empty threat, darlin'. It ain't gonna happen."

"Yeah, lady." Luther sniffed her bare leg beneath her shorts. "We like you and everything, but we're not attacking Johnny for fun."

"At least not in real life," Rex added, panted, and looking from one two-legs to the other. "Dreams are a different thing. And no, you can't blame a hound for what he does in his dreams."

She shrugged. "Well, it was worth a try. And I guess we're both acting desperate right now, huh?"

"It ain't desperation." Johnny strode down the side of the building again. "This is gettin' what I want so I can get the shifters in this bar what they want—mainly not gettin' themselves killed. So either back me up or—"

"What the hell are you doing?"

Johnny and Lisa both whirled to where Charlie stood at the edge of the parking lot, his arms spread in disbelief. Flanking him were a ridiculously tall and skinny Wood Elf man with one green eye and one brown and woman only a few inches taller than Charlie with platinum blonde hair bordering on pure white.

"After the kinda reputation you guys have, I kinda expected you to know how to find the front door. It's over here."

"Charlie!" Luther barked sharply with such excitement that all four paws almost lifted off the asphalt. "You're here! You came!"

"Man, are we glad to see you." Rex chuffed and trotted toward the mohawked dwarf who'd arrived with yet more friends. "And you should quit running away all the time. Whenever you leave, Johnny goes insane."

"Yeah, can you believe he almost blew the back door up? Whew. Good thing you showed up in time."

Betrayed by my hounds. To my cousin. I'd ask if the day could get any worse but that's already a given.

Charlie's shifter friends glared at the bounty hunter after that highly incriminating canine confession.

The biker dwarf snorted and gave both hounds a good scratch behind the ears. "You guys might wanna keep the whole 'what Johnny was about to do' thing on the DL, boys. Transformed shifters are everywhere."

"Oh, sure." Rex sniffed the Wood Elf's shoes and snorted. "DL. Totally. You can count on us."

"We're all over the DL. Hey, Rex. What does that even mean?"

"Don't Lick, bro. Duh."

"Right, right, right. Yeah, that's—oh…" Luther's rear leg pumped furiously as he leaned against Charlie's leg. "It can mean whatever you want as long as you don't stop with the scratching."

Dammit, this ain't what I signed up for.

Johnny whistled with sharp impatience. Rex whipped his head toward his master and sat. Luther's hind leg pumped a few more times even after Charlie removed his hand before he finally turned with his tongue lolling out of his mouth. "Johnny, look. It's Charlie."

"I can see that fine. What are you doin' here?"

His cousin raised his eyebrows. "You sent me a text. I've heard about these LA meetings but never made it to one. It sounded like a fun thing for a Monday night. Are you coming?"

"I…" Johnny looked over his shoulder at the back of the building he'd intended to infiltrate a little more dramatically, then glanced at the ready but still inactivated disk in his hand.

"This is our in." Lisa grinned at the three transformed shifters and headed toward them. "I'm glad you came, Charlie."

"Yeah, good to see you too."

The hounds padded after the group. "Hey, what about us?"

"Yeah, no one ever says it's a bad thing to see their favorite hounds."

"And everyone knows who their favorite is."

Johnny's mouth dropped open when his partner and his trusty coonhounds disappeared around the corner with his cousin.

Sure, he's cleanin' himself up but he's still pullin' the same shit as when we were kids.

When his team didn't come back for him, the bounty hunter strapped the exploding disk onto his belt and sniffed irritably. "Aw, hell."

He hurried after them but didn't dare to break into a jog and risk everyone seeing his urgency to not be left behind.

Fortunately for him, a short line had formed in front of Ford and Jim. Lisa, Charlie, and his two transformed friends were at the end while the hounds sniffed the area, their tails whipping against whatever two-legs happened to get in the way.

Lisa smiled at her partner as he approached and gestured toward the Wood Elf and the blonde. "Johnny, this is Ray and Anna—"

"Great." He stopped inches from his cousin instead and leaned toward Charlie to grumble, "If you were plannin' on headin' out here anyhow, why the hell didn't you let me know?"

The biker dwarf raised his eyebrows but stared ahead at the shifters in front of him. "I don't need a babysitter, 'coz."

"At least we can finally agree on that part. You didn't think I coulda used a heads-up?"

"For what? You said I'm still on the case and it's not like you would have sent me the place and time if you weren't gonna be here yourself."

"Dammit, Charlie. I know what I said." Johnny rubbed his hand down his face then jerked it down to fold his arms. "I'm talkin' about you leavin' me in the—"

"On a case, huh?" Anna smacked Charlie's shoulder with the back of a hand and smirked. "I didn't know you were working steady jobs."

"Oh, yeah." Charlie hiked up the waistband of his jeans, which was required now that his belt had been destroyed in an underground tryst turned accidental prisoner-escape. "I do a little consulting from time to time. I thought I'd give it a try, and you know what? I think I like it and might be good at it too. Wouldn't you say, Lisa?"

She widened her eyes and glanced at Johnny. "You…uh, bring a certain value—"

"Hey, what a nice thing to say. Do you mean it?"

Despite her partner's warning scowl, she nodded. "Yeah, Charlie."

"See? I found something I'm good at that 'has value.'" He hiked his black jeans up again and puffed his chest out. "I'm diggin' it."

"Look at you." Ray chuckled. "Fancy Charlie Walker getting himself consulting jobs. I never thought I'd see the day."

"Oh, yeah. Big changes all around, buddy. Big changes. Just you wait."

Christ, he's milkin' this.

The bounty hunter rolled his eyes. "Sure. He got himself a fancy business card and everythin'."

The shifters completely ignored him.

"What kinda case is it?" Ray asked.

"Classified." Charlie cleared his throat and raised his chin. "It's very hush-hush so I can't talk about it while we're here. But maybe if everything goes the way it's supposed to at this meeting, I might fill you in a little."

Rex snorted. "Not that hush-hush."

"Yeah, you don't have to worry about secrets or anything," Luther added as he tested a discarded gum wrapper before trying multiple times to spit it out again. "Johnny already told the big guys out front everything he knows."

"The truth, the whole truth, and nothing but the Johnny Walker truth. Wait—"

Luther sniggered. "That's not even a thing, bro."

"You're right."

Both hounds burst out laughing and even Johnny's quick snap didn't get them to stop completely.

Charlie turned to Lisa and refused to spare his cousin a single glance. "And they still didn't let you in?"

"Nope. It seems the truth isn't anywhere near as convincing as a lie. Or a little personal leverage." She shrugged. "That was a first."

"Nah, don't worry about it. We'll get you in." He winked at her and hiked his pants up again.

"For cryin' out loud, Charlie. They're sellin' belts two blocks down."

"I'm good."

Johnny gritted his teeth and felt Lisa's warning stare before he even turned to meet her gaze. She nodded toward Charlie in front of her and mouthed, "Be nice."

Since when did she start thinkin' a warnin' like that would work on me?

Despite his frustration, he kept his mouth shut and hooked his thumbs through his belt loops in irritation.

The line of shifters ahead of them were finally admitted to

Reggie's and they stood in front of Ford and Jim again. This time, they were joined by three transformed shifters who didn't have to pretend to be anything else at a meeting like this.

Ford glared at Johnny and scratched his bushy muttonchops. "I know I told you to get lost."

The bounty hunter shrugged and scowled in response. "And I told you we're gettin' in."

"This is a private function. It's a shifter thing."

"Are those rules carved in stone somewhere? 'Cause I don't—"

"Hey, don't worry about it, man." Charlie leaned toward the hairy bouncer and lowered his voice. "Everything he told you is true."

Ford and Jim exchanged mixed glances of confusion and amusement. "Seriously? That he can talk to his dogs, knows sensitive information he shouldn't, and wants to help us."

"In a nutshell, yeah." Charlie tipped his head from side to side. "Of course, he didn't mention me."

"No shit." Ford chuckled. "You're the cousin."

The mohawked dwarf perked up immediately. "Well, I'm much more than that, but yeah."

Rex snorted. "Like this guy's bitch-brother, to start."

"He is!" Luther laughed so hard that he tossed his head and stumbled sideways. When he crashed into Lisa's legs, she grunted and stepped quickly aside to catch her balance before she frowned at him.

All amusement vanished from the bouncer's face. "What the hell does that mean?"

"The crazy witch with the secret club who likes to throw her shoes at hounds," Luther said through gasped laughs.

"Yeah, and herself at dwarves and shifters and shifter dwarves."

"Ha!" The hounds erupted in another round of laughter.

Lisa pressed her lips together as realization and a little horror dawned on the bouncer's face.

We'll never get into this bar, will we?

"Damn. You too, huh?" Charlie laughed and leaned forward to clap a jovial hand against Ford's bulging bicep. "Most people don't believe me when I talk about the crazy magicals I meet all the time, but you do. Ha. She's insane, right?"

Still laughing, he brushed past the burly shifter who seemed frozen stiff by the recent turn of events and waved his friends forward with him.

Ford didn't try to stop them—or Lisa—but he stepped in front of Rex and Luther. "No dogs allowed."

"It's all good, brother," Charlie called as he turned halfway through the door with a grin. "The dogs are with me."

"That's right, shifter." Luther thrust his snout into the air and pranced past the bouncers. "Can't discriminate against hounds."

"Yeah, I'm sure that's a law somewhere. Hey, Johnny. You coming?"

The shifter growled at the bounty hunter and didn't look willing to let him through with the rest of his party.

"Aw, come on. You heard the guy." Johnny pointed at Charlie's back as it disappeared inside. "I'm with them."

"Are you a dog in disguise?"

"Are you lookin' for a fight or what?"

A vengeful sneer curled the bouncer's upper lip. "The dwarf said the dogs are with him."

"Hell, they're my goddamn hounds!"

"Johnny." Charlie poked his head through the open doorway again with a brief nod at the giant transformed shifters and the line behind his cousin, all of whom glared at the bounty hunter. "Quit screwing around and get in here, 'coz. You're gonna make us miss the whole thing."

His fists clenched, Johnny stormed around the hairy bouncer, who didn't try to stop him this time, and into the bar. His teeth ground loudly and painfully in his head.

I'm gonna have a damn aneurysm by the end of the night. This is the last time I try gettin' anywhere through the front door with the truth.

Without bothering to look for Lisa or Charlie, he went straight to the bar instead and rapped his knuckles twice on the wood. "Do y'all have Johnny Walker Black?"

The transformed wizard behind the bar raised an eyebrow. "Not for you. I think you're in the wrong place, buddy."

He grasped the edge of the bar with both hands and leaned as far forward as he could. "I'm already in, buddy. So unless y'all have some secret shifter money and mine's no good here, pour me two damn fingers. Neat. And keep 'em comin'."

The bartender looked at the front door, scanned the crowded establishment filled with transformed shifters and hushed conversation—if any—and retrieved a bottle of Johnny Walker Black from the bottom shelf behind him. He poured like he was sleepwalking and slid the glass toward his unwanted customer. "One drink. Then you need to leave."

"I ain't goin' nowhere." The dwarf downed it in one gulp and thunked the glass down with a nod. "Round two. Go ahead."

"I have to close you out, sir. This is a private fun—"

"I know it's a private damn function and I was invited. Personally. I walked through the door so deal with it and pour me another—"

"Hey, hey." Charlie slid up to the bar beside his cousin and slapped a hand on the wood.

Johnny stared at the bottle of whiskey in front of him and used every ounce of willpower he possessed to not start a drunken barfight with his cousin before either of them had a chance to even get even slightly drunk.

"I'll take care of this, 'coz. The drinks are on me." With a grin, he pointed at the bartender. "Whatever he wants, man. Put it on my tab. And get me a double Hendrix and tonic with lime, two of those light beers you got in the fridge, and a 7 and 7."

Despite the shifter dwarf's chipper demeanor, the bartender continued to frown. "Do you know this dwarf?"

"I sure do. Can't you see the family resemblance?" Charlie chuckled and pulled his wallet out to slide a credit card across the bar. "This guy's taken care of me so many times, it's about time I return the favor, know what I'm saying?"

"You know what's going down here as soon as the doors close, right?"

"Come on, man. Do I look completely clueless? Ha. Don't answer that. And yeah, I can vouch for this dwarf here. This is Johnny Walker."

The transformed wizard shrugged and shook his head.

"So you never heard of him, huh? Yeah, it's all right. He'll keep his mouth shut." Charlie clamped a hand on his cousin's shoulder and gave him a brisk shake. "No one believes him even when he runs his mouth and tells the truth. And keep the tab open."

Wrinkling his nose, the bartender turned to grab the beers and the bottles of liquor for mixed drinks.

Yeah, I wouldn't be fixin' to get caught up in a conversation with us either.

"You don't think that's goin' a little hard there, Charlie?"

Johnny's cousin barked out a laugh. "Relax, 'coz. It's not all for me."

"Even still. You're fixin' to clean your act up. Drinkin' ain't exactly gonna help."

"It's only booze."

"Uh-huh."

Charlie still hadn't looked at him once, even when a crooked smile crossed his lips. "You know what, Johnny? If you can drink and still be the badass bounty hunter you are, I can drink and still be your badass consultant."

"That ain't the same thing."

"Then practice what you preach, man."

The bartender finished the drinks order and set everything on the bar like he was reaching into a catfish hole but trying not to get bitten.

When the bounty hunter said nothing, the shifter dwarf muttered, "Yeah, I didn't think so," and took the drinks before he turned into the crowd gathered around the stage at the far end of the room.

I ain't got a drinkin' problem. He has an everythin' problem.

He downed the second two fingers the bartender reluctantly poured, then snatched the entire bottle of whiskey with the empty glass. "Go ahead and put that on his tab. It'll save you the trouble."

CHAPTER THIRTEEN

Lisa already had her gin and tonic when Johnny found her at the far wall beside the stage with the hounds seated on either side of her. She took one look at the half-full whiskey bottle in her partner's hand and raised an eyebrow. "You know, if you're feeling left out, all you have to do is say so."

"I ain't in the mood, darlin'."

She smirked and sipped her drink. "You're in some kind of mood. Hey, it's a good thing Charlie arrived. We're in with no explosions necessary."

"Uh-huh. And what happens if whoever's fixin' to take this stage real soon decides they'd rather not talk about all the transformed shifter business in front of two hounds and us?"

"I don't think they'd want to disappoint a turnout like this. Look at the place. It's packed."

"They should've set this meetin' outta the city." He poured four fingers into his glass and sipped it this time instead of knocking it all back. "There are too many transformed in one place. They're too much of a target."

"Johnny, there hasn't been a mass attack on transformed shifters since we started this case. Not even by Kaiser." Lisa gazed around the room and ignored the confused and sometimes highly suspicious looks cast at them. "Agnes is good. I'll give her that. But even if we hadn't caught them, I don't think she and Bronson would try to take an entire bar all on their own."

"They might if they went runnin' to Kaiser to tell him their cover's blown."

"I thought we'd already decided that's not very likely."

He sipped more whiskey and grunted. "Neither is us needin' my damn cousin to get into a bar. Or an escaped bounty. Or bein' surrounded by a bunch of magicals lookin' like they wanna rip us apart." With a drink in his hand and the whiskey slowly starting to take effect, a faint smile came easily to the bounty hunter's lips. "I think there's one silver linin' to this."

"Oh, yeah? What's that?"

"We didn't have the time to take your bullet outta that crazy-ass witch's leg."

Lisa threw her head back and filled the bar with her easygoing, ringing laughter. That only drew more weird looks, but it took her a moment to register the many shifters' attentions fixed firmly on her. She forced her grin into a tight-lipped attempt to stop smiling altogether, leaned toward Johnny, and cleared her throat. "Is it weirder that I laughed at a meeting like this or that I laughed at wounding a blood witch with my firearm?"

"It ain't weird at all, darlin'." He slipped an arm around her waist and pulled her closer as he lifted his rocks glass toward the closest staring transformed. "Hell, let 'em stare."

"Right. Your morbid sense of humor finally rubbed off on me." She focused intently on the stage, took the straw in her mouth, and waited somewhat impatiently for the highly antici-pated meeting to start.

Charlie was one of the few magicals who looked like he was happy to be there. He joked with Ray and Anna and brought two other less-gloomy transformed into one of his jokes. Despite his efforts, their slightly awkward laughter ended abruptly when a middle-aged man in a Polo t-shirt and khaki pants took the stage with a microphone in his hand.

The lights above him brightened and he tapped the mic to test it, and the entire bar fell into a tense, anticipatory hush.

"Hey." The shifter onstage took his sweet time to look at every face that stared at him. His eyes narrowed briefly when his gaze swept over Johnny and Lisa, but he didn't seem all that worried about two attendees who by rights weren't supposed to be there. "Thanks for coming, everyone. I also want to thank Mitch for hosting these meetings over the last couple of months here in his fine establishment."

The transformed wizard behind the bar raised a glass and nodded, his smile grim and determined. Others around the room did the same and Johnny frowned.

Damn. He didn't even pull the owner card to get me outta here. There might be a chance these folks are hopin' for some outside help after all.

"And, of course, Ford and Jim. You guys do a hell of a job keeping a close eye on things."

Right on cue, the two giant bouncers slipped through the bar's front door and pulled it shut behind them. Jim stopped to turn the lock briskly in the door before he eased into the crowd to get a better view of the stage.

"My name's Grant Bitterson," the man continued into the mic. "Those of you who have joined us over the last few months or weeks—heck, even for the last meeting or two—already have an idea of what this is all about. And for anyone new here tonight, welcome. You made it at the right time too because we have some major news." Finally, a smile flicked across his lips. "Before we get to that part, though, I want to update everyone with what we know about the current numbers and to pay our respects to those who unfortunately aren't here to see what happens when the transformed come together for a common goal."

Grant removed a folded paper from the pocket of his shorts and filled the bar with the magnified crinkle as he opened it to hold it in front of him. He slowly read the names of the latest transformed shifters to have fallen over the last week—who they were, what they did, when they'd been killed, and where. There seemed to be more names and details than a single piece of paper could hold, and no one made a sound as he worked his way down line by line.

The total count so far was five hundred and twenty-three.

Johnny sipped his whiskey and scanned the bowed heads and pained frowns all around him.

Damn. Twenty more in the last week and the rest of the world ain't even callin' this war invisible. They ain't callin' it a war at all. Folks don't know and they don't care.

After a long, tense moment of silence once Grant finished reading the names, the shifter raised his head and cleared his throat before he lifted the mic again.

"This is how we've started these gatherings every week for months now. It's a way to remember why we're doing this and what's at stake for all of us. If you're here tonight, you already know what's been happening all over the country to first and second-generation transformed. We might not have any real idea why we've been caught up in this war, and for a long time, many of us found it hard to believe there was any hope at all for people like us—*magicals* like us and yes, I know some of you had no part in the magical world until thirty years ago."

He took a deep breath and his eyes widened as he gazed across the crowd again. "You might think you've already given up hoping for a change. For justice. For a chance to live your life however you want without being threatened with your life for not conforming to what someone else wants you to be. But if all hope was lost, you wouldn't be here. None of us would."

Movement stirred at the side of the bar, although the magical who stepped through the crowd and slipped between the transformed was entirely obscured by so many bodies crammed into such a tiny venue.

Grant glanced in that direction and when he smiled, he looked like an entirely different shifter altogether.

Well hell. If a smile wipes a couple of decades off a face like that, I oughtta try it more.

Johnny leaned forward for a better look at the stranger moving through the crowd but couldn't see over the taller magicals around him.

"But tonight," Grant continued, "that all changes. There's nothing I've wanted more than to be able to give other transformed a real reason to hope that goes beyond blind optimism and faking it until we make it. Tonight, we have proof of what's coming. And all I ask is that you listen to what my friend has to say before your draw any conclusions. This is only the beginning. I hope to see every single one of you with us to the very end."

The bar was so silent now that when Luther lowered his head to lick between his legs, the shifter on the stage looked sharply at the hound. Johnny snapped his fingers and Luther whipped his head up immediately. "What? No one's paying attention, Johnny—"

"Shh."

The magical who'd moved through the crowd now finally stepped onto the stage.

"Wow," Lisa whispered.

"It was a decent speech, sure," the bounty hunter replied, distracted by pouring himself another drink from the bottle before he placed it on the table against the wall. "But it wasn't that great."

"I'm not talking about the speech." She tapped his arm and nodded toward the stage.

"What? Oh. Hold on…" He squinted and leaned forward as the newcomer shook hands with Grant and took the mic graciously.

We've seen too many faces with multiple names over the last few weeks. We know that guy.

"Is that…"

"Hello, everyone." The shifter man with salt-and-pepper hair smiled, held the mic with one hand, and rubbed his other palm against the leg of his jeans. "My name is Terrence Caul, and I'm… Well, if I'm honest, I'd have to say I didn't expect to be in LA so soon. But there's no time like the present, right?"

Terrence Caul. That's the shifter runnin' those other secret meetin's in North Dakota.

When Johnny looked at Lisa, she was already staring at him with one of her knowing looks.

Yep. That's him all right. What the hell's going on?

Terrence smiled and gazed around the room before he chuckled softly. "You know, Grant has said everything I would have stood here and told you. Thanks for that, by the way."

Grant raised a fist and some of the gathered transformed responded with soft laughter.

"So I'll cut right to the chase." The speaker transferred the mic to his other hand, dropped the nervous newbie act, and prepared for the big reveal. "I won't say war is coming because it's already been on our doorstep for quite some time. But I will tell you the winds are shifting. We've been running from the natural-born calling himself Kaiser for way too long. We've lost family, friends, neighbors, and what little pride we had to begin with. It's time to take it back. And I—"

"How?" someone shouted. "Man, I don't even know who you are."

"No, you don't. But I'm not the one you need to know."

"Unless you found a way to kill the bastard yourself, you don't have anything else to offer us," another heckler called. The shifters beside him jostled him into silence again.

"Let the man speak!"

Terrence turned toward his supporter and broke into a wide

grin. "Thanks, Charlie. It's weird to see you here but I guess I shouldn't be surprised. Is anyone else opposed to listening through to the end?"

No one else interrupted, and the Midwestern shifter in a plaid shirt and jeans nodded. "Good. Because I've traveled around and shared this with as many transformed groups as I could find. After thirty years, we finally have a reason to stop hiding. No more running because as we speak, Azure is heading this way. She's already close."

The bar erupted into shouts, half of them in earnest to hear more and the other half in angry, protesting denial.

"We don't have time for urban legends, man."

"She's real. My sister said she passed through Kansas not that long ago."

"If we want an army to go up against Kaiser, someone had better give us guns, at least!"

"Shit," Johnny grumbled into his rocks glass. "This ain't how to rally the troops."

"Oh, yeah?" Lisa watched the surprise, hesitation, and curiosity that rippled across the gathered crowd. "Do you think you could do a better job?"

"I thought we'd be gettin' insider knowledge at this damn thing. Not a riot."

She shook her head and waited for Terrence to continue speaking.

The shifter from North Dakota waited for a lull in the din before raising the mic in front of him again. "You can believe what you want. I'm merely a shifter who volunteered as a mouthpiece but there are more of us. Those who have seen Azure believe in what she's doing—gathering the transformed from coast to coast to finally stand against the natural-borns who want to see us beaten into the dust. None of you have to make a decision now but if you want to know more—if you want the proof Grant mentioned—come speak to me after the meeting."

"And how much is it gonna cost us?" a woman shouted.

"Oh, come on, now." Terrence frowned playfully at her. "If I was promoting some kind of self-help seminar, I would have at least brought a few pamphlets."

Those who weren't immediately opposed to his revelation chuckled and nodded.

"The answer is nothing. It costs you nothing but a little of your time and a willingness to fight for what's right with the rest of us. Like I said, if you want to know more, come see me outside. This is big, people. Azure has what we need to end the skirmishes and the more of us who stand at her side, the greater our chances of eliminating Kaiser for good. You don't even have to take my word for it."

"And what if we don't want anything to do with this?" A squat man with crooked glasses pushed the taller transformed next to him away so he could be seen from the stage. "I only want to remember those I've lost and move on with my life. I don't want a war."

"None of us do," Terrence replied. "And if you don't want to join this movement, that's your choice. There are no repercussions and no punishment or hidden fees." A group of young shifters laughed at that. "But if you have even a little aversion to being left out of the magical history books altogether, I'd say to not discount everything yet. Trust me. This will make history."

With a grin, he handed the mic to Grant and hopped off the stage. Some of the transformed closest to him tried to engage him in conversation and ask their questions but he shook his head and pointed toward the front door of the bar.

"I know it's a weird process," he said and drew everyone's attention again. "But Terrence Caul is a shifter of his word. Now, I think it's best if we—"

"Excuse me. Excuse me." A petite woman in a business suit with her hair tied back in a severe bun approached the stage and leaned forward to mutter something.

Johnny rolled his eyes.

Every damn shifter in the place can hear what she's sayin' and we gotta stand here like a couple of clueless idiots.

"Sure, sure. Lena's getting up to share a few extra details." Grant handed her the mic, and the woman immediately launched into a ridiculous tale of he-said-she-said about Tyro sightings all over the country in the last two weeks. Some claimed that he had Oriceran monsters working for him, had connections to the mafia in New Jersey as well as the Yakuza, and had built himself a suit that turned him invisible and enabled him to fly.

"Jesus Christ." Johnny knocked back his second four fingers of whiskey and shook his head. "This went from semi-interestin' to full-on conspiracy theory."

"And it's a little strange how many magicals are sticking around to listen to it," Lisa muttered. "It's certainly confusing."

"I estimate that half these shifters were human thirty-odd years ago. This is what happens when no one's around to tell 'em which magical-world rumors are true and which are complete bullshit."

"They can't all be this crazy. There's no way."

"I've had enough crazy for one case, darlin'. Let's get outta here."

"Johnny." She caught his arm and nodded toward the bar's entrance. "We need to stick around and talk to Terrence after this. If he's right and Azure is heading to California, we need to arrange a meeting with her."

"I ain't joinin' the front lines of transformed shifters who think New Jersey's mafia gives a damn about shifter politics."

"It's not politics when magicals are being murdered."

The bounty hunter snorted and raised an eyebrow. "That's like sayin' all lawyers are heroes and nothin' gets folks' tickin' like payin' taxes."

Lisa froze, wrinkled her nose, and shrugged. "Okay, I phrased that wrong but you know what I mean."

"Uh-huh." He noticed her empty drink and smirked. "You oughtta get yourself another drink while we settle in to wait for our private audience with the Midwestern shifter we met the first time in a barn. It might make it easier for you to say what you mean."

She rolled her eyes. "I don't need another drink."

"Charlie's payin' for all of it."

"Hmm." With a shrug, she patted his shoulder as she moved away toward the bar.

CHAPTER FOURTEEN

It was almost 11:00 pm before the most frightened and most conspiratorial of LA's transformed shifters finally left the bar. It was still technically closed for a private function—evidenced by Jim the bouncer having to turn away a group of college girls barely old enough to drink in the first place—but the transformed moved in and out at will. Most of them returned home but a few stood around to talk and kill time until they were next in line to speak to Terrence Caul personally.

Johnny and Lisa ordered a final round of drinks before they stepped through the back door and into the small courtyard behind the building. A raised patio boasted a small party tent along the rear, where the transformed who wanted more information waited in line to step inside one at a time.

"This is as weird as hell," Johnny muttered as the line finally dwindled only two shifters still waiting patiently for their turn. "It looks more like he's playin' Wizard of Oz than shifter-army recruiter."

"I'm sure he has his reasons." Lisa leaned back in her patio chair and watched a woman emerge from Terrence's private tent and pat her pockets before she walked into the bar. "Although I would have thought having the hounds standing right outside would have given us a little more insight."

Seated beside the tent, Luther whipped his head up and yipped sharply. "We're not useless!"

"Yeah, what he said." Rex sniffed the bottom edge of the tent and trotted from behind it. "No one here says anything, Johnny—"

"Hey." The bounty hunter whistled shrilly and lifted a finger quickly to his lips before he jerked his hand down again.

Luther cocked his head. "I didn't say anything either."

And we ain't gettin' anywhere with two hounds talkin' about spyin' and this whole place crawlin' with shifters who can hear 'em.

A group of shifters burst out laughing at another table across the patio and Lisa raised her drink. "At least someone's having fun."

Charlie grinned and raised his glass toward her before he leaned forward and muttered something to the friends he'd arrived with and the three other shifters he'd drawn into his fun little circle.

"I don't get it." Johnny folded his arms and scowled at his cousin. "He's sittin' there laughin' and jokin' like he ain't got a care in the world. But he ain't looked me in the eye since he arrived."

"I think that's the point."

He stared expressionlessly at her. "Do I need to cut you off the gin for the rest of the night?"

"Very funny. I'm serious, Johnny. He pissed you off, you pissed him off, and now he's dealing with it in his way while getting back on this case with us so we can finish it. Hopefully."

"His way? Darlin', that ain't the way a grown dwarf handles bein' pissed off. What he's doin' is teenage-girl mind games."

Lisa choked on a laugh and almost sprayed her drink over the table. "You only know one teenage girl and when Amanda's pissed, she storms out and breaks a few things she hopefully won't regret later. You two are so alike, I could say it runs in the family."

He scoffed. "Comparin' me to a thirteen-year-old shifter ain't helpin' your case."

"Okay, there is a slight difference. She goes out to break the bones of small swamp critters and you either break open a bottle of whiskey or someone else's face."

"Christ. You make me sound like some kinda violence addict."

"Johnny, you built yourself a bomb belt and wear it everywhere. I think you're past the point of hiding it."

He glanced at his belt and shook his head.

Lisa and her goddamn observations.

"And I reckon you're fixin' to tell me you ain't got a need to act out when you're pissed, huh?"

"Are you kidding?" Lisa laughed and took another long sip. "I have my coping methods, thank you very much."

"Well, since we're layin' it all out on the table, darlin', go right ahead. Enlighten me."

She stared at the tent across the patio and pressed her lips together but couldn't completely hide her smile. "You know that long cabinet in the storage closet on the houseboat?"

"Uh-huh…"

"It's not jammed."

The bounty hunter leaned forward over the table and folded his arms on the metal mesh. "You've been hidin' things in there and lockin' 'em up where I can't see. Uh-huh. So, what? Have you been breakin' a few things yourself when you get angry?"

"No, Johnny. I don't…" She laughed. "I don't lock the bones of my victims or busted vases in a cabinet in our houseboat to get rid of the evidence."

"A likely story."

"When I'm frustrated, I…uh, impulse-buy."

"Aw, hell." The dwarf lurched back in his chair and rubbed his temple. "It's books, ain't it?"

All she had to do was shrug and dart him a sideways glance.

"Dammit, I knew you weren't tellin' me the whole story when you had no problem leavin' all those boxes in the storage unit. And now you're usin' the houseboat as a giant bookshelf?"

"Hey, don't judge me or my library. You have your workshop—"

"Which I built myself."

"And I'm allowed to rebuild my book collection. And no, I'm not paying you rent for the space. It's a cabinet."

"For now. The next thing I know, I'll be turnin' around reachin' for my tools and pickin' up some stupid sappy romance book instead. Then you'll be makin' me sleep on the couch 'cause there ain't room for ten books and two bodies in a double-sized bed."

"See, this is why I didn't tell you." Lisa looked at the few shifters on the patio who now fixed them with intrigued looks. "And I think it's a good idea for you to stop projecting your fight with your cousin onto my reading habit."

"We all have damn habits, don't we?" Johnny shook his head, poured himself another four fingers from the bottle of whiskey on Charlie's tab, and lifted the glass to his lips. He paused when he felt his partner's stare on him again. His gaze darted around the table before it settled on her. "What?"

"Were you being facetious or did that go right over your head?"

He stared at her as he sipped his drink slowly.

I think she can handle not knowin' that one all on her own. We can trade secret books for not-so-secret booze. Fine.

Lisa rolled her eyes playfully and returned her attention to the tent. "Hey, the line's gone."

"Great. Time to have us a little—"

"Johnny!" Luther bayed wildly before he raced across the patio. "Johnny, hey. The barn shifter told us to tell you—"

"Come on back!" Rex shouted in front of the tent entrance.

"Bro, I was about to tell him."

"Yeah, and I told him first."

Luther sat and licked his muzzle. "Johnny, we're gonna talk to him, right?"

"Yep." The bounty hunter stood and headed toward the tent.

As Lisa followed him, she caught Charlie's gaze and nodded for him to join them. He didn't look nearly as excited about talking to a shifter he already knew as he did sitting at his table to keep telling new friends old stories. Still, he picked his drink up and stood to join the team.

Because he's on the case and that's why we're here.

Lisa smiled and ignored Johnny's scowl of disapproval before he whipped the open flaps aside and stepped in.

There's no way working on a case like this won't settle whatever's going on between them. We'll need all the help we can get before the end.

The hounds raced inside when she held the flap aside. Terrence Caul stood behind a short display table with his hands thrust into the pockets of his jeans. "It's good to see you again. Both of you. You know, when I hadn't heard anything after the last time we spoke, I assumed you hadn't found anything."

"We could say the same about you," Johnny replied as he shook the man's hand. "It was quite a surprise to see you in the city instead of out in the boonies."

"Tell me about it."

Charlie finally joined them and the transformed shifters grinned at each other before Terrence stepped around the table to wrap the mohawked dwarf in a quick hug. "Charlie. It feels like everywhere I go to give a speech and hand information out, there you are."

"What can I say? I get around."

Rex snorted and sniffed at a few crumbs on the patio's wooden slats. "You can say that again."

"Yeah, Charlie has a weakness for witchy two-legs."

"Bro, is there any other kind?"

"How should I know?"

Terrence smirked at the hounds but his slight frown betrayed his confusion. "Witches, huh?"

The biker dwarf shrugged. "Would you believe I had no idea a place like The Devil's Playground existed?"

"The Devil's Playground? I haven't heard of it."

"Oh, man. Lemme tell ya. The witch who runs it? Whew. Most people would probably say she's scarier than the blood witch, but I gotta say—"

"Blood witch." Terrence's eyes widened and he turned to Johnny for answers. "Is that—"

"Kaiser's shifter hunter? Yeah." The bounty hunter nodded. "We had a few run-ins with her. She's damn near impossible to take down and keep down."

"That's…" The shifter man's smile morphed into a grimace. "That's not exactly the kind of news I hoped to hear after finding the three of you in LA."

"That doesn't mean we're giving up," Lisa added. "If anything, we'll only double down from here on out. And we've found some things in the last few weeks that shed more light on these skirmishes than we expected. I wouldn't necessarily say they explain what's happening, but it's a good start."

"I'm glad to hear you've found more information. Honestly, I was sure Charlie was leading you both on a wild goose chase."

Johnny grunted. "Yeah, so were we."

Terrence's eyes blazed with a renewed excitement. "As harsh as it might sound, though, I think the time for explanations is over. We're looking at taking real action against Kaiser and his band of murderers—which I'm sure you realized when you heard me talking onstage."

"Only Kaiser?" Johnny folded his arms. "Nothing about Tyro yet?"

"They may or may not be connected. Who knows? But

Kaiser's the real problem. We're fairly certain stopping him will get rid of the Tyro problem altogether, whoever he is."

They have no damn idea who Kaiser and Tyro really are or how they're connected. It sounds like they ain't too concerned about finding out one way or the other either.

The bounty hunter exchanged a glance with his partner and Lisa pressed her lips together.

Sure. We'll keep that to ourselves. The last thing we need is an army of transformed goin' after Bronson Harford and blowin' this whole thing to hell before we have a chance to find out the rest of it.

"I'm guessin' this Azure is the one spreadin' all the confidence, huh?"

Terrence gestured toward the thin stack of flyers on the table and Lisa took one.

Johnny snorted. "I thought you said you weren't sellin' self-help conventions and givin' out flyers."

The shifter shrugged. "It's easier to weed out those who are genuinely interested that way. This isn't exactly something we can simply throw around unless transformed are willing and able to seriously consider what we're doing."

Lisa held the flyer out toward Johnny. "So Azure's real. Not merely a face for this resistance of yours with a name but no substance?"

Terrence chuckled. "She's real, all right. And from what I've heard, she's a force to be reckoned with."

Charlie scratched the shaved side of his head. "You haven't seen her in person?"

"Not yet. I know, it's a little misleading. Me out here, standing on stages and trying to bring hope and agency to all the shifters who haven't exactly had much of either. But many rumors are circulating through the transformed communities."

"Uh-huh. Like Tyro can fly and has connections with the Yakuza." Johnny scoffed. "Hear one crazy theory and you've heard 'em all."

The man nodded. "I know it feels like a long shot but I've sat down with three different transformed who have seen Azure. Right after the three of you stopped at Emmitt's property, in fact. It was crazy timing, all things considered."

"It sure as hell sounds like a coincidence."

"I don't think it is. The shifters I spoke to—those who have seen her—believe in what Azure's doing and I believe them."

"So you've traveled from North Dakota to rally transformed around this Azure magical…" Lisa bit her lip and frowned. "You haven't told any of them you haven't seen her, have you?"

Terrence laughed. "That's not exactly the best way to instill the most confidence and get them to step out of their shells. Everyone's scared and no one wants to stick their neck out unless they have a reason to trust that the guillotine won't come down on top of them. Especially when the proverbial chopping block is all but invisible."

Johnny looked at the flyer again. "Have you seen any pictures of her?"

"No."

"Does anyone know who she is?" Charlie asked. "And where she came from? Who she was before she chose that name? Don't get me wrong, it sounds cool and has kind of an ice-queen vibe to it, am I right?"

The bounty hunter frowned at his cousin and shook his head, but the shifter dwarf either didn't see or was still giving him the cold shoulder.

"All I've heard is how powerful a speaker she is." Terrence clasped his hands behind his back and shrugged. "And that she's been through more than her fair share of hard times, as a transformed or otherwise. Look, I know this might sound like a complete hoax but it's not. Transformed are coming together with Azure, and we'll finally put an end to this."

"How's that, exactly?" Johnny folded the flyer and shoved it into his pocket.

"The most I can tell you is that she has what they're calling a secret weapon."

Lisa widened her eyes. "Are we talking about an actual weapon here? Because that changes things a little."

The shifter frowned. "I don't think it changes anything."

"You can't have a bunch of rallied shifters lookin' for vengeance and callin' it justice runnin' around with an actual weapon of mass natural-born destruction," Johnny pointed out bluntly. "You can see how that makes this problem bigger than it already is."

"Weapon or not, we'll do what we have to do to stop the indiscriminate murders and the threat against all our lives. It's already become far enough out of hand."

"Terrence." Lisa spread her arms placatingly. "We promised to look into this and help the transformed as much as we possibly can, and we're very close to finally making that happen. But I have to be honest with you. Bringing all-out war to Kaiser and his organization, no matter the reasons, won't help anyone. And if that's the case, we can't simply stand aside and let this play out the way it sounds like Azure is hoping."

Terrence lowered his head. "That's fair. I appreciate the heads-up but this isn't my call to make."

"What kinda weapon, Terrence?" Johnny asked.

The shifter studied him for a moment, then shook his head slowly. "The way I understand it, this is Azure's version of the weapon Kaiser's fired on the transformed all along."

Charlie sucked in a sharp breath. "The shifter hunter."

"Agnes?" Lisa wrinkled her nose. "Azure has another blood witch on her side to fight for the transformed?"

"I don't know the specifics," the man replied. "I had the same thought and I wondered if any of this would work. But honestly, it sounds more like Azure's secret weapon is knowledge. How to find Kaiser at his weakest and how to stop him. It may or may not be with actual violence, but with enough transformed behind us to take this to the bastard calling the shots and deciding which of us live and die, his options are limited after that either way."

"So Azure knows how big his operation is and how far it extends," Johnny said. "Is that it?"

"Everything I've told you is as much as I know." Terrence pointed at the stack of flyers. "But if you want to know more, feel free to attend the conference. The word is Azure will map out more of her plans there now that she's gathered enough transformed to join the cause."

"How many?" Lisa asked.

The shifter man shrugged. "Hundreds. Maybe thousands. Which, again, you'll be able to see for yourselves at the conference."

Johnny considered this for a long moment, then turned to the shifter and raised his eyebrow. "Are you handin' out VIP passes?"

Terrence laughed. "Even if I were, you don't need one, Johnny. You got yourselves into a private transformed function at a bar in LA and a magically secluded meeting on Emmitt's property in North Dakota. I'm sure you won't have a problem getting into this too."

Charlie grinned at Lisa. "I got you."

"Okay." She nodded at Terrence. "You have our numbers, so let us know if anything changes."

"You bet. Honestly, it's good to see you guys again. Especially in one piece."

"Yeah, you too." Johnny shook his hand again and Charlie leaned forward to clap a hand on the other shifter's shoulder.

"So this is your first time in LA, huh? I'm telling you, man, this place has everything."

"I'm sure it does. Stay safe, Charlie. See you on the other side."

"Yeah, you too."

The bounty hunter snapped his fingers and pulled the tent entrance aside. The hounds padded dutifully after him.

"Later, shifter."

"Hey, if you see any witches in trench coats, run."

Terrence's soft laughter followed them out of the tent, but he stayed inside in case any other wary but still curious transformed in LA finally found the courage to listen to what he had to say.

Charlie shoved his hands into his pockets and leaned toward Lisa. "Is there a reason we didn't tell him about Tyro and the witch and Addison Taylor maybe being alive? 'Cause hey, I could have told the hell out of that story."

"No one knows who she is," she muttered as she looked over her shoulder at the tent. "No one knows who Tyro and Kaiser are, either. And there are way too many rumors going around for us to start spreading that news without any actual proof."

Johnny grunted. "Which we would have if the witch hadn't—"

"Hey, when are you gonna quit trying to blame me for that, huh?" Charlie whirled on his cousin and gestured impatiently.

"Oh, now you're ready to look me in the eye, huh?

"I said I was sorry."

"And I ain't said shit about you bein' the issue right now." When he felt Lisa's warning gaze on him again, Johnny gritted his teeth and stared at the back door of the bar.

Hell, I gotta patch this up before we keep goin'.

"Listen, Charlie. The way I see it, there ain't much anyone can do to keep Agnes locked up or off her feet for longer than we managed. You're good at screwin' things up, sure."

"Johnny…" Lisa heaved a sigh.

"Well, I ain't fixin' to lie to him, darlin'." He nodded at his cousin. "But it ain't like we're the only ones who let that witch get away. As long as it doesn't happen the next time we cross paths with those two, we'll call it good and move on."

"Honestly?" Charlie leaned away and regarded him with the barest hint of a smile playing on his lips. "Do you mean it?"

"Sure."

"Cool. Then we're good." His cousin extended his hand and

Johnny only took it because Lisa's intense stare made his skin itch.

"Sure."

"All right." With a grin, the biker dwarf downed the rest of his drink and turned in a circle to survey the bar's back patio where only a handful of transformed remained at a table and talked in low voices. "So now what?"

"Now we have to find out what this secret weapon is." Lisa glanced at her partner's pocket. "Azure's closer than we thought. Not only geographically, but she might be on to something."

"Uh-huh. And how many leaders of any army have gone in sayin' they have all the answers and secret weapons and ways to win a goddamn war without havin' any of it for sure?"

"It's worth looking into, Johnny."

"I know. The least we can do is get into this conference, hear it all for ourselves, and see her with our own eyes."

"Then get a private meeting with the leader of the transformed army and find out for ourselves if Addison Taylor is as dead as everyone thinks she is."

"That too."

"Great." Charlie placed his empty glass on the table and clapped in excitement. "So where are we going?"

The bounty hunter's grimace made his thick red mustache bristle. "Vegas."

"Are you kidding me? I love Vegas! Man, you wouldn't believe—"

"I'm tellin' you right now, Charlie, if you can't hold yourself together while we're there and stay outta trouble, I'll handcuff you to a hotel bathroom and leave you there until we're done."

Lisa looked warily at him. "You have handcuffs?"

"I'll use yours."

"Wow."

"Don't worry about me, 'coz. I can handle myself in Sin City."

"See, that's what I'm talkin' about. We have different definitions of handlin' yourself."

Charlie laughed and brought his hand down hard on his cousin's shoulder before he shook him in his excitement. "Relax, man. We'll go with your definition. Grumble everywhere we go, mean-mug the locals, and be the most boring magicals who ever stepped foot in Las Vegas. If you can do it, how hard could it be?"

Johnny's upper lip twitched and he shrugged out from beneath his cousin's hand and stormed toward the bar's back door to return to their rental out front.

"Ha." Completely unfazed, the biker dwarf rubbed his hands together and giggled as he headed after his cousin. "Vegas, baby. Oh, yeah."

CHAPTER FIFTEEN

Azure's big reveal detailed on the flyer wasn't until Wednesday night, and while Charlie presented an incredibly long list of all the reasons why they should let him ride to Vegas ahead of time so he could "scout the area," the bounty hunter wouldn't budge.

Instead, they stayed another two nights at the Residence Inn. Both partners tried not to lose all patience at having to share a hotel room with an overly excited transformed dwarf who regaled them with tales of Vegas "from his old life," bogarted the TV remote, and didn't see the problem with leaving his wet towels on the bed or the wrappers from candy bars and to-go meals all over the countertops. Only when Johnny received a text from Felix did he remember having sent a slew of messages to his pilot's phone only days before.

Ready to go at LAX.

"That's it?" He snorted. "The man finally saw all the missed calls and texts and he doesn't say a thing about the emergency part."

"Well, you did tell him he could take a vacation without being on call," Lisa said as she finished packing her overnight bag for yet another flight across state lines. "And how many times have you told Felix it's an emergency when it wasn't?"

He heaved his duffel bag over his shoulder and grunted. "Once or twice."

"Well then, you're now the dwarf who cried emergency. At least we have the jet ready to head out."

"I wonder if Felix likes Vegas."

"Everyone likes Vegas, 'coz." Charlie finished gelling his mohawk and turned away from the mirror over the couch. "Everyone."

"I wasn't talkin' to you."

Felix didn't seem surprised in the least to hear the plans had changed from flying four hunted transformed to the Everglades. He didn't mention not responding to the emergency texts either. When they landed at the private airstrip in Las Vegas and prepared to debark, Johnny couldn't keep his curiosity at bay.

"You did get my messages, right?"

"Eventually, sure." The pilot gave his eccentric employer a small smile. "And I was on vacation."

"Yeah, but emergency means emergency."

The pilot chuckled and nodded good-naturedly. "Sure. Sorry I didn't bite, Johnny. I know you'd call and leave a voicemail if it was that important."

"I—" He paused and scowled at Lisa as she passed him on her way to the staircase out of the jet, her roller suitcase in one hand and a smirk playing on her lips. "Right." He pointed at Felix. "Real emergencies leave voicemails. I have no idea how long we'll be here, so hang tight, huh?"

"No problem, Johnny. I have a few friends in Vegas. I'll find a way to pass the time."

"Good." With a curt nod, he turned quickly and followed the hounds and Charlie down the temporary stairs and onto the tarmac.

So words done lost all their meanin' if they ain't left in a voicemail.

Christ, this modern-tech crap is suckin' all the life outta the under-standin' between a dwarf and his jet pilot.

Lisa waited for him to catch up with her and smiled as she pulled their rental reservations up on her phone. "Are you okay? You look a little—"

"Don't say a word, darlin'. I know damn well what has you so tickled. Point taken."

She lowered her head and stifled a laugh before they headed toward the Vegas strip almost nine miles from the North Las Vegas Airport. "At least we can spend a little time in Vegas."

"I ain't a fan."

"Why not? Are there too many tourists?"

"Naw." The bounty hunter glanced across the street that separated the airstrip from the heart of the city and pressed his lips together. "There are enough ways to avoid the real tourists if you know where to go. Even in a place like this."

"Then why do you look so disappointed?" She fought back another laugh as the hounds raced forward to run circles around an invigorated Charlie, who started the engine of his unloaded Harley to ride it down the side of the airstrip. "We might have some time to try the slot machines. I've never done that before."

"I ain't the gamblin' type, darlin'. Don't get me wrong. I've had a time of it comin' out here once or twice before. No one gives two shits if I pickle my brains and spill 'em all over the floor. Plus, I have a few friends here."

"Friends in Vegas? Again, I'm confused about why you look so uncomfortable. Especially after the strange but very 'you' reasons for enjoying this city."

"Hell, it's…" He ran a hand through his hair and exhaled a massive sigh. "I could run around here makin' a fool of myself. I'm not sayin' I do or I even want to. But it would be fine 'cause there's always someone here puttin' on some kinda shindig or show or what have you that's a hell of a lot weirder than anythin' most folks get involved in."

"Uh-huh. So Vegas-weird isn't weird in comparison. Is that what you're saying?"

"Sure. Except this time, we're the ones showin' up for the weirdest part."

Lisa laughed. "You think this convention is going to be the weirdest thing we'll find in Las Vegas."

Johnny glanced at her and raised an eyebrow. "A horde of hunted, angry, scared, ready-to-wage-war transformed shifters gatherin' to hear one of their own talk about her secret weapon against the natural-born playin' god. And their leader may or may not be Bronson's fiancée, the girl who died and started this whole war in the first place before comin' back from the dead to raise hell against him without knowin' it. That doesn't sound as weird as hell to you?"

"Well, when you put it that way, it's a little…niche."

"Uh-huh."

Lisa pressed her lips together to try to force the smile from her face. "But that doesn't make this the weirdest thing in Vegas."

"Charlie gettin' us into the private conference so we can talk to a magical everyone else thinks is dead? If it ain't the weirdest thing goin' down tonight, prove me wrong."

"Hmm. Yeah, I won't make any bets."

"That's what I thought."

They collected their rental and Johnny gave his cousin the address of the next location where they would meet with an added, "Stay there and wait for us or I'll kill you," thrown in for good measure. Lisa stared out the passenger window at the tall buildings and all the flashing lights and buildings they passed. "You said you booked us a hotel, right?"

"It's taken care of, darlin'."

"Okay, but you still haven't told me where we're staying. Is it the Bellagio?"

"No."

"Caesar's Palace? I've always thought it would be super cool to stay there for at least a night."

"It ain't the Palace."

"The ARIA? The Cosmopolitan? Oh, my gosh, is it the MGM Grand?"

Rex snorted. "Sounds like a dump."

"Bet it smells like one too," Luther added.

"No, no, and no." Johnny shook his head and glanced in the rearview mirror. "We're makin' a quick stop first. Before the hotel."

"To do what, exactly?"

"See a few guys about the magical parts of Vegas."

She turned away from the window to stare at him. "Since when does Johnny Walker need a tour guide?"

"Do you honestly think that's where I wanna make our first stop?"

"Well, I don't know. You won't tell me anything."

"Trust me, darlin'. Nothin' I can tell you is anythin' close to the real deal. Just wait."

"That's the worst thing to say to someone who's already curious and impatient."

Johnny smirked and didn't say another word.

Charlie was waiting for them when they pulled up in front of a low, squat, nondescript building on West Chicago Avenue. Of course, the dwarf had already struck up a conversation with a group of young women in standard Vegas heels, short skirts, and layers of makeup. They giggled and twirled their hair as he told some extravagant story while he waved his hands enthusiastically. He stopped when he saw Johnny, Lisa, and the hounds getting out of the rental.

"I gotta run, ladies."

"Oh, come on." A leggy blonde with a rainbow backpack tried to step in front of him and pulled her phone out. "We're going dancing tonight. You should come with us."

"As much as I'd love to, I truly can't—"

"Hey." Johnny stormed toward them, already glowering despite the coy looks and approving smiles the women now turned on him too. "Y'all step aside. Whatever y'all are sellin', he ain't interested."

"Selling?" The brunette with massive silver hoops in her ears looked both insulted and amused. "Not everyone in Vegas is trying to sell something."

"Come on, Johnny." Charlie gestured toward the young women. "Are you trying to say there's anything about these beautiful women standing here with me for an innocent conversation that's even remotely dangerous?"

The bounty hunter studied them quickly.

There is no way in hell they're old enough to drink or be in Vegas at all.

"I ain't answerin' that. Go on. Get outta here."

"We only wanna have some fun." The third woman with light-brown hair coiled in a bun on top of her head stepped toward Johnny and touched his arm. "That's why we're all here, right?"

"I said he ain't interested. Neither am I."

"It sounds like you need a little something to help you unwind," the blonde said. "We brought party favors. You should come with us and party."

"Oh, yeah?" He gave her a crooked smile and gestured toward Lisa. "You gonna invite the federal agent standin' behind me too?"

Every smile vanished from the young women's faces and they scowled at Lisa before they hurried down the sidewalk.

Charlie gaped after them and looked like he'd been punched in the gut. "Oh, man…"

"That's enough." Johnny grasped his cousin's shoulder and spun him before he shoved him toward the front door of the building. "Ten minutes in Vegas and you're already settin' yourself up for failure."

"Hey, man, they walked up to me." The shifter dwarf rubbed his arm. "You said to wait here and that's what I did."

"Uh-huh. Forget the handcuffs. Maybe I oughtta put a boot on your damn bike instead."

"Aw, come on, Johnny. I didn't even do anything."

"And you won't. Let's go."

The mohawked dwarf stopped in front of the building's entrance and looked at the faded sign over the door. "Henderson & Hawk? What is this place?"

"Keep your mouth shut and you'll find out."

"Johnny." Lisa shook her head as she studied the building's front façade. "I'm not interested in a repeat of The Devil's Playground. Especially not in Vegas."

"It ain't anywhere near the same thing, darlin'. These fellas are professionals. It doesn't look like it from the outside but that's Vegas, ain't it?"

"What is it?"

"Well, that would ruin the surprise, wouldn't it? Let's go." Johnny tugged the door open and whistled for the hounds. "Y'all keep your paws to yourself. Understand?"

"You bet, Johnny."

"Paws on the floor. We got it." Luther paused outside the door to sniff a spilled and dried pile of something bright pink and sticky. "What about our tongues, though?"

He snapped his fingers. "Luther. I'm only gonna tell you this once. Spills on the sidewalk are off-limits here."

"Okay, but what about—"

"All of 'em. The last thing I need is my coonhounds runnin' round as bent as the other crazies here."

"It smells like bubblegum, Johnny."

"The chances are it ain't. Get inside."

The hound trotted dejectedly through the door and Johnny brought up the rear of the party to step into a store very different than Kennedy's specialty shop above an underground club.

Brightly lit glass jewelry cases lined the walls, filled with jewelry, watches, knives, an assortment of antique pins, two tiaras that were obviously fake, and an entire shelf of trading cards of every conceivable collection. A row of glinting guitars hung above the register counter, surrounded by vintage hats and leather jackets. The rest of the shelves built into the wall were crammed with more random junk—electronics, kitschy tin boxes, and more antique knickknacks.

The bounty hunter strode directly to the register counter and slapped his hand on the metal bell. The ensuing ding was deafening, and Charlie jumped before he spun to look at him. "What the hell?"

"What?" He shrugged. "How else am I supposed to get their attention?"

"Who has a bell that loud?"

"Henderson & Hawk."

Lisa perused the shelves. "You brought us to a pawnshop."

"Somethin' like that, yeah."

"Ooh, hey. Johnny." Luther trotted up to his master, his tongue lolling. "I know. You're gonna sell the shifter dwarf."

"Say what?"

Charlie's eyes widened. "What?"

"Now where the hell did you get an idea like that?"

"We saw it on some show, Johnny. That's what pawnshops are for, right?" Rex leaned toward a display of tiny porcelain dogs and dog bones before he pressed his nose against the glass and snorted. "You take in what you don't want and get money for it."

"No one pawns their cousin." Johnny clicked his tongue, then smirked. "Although I reckon you might be onto somethin' with that."

"No way." Charlie pointed at him. "That's illegal."

"Somethin' bein' illegal never stopped you."

"That's totally dif—"

The bounty hunter banged on the metal bell again and his

cousin clapped his hands to his ears with a snarl. "Stop doing that!"

"It's a bell, Charlie."

The door behind the counter swung open and an Atlantean with eerily tanned skin wearing a slate-gray business suit and a fedora over his two-foot-long hair snakes entered the room. A gold tooth winked under the bright lights when he spread his arms and grinned. "And I'm too slow for Johnny Walker."

"Silas." Johnny raised an eyebrow. "After all this time, I thought you would have looked older by now."

"Neither one of us is getting any younger." With a laugh, the Atlantean stepped out from behind the counter and wrapped the bounty hunter in a crushing hug. His snakes hissed and shied away before the dwarf managed to pull himself out of his old friend's embrace.

"Still with the hugs, huh?"

"You know me. Everyone's a friend until they aren't." Silas' grin widened when he saw Lisa and he scrutinized her with great interest. "Especially you, beautiful. What's your name?"

"Lisa."

"Well, bring it in, Lisa." The Atlantean opened his arms to hug her too but she stepped back and extended her hand instead.

"I'm also not that into hugs."

"Ha! And you're faster than the dwarf." They shook and the snakeheads at the end of his hair trembled violently before they fell limp. "Now what in the world would a gorgeous Light Elf like yourself be doing running around with this dwarf in Vegas, hmm? Are you back in the game, Johnny?"

"What game?" she asked.

"I told you I was out and I meant it." Johnny pointed at his friend. "So don't even try."

"Well, I can't imagine why else you'd be here." Silas leaned toward Lisa again and wiggled his eyebrows. "Whatever he promised you, I bet I can beat it—"

"She's my damn partner, Silas."

"Oh, yeah? In more ways than one, I bet."

She smiled caustically. "You're a real charmer, aren't you?"

"You have no idea." He removed his fedora, slid his hand along the snakes on the top of his head, then chuckled and replaced the hat. "So why are you here?"

"To sell his cousin," Luther added nonchalantly although the Atlantean couldn't hear him. Charlie, though, gave the hound a scathing glare.

"I thought you and Mitch might have a few open rooms." Johnny turned as the shop's owner moved behind the counter. "For the three of us and two hounds."

"The three of…" The proprietor finally noticed Charlie and studied him carefully. "Where did you come from?"

The mohawked dwarf spread his arms. "I've been here the whole time."

"And you're with him?"

"I don't know why that's so hard to believe."

Silas wrinkled his nose, then shrugged. "Hey, what Johnny wants with two partners is none of my business."

"I'm his cousin."

"He's not my partner," Johnny clarified. "We're stoppin' here for a conference and need a place to stay."

"And you came to your old friend Silas so he could set you up with something real nice." The Atlantean pressed a manicured hand over his heart and lowered his head. "I'm touched. Truly. It would have been nice if you'd called first, though. It's been too long, Johnny."

"It was a last-minute decision." The bounty hunter shrugged and nodded at the door behind the counter. "I thought I could still count on you."

"Oh, absolutely." Silas clapped briskly and startled all of them by bellowing, "Mitch!"

Rex yelped and skittered across the floor before he turned to glare at the Atlantean. "Hey, snake-guy. You trying to give us a heart attack or what?"

Charlie was already puffing out quick breaths and rubbing his chest. "Tell me about it."

Luther padded toward them, his head low and his tail between his legs. "This guy's crazy. We should get outta here."

Johnny lifted his index fingers, and both hounds sat immediately. Charlie looked from one hound to the next before he folded his arms.

When there was no reply from the summoned Mitch, Silas rolled his eyes and thumped both hands on the counter. "Mitch, you useless hunk! Get out here!" He tilted his head to listen for his business partner's approach, then tsked and smiled tightly at Johnny. "He's been ignoring me since I sold that videogame console. I got top dollar for it and he's pissed because he can't play in the back when we're slow. Give me a minute."

With a dramatic sigh, the Atlantean whirled, jerked the door open again, and bellowed, "Mitch!"

The door swung shut behind him and the shop fell into a tense silence.

"Videogames." Charlie looked confused. "He's not keeping a kid back there, is he?"

"Do you think I'd hang around an Atlantean who locks a kid in the back of a pawnshop and talks to them like that?"

The mohawked dwarf shrugged.

"Silas Henderson and Mitch Hawk. Business partners and no, one of 'em ain't a kid."

"Johnny." Lisa leaned toward him, her eyes wide. "I don't think renting a room in the back of a pawn shop is the best idea."

"Huh?"

"Honestly, he kind of gives me the creeps."

"Hell, that's Silas. It's hard to trust anyone workin' on the strip unless you're payin' 'em more than they're worth, but I trust these fellas. And we ain't stayin' in a pawn shop, darlin'. This ain't a hotel."

"Then what rooms were you referring to?"

"You'll see."

"Yeah, I got a question too." Charlie headed slowly toward them and cast wary looks at the door into the back. "What did he mean by 'back in the game?'"

Johnny snorted and shook his head. "Nope. We ain't goin' there."

"I'd like to know the same thing," Lisa added and folded her arms. "What exactly did you have to get out of?"

"Have I gotta remind y'all that what happens in Vegas stays in Vegas?"

Charlie spread his arms in a "duh" gesture. "We're in Vegas, 'coz."

Luther sniffed heavily under the edge of the closest display case, leapt away immediately, and shook his head with a snort. "And this place stinks. The bad kind, Johnny. Not like the bubblegum outside."

Rex chuffed and turned toward the back of the shop, one paw frozen in mid-step and his tail sticking straight out behind him. "I saw a rat."

"Rat? Where? I'll get it first—"

Johnny snapped his fingers. "Y'all stay put."

"But it's a rat—"

"Hush."

"Johnny." Lisa raised an eyebrow. "You're avoiding the question."

"I ain't avoidin' it, darlin'. I merely ain't fixin' to answer. It was a long time ago and I'm leavin' it at that."

"But you brought us here to an old friend who looks and sounds like he's into some very shady business."

Charlie snorted. "Talk about people, places, and things."

"Say what?"

His cousin shrugged. "That's one of the things they say in the twelve-step groups. You know, get rid of all the old stuff from your old life to—"

"Since when did you start goin' to meetin's?"

"Six months ago." The shifter dwarf looked warily at Lisa but her reassuring smile seemed to put him a little more at ease. "They help. Kinda."

"You're still drinkin'."

"Drinking is not my problem, 'coz."

Lisa nodded slowly and her smile grew. "Now it makes far more sense."

Both Walker dwarves looked at her and said at the same time, "It does?"

"Yeah." She gestured toward Charlie. "That's where he was trying to go the other day. To see a few friends."

"Before Agnes and Bronson snatched him off the road?" Johnny scoffed. "Naw."

"Huh." Charlie scratched his head. "I didn't think it was that obvious."

"See?" Lisa patted her partner's shoulder. "He's trying."

"Well hell. That—" The bounty hunter frowned at his cousin. "I guess it's…"

"A surprise. I know." Charlie sighed. "Whatever. I can put all that on hold, though, because I'm your consultant on this case and that's more important."

"Don't push it, Charlie."

"You know you need me."

The back door whipped open and banged against the wall, which made them all jump and turn toward the counter, A wizened, bent half-wizard with gray hair sticking straight up from his head shuffled into the shop. His comically enlarged eyes widened behind the ridiculously thick lenses of his glasses and he wagged a crooked finger at Johnny. "You."

"That's right."

The newcomer wheezed a laugh, choked, then cleared his throat and chuckled again. "You're throwing the snake for a loop, you know that?"

He shrugged. "That's his problem. Not mine."

"Yeah, yeah, yeah." The old magical scrutinized Lisa in silence, then spared only a glance for Charlie and the hounds. "Come on back. We'll find you something."

Without waiting for a response, he disappeared behind the door again.

"That two-legs smells like fertilizer and cigarettes." Luther sniggered. "So what kinda shit is he smoking?"

Rex howled with laughter and trotted in a slow circle as he shook his head.

"Nothin' that's good for hounds, I'll tell you that much. Come on."

"Seriously, though, Johnny." Rex trotted behind his master. "Who's the walking skeleton?"

Lisa squinted at the door behind the counter. "I'm wondering the same thing."

"That's Mitch."

"That's the 'useless hunk' the other guy was screaming at?" Charlie asked. "Who plays video games?"

Johnny rapped his knuckles against the countertop, opened the door, and gestured for everyone to step inside first. "He does much more than that. Wait until you get a good look at him from head to toe."

His partner slipped past him into the dark hallway beyond the door and muttered, "I'm not sure I want to."

"Trust me, darlin'. If you want the best in Vegas, these are the fellas to get the job done."

CHAPTER SIXTEEN

When the door closed behind them, Johnny and his team were cast into complete darkness.

"Johnny?"

"Give it a sec, darlin'."

"This feels exactly like the kind of place you don't want to walk into in this city."

"One sec…"

A bright blue light clicked on overhead, followed by another. Then, a path of multi-colored neon lights lit up and spread away from them down the slight decline of a black-carpeted ramp, illuminating both the floor and ceiling ahead of them. The lights strobed away from them repeatedly, and the faint beat of music from somewhere ahead rose toward them.

"A spaceship theme in the back of a pawnshop, huh?" Charlie chuckled and brushed past his cousin to lead the way. "I can dig it."

"What's going on?" Lisa whispered as they followed the shifter dwarf, his silhouette rhythmically lighting up with color before it darkened again beneath the lights.

Johnny shrugged. "So they're a little eccentric. It's part of the gig."

"What gig?"

"I told you it's better to see for yourself."

"That's not—"

"Hey, hey." Mitch appeared at the bottom of the ramp and snapped his fingers urgently as Charlie peered through the open doorway on their left. "That's not for you. Get over here and don't touch anything."

Charlie raised both hands. "I didn't."

When the two partners reached the end of the ramp, she couldn't help but glance through the same door. Dozens of computer monitors rested on long rows of tables, each of them split into six different sections showing live footage of casinos and gambling halls. The same multi-colored lights in the hallway were wrapped around certain groups of monitors to color-code them.

"So your friends own a casino."

"Not exactly." The bounty hunter gestured after Charlie and Mitch, who'd turned down a branching hallway lined with metal railings along the walls.

"So…what? They run security?"

"Ha. No."

"Johnny."

"That ain't what we're here for. Come on."

Lisa looked over her shoulder at the room of monitors. "You know I won't let this go."

"I'll fill you in later."

"You won't tell her a thing," Mitch called over his shoulder as he shuffled along the worn black carpeting. "But if the lady wants to know, I'm happy to give her the tour."

"No way in hell, Mitch."

The half-wizard wheezed another laugh and turned the next corner. Charlie looked back at Johnny with a questioning expression and pointed at the doorway where their guide had disappeared.

"Go ahead."

"Hey, Johnny." Luther sniffed the edge of the carpet and his tail thumped sporadically against the wall. "Smells like other hounds were here. A long time ago."

"Yeah, angry hounds."

The bounty hunter grimaced. "That was a long time ago too."

"What are you talking about?" Lisa asked.

"It was a bad business. Before Silas and Mitch bought the property and did all their remodelin', there used to be a fightin' ring down here."

"For hounds?" Rex stopped short and whined. "Who would do that?"

"A group of no-good morons who didn't last long. That's who." They turned the corner where Mitch and Charlie had disappeared and he leaned toward her to mutter, "If I were to call it anythin'—and I ain't sayin' I am—this might be the first job I ever did as a bounty hunter. Before I was a bounty hunter."

"Wait, seriously?"

"Sure. I had a run-in with the loan shark runnin' the place upstairs and openin' the back up for hound fights at night. I shut his business down and sent him packin'.'"

"You owed money to a loan shark."

"Naw. Silas did. He'd already paid the guy off too, but the asshole wouldn't quit squeezin' him for more so I helped out."

"So you and Silas were friends before all this?"

Johnny snorted. "Naw. I simply have a thing for helpin' the little guy out from under the rocks crushin' him."

"Without any kind of payment or making a deal?"

"I wouldn't say that. We helped each other out."

Lisa responded with a frustrated laugh. "You won't tell me any more than that, will you?"

"Not right now."

They passed through another door and into a room where Charlie and Mitch stood at a balcony railing and gazed over what looked like it had once been an amphitheater. The entire area was lit by the same strobing colored lights, the ramps and stairs leading to the circular arena below were also covered by black carpeting, and all the walls were painted black. A dozen open doorways lined the perimeter of the amphitheater, interspersed between the rows of stadium seating, and each of them was outlined by strands of the same lights that had marked the computer monitors in corresponding colors.

At the center of the open space below, Silas stood in front of a podium that had been refitted into a control panel on the top. He grasped both edges of the podium's surface, his head bowed, and didn't move.

"What's going on?" Charlie whispered.

"Shh." Mitch turned away from the railing to look at Johnny. "He's almost done."

"Hey, look, Johnny. Another ramp." Luther started to walk down but a snap of his master's fingers made him stop. "What? It's for walking on."

"Sit."

"Aw, come on."

A soft hiss rose from the bottom of the amphitheater and echoed toward them, joined by another and then another. Beneath the flashing lights of each doorway around the perimeter, thin, dark shapes moved along the floor.

"Snakes." Rex poked his snout through the spaces in the railing and looked from one doorway to the next. "Those are his snakes."

The bounty hunter peered over the railing as well. Two of Silas' hair snakes slithered down every branching hallway and moved quickly beneath the strobing colors that illuminated their slick, glistening scales.

They all converged upon the Atlantean standing in the center of the room, and only when every single one of them had slith-ered up his pant legs and the podium and finally to his head did he remove his grasp from the podium's edges. He retrieved the fedora and secured it on his head again.

"Your friends get into some freaky stuff, 'coz," Charlie muttered and shook his head slowly.

"Freaky?" Mitch turned toward the mohawked dwarf and wagged a crooked finger in his face. "This is business, son. By the looks of you, I'd say you could learn a thing or two about getting things done."

Johnny snorted.

Charlie returned the bent old half-wizard's stare and broke into a crooked smile. "Says the old-timer wearing glittery plat-form shoes."

"Says the guy who gets things done."

Down below, Silas turned away from the podium to face his guests on the balcony and spread his arms with a wide grin. "What sounds better to you, Johnny? Mandalay Bay or The Mirage?"

The bounty hunter turned toward Lisa and raised an eyebrow. "It's your call, darlin'."

"Um…no. Whatever you guys are planning to do to either one of those hotels, I won't be a part of it."

"He's talkin' about a room." The bounty hunter chuckled. "Usually, there ain't more than one option."

"You're serious?"

"Uh-huh."

A hesitant laugh escaped her and she shook her head. "Well, we'll end up at Mandalay Bay anyway."

"Mandalay Bay it is!" Silas clapped and the echo magnified around the amphitheater. "Well don't just stand there. Come on, Johnny. You know the drill. And if you don't mind, I'd rather get back to my work around here that actually pays."

"Naw, you can't make me out like a free-loader. This is still covered under your IOU."

"If you say so."

"Come on, darlin'." He took Lisa's hand and led her down the curved ramp toward the center of the amphitheater. "We'll go get us a room at Mandalay Bay."

"And then you'll tell me what's going on down here," she muttered and smiled tightly at Mitch as he grinned and wiggled his fingers at her in goodbye.

And why he's friends with two creepy magicals who run this weird place under Las Vegas.

"Johnny," Charlie called and leaned over the railing. "Hey, that includes me too, right?"

"If you wanna stay down here with these fine fellas on your own, Charlie, be my guest."

"Nope. I'm coming." The mohawked dwarf skirted past Mitch and hurried down the ramp with the hounds on his heels.

"Good choice."

CHAPTER SEVENTEEN

Once they were situated in their suite at Mandalay Bay and Silas had returned to his underground hub beneath the pawnshop, Lisa paced across the living area, her brows contorted in a deep frown. "That was way more than I wanted to know about who your friends are and what they do in Vegas."

"That ain't all they do. Only part of it."

"It has to be illegal."

"Lisa, you're overthinkin' it."

Charlie sat in the plush armchair beside the far window and crossed one leg over the other. "I kinda have to agree with her on this one. And you can't argue that there isn't a seriously shady side to what we saw."

"Y'all have the wrong idea about the whole thing." The bounty hunter opened the bottle of Johnny Walker Black Silas had presented to him before they'd entered the hotel's service elevator and took a rocks glass from the cabinet. "It ain't like anyone's gettin' hurt. No one's bein' stolen from. All the money goes to the right places."

"You didn't pay him, Johnny."

"Well, when it's me, it's outta Silas' pocket. I helped him build the place."

"Yeah, that's what's weird to me." Lisa spun, darted him a disapproving scowl, and continued to pace. "You helped a few magicals however long ago settle their debt with a loan shark moonlighting as the guy hosting dog fights underground. Then you helped them turn that creepy arena into…I don't even know what you'd call it."

"Tunnels works," Charlie suggested.

"Sure. Fine. Creepy tunnels. But… Okay, was the mini subway already there or did you build that too?"

"What can I say, darlin'?" Johnny took a long, slow sip of whiskey. "The place had good bones."

"I simply… Every single tunnel had a tiny self-powering subway to every major hotel in Vegas? Do you know how insane that is?"

"It's a hell of a perk for the right clientele."

"It's dangerous, is what it is. Someone could do some serious damage to the entire city if they got ahold of Silas' premises."

"That's not gonna happen. They have security."

"I didn't see any."

He smirked at her. "That's the point. Listen, it ain't a hundred percent on the up-and-up, sure. But Silas is good at what he does. Do you know how hard it is to find a decent room in the best Vegas hotels at the last minute?"

"At the end of the summer?" Charlie sighed. "Almost impossible."

"So how exactly did he get this one for us, huh?" Lisa folded her arms. "Because I can't shake the feeling that we screwed something up for someone else because we wanted a nice hotel."

"Look, it's all about the timin'. He sends his snakes out here and they find out who's comin' into what room when. He makes a few extra bucks on the side by gettin' magicals who know what he does into the rooms they want for a short stay.

We only have the place for twenty-four hours and that's all we need."

"What if someone arrives early and we're illegally in their hotel room?"

"I've never seen it happen."

"He does the same thing for the casinos and restaurants and stuff too, right?" Charlie shifted in the armchair. "That's what all those monitors were for."

"Okay…" Johnny cleared his throat. "They have a little side business goin' on, but I ain't gonna judge."

"A side business on top of their side business?" Lisa laughed in disbelief. "Which casinos are they working?"

The bounty hunter squinted at the counter. "All of 'em."

"Johnny."

He knocked his drink back and poured another. "On rotation. I think."

"This is why you wouldn't tell me what you were up to before I got to 'see it for myself.'"

"Silas and Mitch have numerous other enterprises under their shop—slot machines and even shows when they can get an act in time. Hell, you wouldn't believe the gift shop—"

"That's not funny."

"Fine. You wanna find us a hotel room close enough to this one from where we can keep an eye on things before and after this conference with Azure? Go right ahead."

"Oh, yeah. I will." She whisked her phone out of her pocket and stormed into one of the suite's bedrooms to do exactly that.

Johnny shook his head, took his glass with him, and sank into the couch across from his cousin in the armchair. "I'd better not hear about you huntin' Silas to get somethin' else outta him."

"What?" The shifter dwarf wrinkled his nose. "Me? Come on. Why would I do something like that?"

"You tell me."

"Johnny, I'm sticking to you like a duck on a cracker."

"I sure as hell hope not."

The mohawked dwarf snorted. "Like gum on a shoe. Like white on rice. Like fleas on a hound."

"Speak for yourself," Luther said from the opposite bedroom. "I haven't had fleas for months."

"He means weeks," Rex added.

Charlie peered into the open room. "Hey, that's my room."

"The door was open." The hound poked his snout around the doorway. "And the bed is nice."

"Well, you're not sleeping on it. Get out of there."

Luther sniggered. "It's way better than all the lumpy mattresses we've been sleeping on lately. What was up with that, Johnny?"

"Yeah, were you trying to punish us?"

"That's enough." The bounty hunter snapped his fingers and sipped more whiskey. "We'll sit tight until it's time for that conference and then we see Azure for ourselves. Maybe we can talk some sense into her."

"Do you think she knows about Bronson?" Charlie asked. "That he's Tyro, I mean."

"I have no clue. But whoever she is, I reckon tellin' her, at the very least, is the best card we have to play." He turned toward the other bedroom.

Lisa stepped slowly into the living area, her lips pressed tightly together as she slid her phone into her back pocket.

"Did you find somethin', darlin'?"

She glared at him. "No. But I want to be out of this room before the twenty-four hours are up. First thing in the morning—if I can even get to sleep knowing we aren't technically supposed to have this room."

"No one else is usin' it. Come have a seat."

She ignored the invitation, went quietly into the kitchenette to find another rocks glass, and poured herself a stiff drink out of Johnny's whiskey bottle. "This place has restaurants, right?"

He chuckled. "I think so."

"Good. Then we should get something to eat before we have to sit in another room full of transformed shifters who don't want us there."

"And drinks," Charlie added.

"We have drinks right here."

"Ew, no. Come on, 'coz. That's all crap."

Johnny lurched forward on the couch and leaned toward his cousin with his glass raised in warning. "Watch it."

"Jeez, okay. Touchy. How about I'd rather let you drink your private bottle in peace without your cousin mooching off you? Is that better?"

The bounty hunter lifted the glass slowly to his lips and fixed him with a deadpan stare. "It's a start."

Mandalay Bay's Rí Rá Irish Pub, which should have been low-key enough, unfortunately refused to seat the team with two coonhounds accompanying them. The hounds grumbled about discrimination and Lisa was too worried about calling attention to themselves and the fact that they weren't technically guests at Mandalay Bay to let Johnny try to weasel his way in. Instead, they ordered their dinner to-go and took it with them to the large open area in the lobby to eat it there in front of everyone.

She studied the swarms of people and magicals who milled around the hotel on their way to restaurants, casinos, and other events in the same location. With a grimace, she wiped her mouth with a napkin and muttered, "This feels like a stakeout with a giant neon sign over our heads that says, 'We're looking for criminals.'"

Johnny swallowed his Reuben and chuckled. "It ain't either of those things. Whoever Azure is, I don't think she's exactly a criminal."

"Not yet. But if she's trying to bring an all-out war into broad daylight?" She shrugged. "If she is who we think she is, we have to be very careful about what we tell her."

"We'll have to test that ourselves when we get there."

Luther sat at his master's feet and stared at his to-go box. "Hey, Johnny. You gonna share?"

"You already have your own."

"Yeah, and it's gone."

The bounty hunter dropped a glob of sauerkraut onto the floor and looked around.

"Yes! You're the best, Johnny."

"Hey, what about me?" Rex trotted toward them and cocked his head. "I'm your favorite."

"Bro, you wish."

"Go ask Charlie." Johnny nodded at his cousin, who paused halfway through chewing a giant mouthful and frowned.

"Charlie. Hey. You got any leftovers?" Rex sidled up to the mohawked dwarf and sniffed him. "I can help. You know, if you're full, or you don't like something, or you feel like being a cool two-legs and helpin' a hound out with a little extra some-thin' somethin'—yes! Thanks for the—" The hound snorted at the offered snack in Charlie's hand. "One French fry? That's it?"

The biker dwarf raised an eyebrow. "Do you want it or not?"

"Yeah, I'll take it. Man, you're stingier than Johnny."

Lisa watched the entire exchange with a private smile. "What happened to your 'no feeding the hounds' rule?"

Johnny cleared his throat. "I'm only tryin' to help him feel useful."

"Gee, thanks, 'coz. Do you want me to shine your shoes next?"

"Hey, look at that." She nodded toward the front of the hotel and a group of curious-looking newcomers who moved slowly through the doors. "If I were a transformed walking into a conference that might or might not be a complete hoax, I'd prob-ably have that same wildly lost look on my face."

"Uh-huh." The bounty hunter wiped sauce from his beard with a napkin and shoved his empty to-go box into the bag beside him. "I suppose it's almost showtime."

Lisa glanced at her watch. "The flyer said eight o'clock, right?"

"Yep."

"Five minutes to go, and we've only seen half a dozen shifters head toward the event. Are you sure we're at the right place?"

"It ain't like this is a Madonna concert. I assume fewer folks are willin' to buy into this whole Azure business than those who think stayin' home and not runnin' out to get killed is the better option."

"Terrence didn't seem to think so. Let's go double-check."

"Sure." He pulled the flyer from his pocket and handed it to her. "Go ask the front desk if the secret shifter war meetin's been changed to a different conference room."

She rolled her eyes, snatched the paper from him, and turned toward the desk.

Johnny cleared the remains from their to-go dinner and handed Charlie all the trash.

"Hey, what gives?" The mohawked dwarf struggled to hold the empty bags and boxes and glared at his cousin. "The trashcan's right there."

"You're closer." Ignoring the groans in response, the bounty hunter watched Lisa's quick and uneventful interaction with the young woman behind the help desk before he snapped his fingers. "Come on, boys. They might not serve hounds at a table but no one's keepin' us outta this next part."

"You think they'll have snacks, Johnny?"

"Yeah, a whole room full of shifters? They have to have food. We got snacks last night at the bar—"

"Who the hell fed y'all on the patio?" Johnny growled.

"I dunno. Some shifter."

"More than one, Johnny. They were happy to share."

"Yeah, and we were happy to help."

"I bet you were." He tsked. "Y'all stay with me. I ain't fixin' to lose y'all if this meet and greet goes south."

"Lose us in a crowd of eight shifters?" Rex snorted. "You're setting the bar a little low, Johnny."

"Yeah, even for you."

Charlie snorted a laugh and covered his mouth quickly with a fist when Johnny turned to scowl at him. Lisa joined them in the hall as they headed toward the original conference room.

"This is the right one." She slid the flyer into her pocket. "The woman at the desk made it sound like there wasn't much of a response for the conference, though."

"There's no way in hell she knows what's goin' down in that room."

"No, but someone did book the venue about a month ago and no one's called to change the date, time, or location. I couldn't get a name, but if this is what was on the flyer Terrence was handing out, the details for tonight haven't changed."

"Huh." The bounty hunter turned to scan the hotel behind them, then peered down the hall in front of the conference room. "I assume we'll have enough time afterward for some Q and A with Azure too. Startin' with, 'Where's this army your foot soldiers keep spoutin' off about?'"

"Well, let's see how this goes first before we pose insulting questions and try to tear her apart." Lisa paused and pointed at her partner. "Metaphorically."

"I know you meant interrogate, darlin'."

"No, that's not exactly what I meant."

Charlie paused and sniffed the air. "It smells right."

"What's that?"

"He's right, Johnny." Luther zigzagged across the carpeted floor. "Yeesh. There's booze, sweat, old food, shoes, and cigarette smoke all over everything."

Johnny scoffed. "That's Vegas, not the floor. One would think they would have remodeled the stink with the rest of it."

"That's not what I meant," his cousin said and nodded toward the conference room.

Rex followed the same trail and sniffed madly at the bottom edge of the door. "Those scared-looking shifters went in here, Johnny. That's what he means."

"Yeah, them and…someone else."

"Lots of someones, Johnny."

"All right. Quit tryin' to work it out before y'all bust yourselves. Y'all are simply smellin' the last few weeks of foot traffic."

"I wouldn't be so sure about that," his cousin muttered as he came up behind them. "Unless this isn't the first transformed convention in the last few weeks."

"Please. We've been sittin' right there watchin' folks come in and out of this hotel for the last couple of hours. There ain't no way the place is already packed."

"Which might explain why they don't have any bouncers here." Lisa regarded the door warily. "Something doesn't feel quite right."

"Half a dozen shifters, darlin'. Ten tops." Johnny grasped the door handle and pulled it open. "The only thing that ain't right about this is that Terrence and all the other go-getters have been talkin' up a bigger game than they can deliver."

They filed quickly into the conference room and he intended to turn to make sure the door was completely shut again but was too distracted by the mass of shifters in the rows of chairs that filled the entire conference hall from wall to wall. "What the —"

"Wrong room, pal." A sneering transformed Kilomea clutched a fistful of his collar and jerked him toward the door. "This is a private party."

"I was invited." He jabbed his fist into the beefy inner elbow to break the magical's hold on his shirt, then stepped away and raised both hands. "You touched first."

"It's cool, man," Charlie interjected. "Seriously, it's cool. They're with me."

The Kilomea scrutinized him in silence and sniffed the air. "You're fine but they have to leave."

"No, I'll vouch for 'em." Charlie slung his arm around Johnny's shoulders and grinned. "He's my cousin."

"Mazel tov. Get out."

"Hold on." Lisa pulled the flyer from her pocket and handed it to the transformed Kilomea who acted as a bouncer. "We're on your side. And we only want to help, okay?"

"Where did you get this?" He snatched the flyer from her and held it up to the light. "This isn't for you."

"We know this is a closed conference." She spread her arms in a placating gesture. "But we got that from Terrence Caul in LA two nights ago. He's one of the transformed spreading the word about—"

"I know who he is." The Kilomea cocked his head at Rex and Luther, both of whom remained perfectly silent as they gazed at him and panted happily, their tails thumping against each other. "Are these your dogs?"

"They're with us, yeah." Johnny nodded at the hounds. "And they'll tell you the same."

"Uh-huh." The unconvinced magical pursed his lips around his giant protruding eyeteeth. "If you didn't have mute dogs."

They choose now of all damn times to not say a word? Unbelievable.

"The hounds stay with me."

"And we truly are here to help as much as we can," Lisa added and plastered on a reassuring smile.

The Kilomea scratched the back of his neck. "Did you tell anyone else you were coming here?"

"No."

"Not a soul," Charlie added. "You could slit our throats and throw us in the dumpster out back and no one would even know we were missing."

Johnny and Lisa both stared at him in disbelief.

"Oh, come on. It's all hypothetical."

The agitated bouncer sighed heavily and shoved the flyer into his pocket. "Take a seat in the back. If you can't keep quiet, I know exactly where the closest dumpster is."

"Thanks, man." Charlie patted his arm and instantly pulled away when he was growled at in response.

"Not a sound," Lisa promised. "Thank you."

They moved along the last row of chairs. Three empty chairs were grouped at the very end and they sat quickly before the Kilomea changed his mind.

Johnny folded his arms and shook his head. "No wonder the seats were open. We have the worst view in the whole damn room."

"Well, we are technically bystanders."

"Darlin', after what we've seen in the last couple of weeks, we're a hell of a lot more involved than anyone else here. This ain't a tourist attraction."

"You have a point." She crossed one leg over the other and scanned the massive gathering of transformed shifters crammed closely together to get a glimpse of Azure. "There has to be at least two hundred here. Maybe two-fifty."

Charlie leaned forward to peer past her and smirk at his cousin. "Ten tops, huh?"

"Obviously not." He tugged on his beard. "What I wanna know is where the hell they all came from. They can't be campin' in an event room at Mandalay Bay."

"Oh." Lisa tapped his arm and pointed at the door slightly to the left of the stage at the far end of the room. A large group of wide-eyed, hand-wringing, skittish transformed filed through and searched urgently for open seats while they muttered to one another.

"It's a back-door party." Charlie nodded and grinned. "Smart."

"Uh-huh. If you were scared for your life but wanted to hear one of your own talkin' about the end to bein' scared, I imagine you'd be slippin' through back doors too."

"Speak for yourself, 'coz. I don't have anything to hide."

"It might be part of why you were snatched off the highway." His cousin scoffed and shook his head.

Lisa tapped her fingers against her lips and studied the transformed as they settled in their seats. Most of them looked completely lost and understandably nervous, and the scattered pockets of magicals who held low conversations in small groups were few and far between. "You know, I didn't fully understand why they'd call this kind of meeting in Vegas, of all places. But now it makes sense."

"Sure. What better place to air all your dirty laundry out in the open without anyone judgin' you for it?"

"I was talking about the low chance of an attack, Johnny."

"So was I. Even if Kaiser and his crew caught wind of this goin' down tonight, they can't attack. The whole damn city would know about it. Especially in a place this size."

"It's smart when you think about it. Right under everyone's noses."

Johnny swiped his beard, scowled at the sauce he'd missed from dinner, and wiped it on his jeans. "Hopefully, whatever Azure's fixin' to say tonight is even smarter."

"We're about to find out."

CHAPTER EIGHTEEN

They waited another ten minutes before the overhead lights dimmed more than halfway. A hush settled over the transformed gathering and ended the last snippets of conversation and whispered speculation. A short, petite figure too dark to make out emerged from behind the curtain and stepped toward the front of the stage. Another ten seconds of dramatic pause ticked past before the intensely bright lights at the edge of the stage clicked on.

Johnny narrowed his eyes.

That ain't Addison Taylor. Kennedy can't be that blind.

The transformed woman who stood at the edge of the stage wore a microphone headset, the red light a bright dot beside her ear and halfway hidden behind long, thick black curls. She spread her arms slowly and scanned the dimly lit faces in the crowd. "Welcome."

No one made a sound.

"There had better be more to the show," Johnny muttered.

Lisa nudged him with her elbow and shook her head.

"I know you've come a long way to be here tonight," the woman continued. "We all have. So on behalf of every transformed who's helped to put this together and all those who have spread the word to get you into this room, I want to say thank you for being here. Thank you for standing up against all odds despite not knowing what tomorrow will look like—or if it even exists at all. You're all safe here for tonight, I can promise you that."

A slow smiled spread across her lips and she took a deep breath. "But it's not my promises you came to hear. You came to see Azure with your own eyes and hear her words for yourselves, so I won't waste any more of your time."

She stepped aside and gestured toward the curtain at the back of the stage, and the bright lights winked out again.

Charlie stifled a laugh. "I didn't know we came to see an actual performance. But that's Vegas, right?"

"Quiet," Lisa chided and turned in her chair to glance at the Kilomea bouncer who might or might not have been watching them in the darkness.

Slitting our throats and throwing us in a dumpster might be off the table, but I do not want to be kicked out of here before we have a chance to talk to her.

The slow, clicking echo of footsteps across the stage filled the room and another dark figure stopped at center stage.

Johnny's leg bounced up and down in agitation until Lisa set her hand on his knee to stop him. When he glanced at the hounds, he found them curled together on the floor beside his chair and shook his head.

This ain't the time for a nap.

"I know you're all eager to see what this is about." The second woman's low, articulate voice filled the conference hall. Chairs creaked as the crowd shifted and leaned forward, trying to get a better look. "But I want you to hear my words before anything else. We're all in the dark together and have been for a long time. To those who remember the days before transformed even existed, thank you for paving the way. To those of you who, like me, were born to this, it's time to take a stand before the next generation finds themselves in our shoes.

"I used to think I wouldn't be caught up in all this. That my family had kept me safe. That my friends and those I cared about were too far removed from the power-hungry grasp of the natural-born shifters who want to take our freedom and our choice from us. I almost believed that things would get better, not worse—until I became Kaiser's next target and barely escaped with my life."

"That sounds more like what we were waiting to hear," Lisa muttered.

This time, her partner shushed her.

The transformed woman on the stage continued to speak in the semi-darkness about how she'd overcome the odds and survived. She told them how strangers had taken her in and nursed her back to health before they were eventually approached by Kaiser's mouthpieces wanting to make them an offer. Her entire world had changed yet again when those who'd given her a second chance at life were taken away from her simply for wanting to be who they'd always been without giving into someone else's demands.

The tale was moving and soon, the conference hall filled with muttered assent as the audience nodded, held tears back in the darkness, and settled into this strange form of storytelling.

Another very smart move.

Johnny looked around and most transformed sat with their heads bowed and their eyes closed.

Gettin' rid of the distraction of what she and everyone else looks like makes a speech that much more powerful. Especially one like this.

Even without a face to put to the name, Azure said everything the transformed wanted to hear. She'd related her experiences that could have been matched by any of theirs and slipped in enough detail to make it all sound entirely plausible and even inspiring.

She went on to explain how she'd traveled the country talking to other groups like this one, asking them to join her and the growing numbers of those who were no longer willing to be subjected to Kaiser's demands.

"But it won't stop with Kaiser," she added and her voice deepened. "I thought about trying to eliminate him on my own, silently and quickly without anyone ever knowing I'd been there. I worked out how to do it and still, I couldn't. Because without taking a stand together and without making a statement that is impossible for the rest of this planet to ignore, this will keep happening to us.

"We're the magicals who weren't supposed to be what we are. We weren't even supposed to exist, and that's not something easily forgotten. It means that we have to make it even harder to forget that we won't allow this to continue anywhere near as long as the natural-borns have been pushed aside by the rest of the magical world."

Charlie perked up and his eyes widened. "That sounds promising."

"Yeah," Lisa whispered, "like an intro to whatever weapon she has."

"Y'all hush up." Johnny leaned forward and frowned intently as he strained to hear what came next despite the microphone being perfectly loud enough.

"What I'm about to tell you may sound like the raving of a transformed woman who's already lost her mind," Azure continued. "But bear with me. I thought there was something wrong with me when I discovered what I also assumed was completely impossible, exactly like everyone else—a secret no one else had. I thought it was mine alone. But the more transformed I spoke to and the more I opened up and shared my story, the more I realized how many others shared this secret with me. Not all of them and I couldn't tell you how or why any of us can do what we can do. I can, however, show you that the impossible is possible."

The conference hall filled with tense silence again. The overhead lights dimmed completely.

Johnny looked around and scowled at the ceiling.

More show tricks. Great.

At first, he thought the faint red glow coming from the stage was merely a stage tech's light or the glow of a device being moved around. But in seconds, the red light flared into a crackling blaze and split in two before it stretched apart like a poured line of gasoline being set ablaze.

The crackling red lines of magic illuminated Azure's face in the darkness. Her eyes flashed silver as a ghostly silver outline of a wolf's head rose around her head like a halo.

Someone in the crowd cried out in surprise as two more sources of red light beside Azure lit up the stage, followed by two more. All five transformed displayed the red crackling magic that blazed across their arms and hands with five faint outlines of wolf heads around theirs.

In the next second, all the magic summoned by the transformed shifters who shouldn't have been able to cast it snuffed out. The overhead lights clicked to full brightness and the entire crowd flinched and shielded their eyes.

After that, all hell broke loose and even Johnny wasn't sure whether the infamous Azure could bring it under control again.

"How did you do that?"

"What does this mean?"

"Tell us the truth!"

"She thinks we're stupid. Who would believe this?"

Cries of confusion and outrage mixed with calls for more answers and explanations as the transformed leapt from their chairs and clamored to be heard.

"They can't seriously expect her to answer all that," Lisa muttered and stared at the shifters in front of them who'd stood but didn't seem quite ready to throw their accusations out.

"She ain't tryin' to answer questions." Johnny held his hand out toward the hounds, who'd scrambled to their feet when the yelling started and now watched the excited crowd as they crouched, ready for action at their master's word. "She's tryin' to make a point."

"Yeah. A point." Charlie slapped his cheeks with both hands and dragged his palms down his face. "Holy shit. Transformed can do magic. How the hell didn't I know this?"

"If what she said is true, she doesn't even know." The bounty hunter stood slowly and gestured for the others to join him.

"Where are you going?" Lisa asked.

"To get a better view and I need your eyes on this too, darlin'. Come on."

She pushed quickly to her feet and caught a completely baffled Charlie by the wrist to haul him away with her.

"I can't believe it," he muttered. "That's a thing? How come I can't do…that?"

"Yeah, I was surprised when I learned that too."

"Wait, you knew about this?"

Lisa shrugged and finally released him. "We found out about natural-born shifters having magic a few months ago but it didn't look anything like that."

"And you guys didn't think it was important to tell me?"

"Quiet." Johnny had stopped beside the door through which they'd entered and nodded toward the stage. "We don't have much time to get a good look at things so pay attention."

"What are we looking for exactly?"

"Anythin' and everythin', darlin'." He folded his arms and stared intently at the stage. "Props. Lights. Special effects."

"This isn't a theater, Johnny."

"I know that."

"Hey." His cousin stepped in front of him and fixed him with an offended look. "You knew shifters had magic?"

"Sure. Kids, right? They teach you somethin' new every day."

Johnny shoved his cousin aside and scrutinized Azure standing front and center on the stage.

She didn't look like a performer who'd unleashed a massive uprising in her audience. The woman stood with her arms at her sides and gazed calmly across the sea of animated transformed faces as the crowd shouted and called for more answers.

But they ain't leavin'. And she knows they won't 'cause she set the bait and they all took a bite without even knowin'.

Now that the lights had turned on, it was easy to make out her features. Her blonde hair was pulled tightly away from her face into a smooth, sleek bun at the back of her head. She wore all black, exactly like the other volunteers who'd joined her on the stage to give their unexpected magical demonstration. Her eye makeup—applied more like warpaint than actual makeup—was so intensely dark that it was impossible to tell the true color of her eyes from across the room. It also made her that much more diffi-cult to compare to the photos the team had seen of Addison Taylor.

"What do you think, darlin'?"

Lisa shook her head. "I think she's an incredible storyteller who knows how to work a crowd. And there's no way to tell who she is under the costume."

"Yep."

Charlie scoffed. "No way. No way is that her."

"And why's that?"

"You guys, I've seen Addison. I knew her. Not super-well but we hung out in the same places. There's no way that's her."

"Because she looks different or because you didn't know she could put on a magical light show?"

"I…" The biker dwarf folded his arms and stared at the stage. "Both?"

"That ain't good enough." Johnny tilted his head and scanned the rest of the transformed in the room, who had begun to settle now under Azure's unwaveringly calm presence. "We're seein' this through to the end and I aim to find out exactly what's goin' on."

"Yeah, I don't think that was real magic either."

Lisa leaned away from Charlie to look sternly at him. "That was most certainly real."

"Oh, you're the expert now, huh?"

"She's not a magician making a living on performances and tricking an audience into seeing what they don't want to believe. She's unveiling her secret weapon."

"What, you mean mass hysteria?" The shifter's voice broke at the end of his shout and he cleared his throat quickly.

"Naw." Johnny smirked as the tension faded slowly from the gathered transformed and they settled to wait for what came next. "The secret weapon is her and the others who can do what she did. Kaiser had the upper hand with a blood witch at his beck and call. Now the transformed have a leader who can fight Agnes on her own, magic against magic—and then some."

Lisa drew a deep breath. "Plus an army of displaced magicals willing to do whatever it takes to stop the skirmishes and protect themselves. It's not a giant bomb but they could still do some serious damage."

"Uh-huh. Which is why we're stickin' around until the end. Whoever she is, we're havin' a little sit-down with Azure, whether she wants to or not."

Luther sat to scratch behind his ear. "Will there be snacks, Johnny?"

He ignored the hound and couldn't take his eyes off the shifter woman who stood tall and proud in the center of the stage.

That's the makin' of greatness right there. We only gotta find out if we're dealin' with a righteous leader or a vengeful warlord and what to do about it.

CHAPTER NINETEEN

Once the room of shifters had calmed on their own and most of them had returned to their seats, Azure made another brief address.

"If you want to know more—if you want to do more—talk to Rebecca. We have a secure system for getting your information and when we're ready to move, you'll hear from us. Maybe even before then so be ready. We're closer than you think."

With that, she nodded at the black-haired woman who'd introduced her, then spun and disappeared behind the curtain.

Slowly at first and with understandable hesitation, the shifters closest to the dais rose from their seats and approached the stage. The others followed until a swell of anxious, eager transformed gathered on the far side of the conference hall.

Not everyone was as convinced by Azure's demonstration, and a thin stream of angry and terrified magicals battled against the rush toward the stage to move to the door leading to the rest of the hotel.

Johnny snapped his fingers and hurried along the wall. "Come on."

"What, to charge through all these magicals and demand an audience?" Lisa hurried after him and the hounds.

"No one will notice a thing. That's the point."

"I don't—Charlie!"

Johnny's cousin jumped and scurried to catch up with them. "What's wrong?"

"Keep up, okay?" She nodded at the bounty hunter who stormed along the wall, intent on reaching the stage. "He's on a rampage."

"Uh…maybe we should just put our names down like everyone else and wait for—no? Okay, yeah. I'm coming."

Johnny's assessment was completely accurate. No one noticed two dwarves, one Light Elf, and two hounds who skirted the back of the stage. A simple wooden staircase was the only thing directly behind the curtain but he didn't bother to stop and investigate the pop-up performance gear. He slapped a hand against the door leading out of the hotel and strode outside into the back lot.

Lisa barely caught the door before it smacked her in the face and she pushed it open angrily before she jogged after her partner. "Johnny."

"There." He pointed at a large, nondescript black RV on the other side of the lot. "Transformed party bus."

"We have no idea that's hers."

"Rex. Luther." Johnny raised his eyebrows at the hounds. "Go ahead."

"Easy-peasy, Johnny." Luther pressed his snout immediately to the asphalt and sniffed in a circle.

"Yeah, we got this," Rex added and did the same. "When everything smells like weird magic, follow the—"

Both hounds spun to face the RV and uttered bloodcurdling bays.

"Found her, Johnny!"

"Party bus like you said!"

The bounty hunter met Lisa's gaze and gestured toward the RV. "Now we know."

"Want us to go say hi first?" Rex asked.

"Yeah, we can warm her up for you. Not everyone likes you."

"But everyone likes hounds."

"Naw, we're doin' this together."

"Hold on." Charlie moved around his cousin and raised both hands. "Listen, I thought this whole Azure business was a little too much too. Like a parlor trick, right? But after all that?" He looked over his shoulder at the RV and swallowed. "Okay, real talk, 'coz. I'm terrified."

"Good. It means we're gettin' somewhere."

"Yeah, but if she…you know, attacks us?"

"I think we have a fifty-fifty chance. If Kennedy was right and this is Addison Taylor playin' transformed spearhead, we're fine."

"Uh…" The shifter dwarf hurried after his cousin when Johnny stalked past him. "How's that exactly?"

"She'll recognize you."

"Yeah, but what if she doesn't?"

"Come on, 'coz." The bounty hunter clapped a hand on Charlie's shoulder and returned one of the vigorous shakes he'd been getting for weeks. "Go heavy on the charm. It's what you're good at, right?"

"I'm…well, yeah, but not like this."

Lisa shook her head and increased her pace as Johnny marched to the RV's side door.

This could go wrong in so many ways. And we still can't walk away.

"Get on up there." Johnny shoved his cousin toward the door. "Go ahead."

"Okay, look. If you're trying to get back at me for…whatever, I get it. Point taken. But I'm not a front-lines kinda dwarf. You know that."

"You are now." He pointed at the door. "Go."

Charlie looked pleadingly at Lisa and his shoulders slumped. When she shrugged and couldn't find a reason to back him up instead of her partner, he sighed in resignation, gritted his teeth, and turned to knock tentatively on the door.

Rustling movement came from inside, followed by a few quick footsteps. The bounty hunter tugged his partner aside so they weren't directly in front of the door and snapped his fingers to draw the hounds with them.

Charlie cleared his throat. "Hello?"

The RV remained silent.

"I'm, uh… Look, I know it's a little weird that I came out here and I know we're supposed to sign up inside or whatever. But I—"

The door opened, and a completely altered version of Azure looked at the shifter dwarf. "I'm sorry. You must be looking for someone else."

"Wait—wait. Hold on." Charlie held the open door and studied the woman's features. Remnants of the dark eye makeup were still smeared around the corners of her eyes and she'd let her hair loose from the severe bun. He inclined his head and laughed self-consciously. "Have we…met before?"

"Nice try." She scanned the parking lot. "You'll have better luck with that line on someone who's interested." She tried to jerk the door out of his grasp but Johnny took the opportunity to step beside his cousin and hold the door too.

"How about now?"

"What—"

"Azure, right?" Lisa stepped behind the dwarves and tried to hide her surprise at the fact that the woman who gaped at them looked exactly like the photos of Addison Taylor. "New life, new name. We get it. At least you don't have to change your initials."

Johnny snorted. "Do you think she's keepin' Taylor as a last name? Or simply dropped the second half altogether?"

"I don't know, Johnny." She shrugged. "But I bet she's willing to tell us all about it in private."

The woman who could only be Addison Taylor widened her eyes and glanced around the parking lot again. "Look, whoever you are, I have no idea what you're talking about."

"Huh. So then it won't mean a thing if we tell you we've been spendin' some time here and there with your fiancé—ex-fiancé, I mean. I wonder what Bronson would think if we told him you're holed up here in an RV—"

"Stop!" The transformed woman bit her bottom lip and released her hold on the door slowly. "Please, stop talking."

"Sure. How about an invitation to step inside?"

She took two steps back and gave them a brisk wave forward. "Hurry up."

"Thank you very much." Johnny stepped around his cousin to climb the two steps into the RV.

Charlie looked at Lisa, wide-eyed and visibly nervous, and she waved him forward before she followed him inside. The hounds leapt into the vehicle and the woman pulled the door shut swiftly, locked it, and peeked through the thick curtains that blocked the windows.

Johnny gazed around the RV and nodded in approval. "Very nice. You don't mind a few hounds in here, do ya?"

"I assume you're only referring to the two dogs."

"That's right, lady." Rex sniffed along the edge of the partition separating the back from the front driver and passenger seats. "We're the only hounds around here."

"Only hounds on the party bus, too." Luther sat in front of the woman and looked at her with wide eyes. "You got any treats in here, lady?"

The bounty hunter snapped his fingers. "That's enough."

Azure blinked quickly and frowned. "I'm sorry?"

"I was talkin' to the hounds." He shrugged. "Yeah, I can hear 'em, and no, I ain't a shifter. My cousin is, but you already knew that 'cause the two of y'all already met. Oh, and Lisa here can hear the hounds too but that's a long story for another time. So hey, now that our little secret's outta the bag, why don't we all sit down and you can tell us yours?"

"I—"

"Addison." Lisa nodded at the woman who stared at her in what looked very much like terror. "We know. Don't worry, we're not here to expose you. But we do need to sit down and have a talk."

"How…" Addison puffed her cheeks out for a long, slow exhale and stepped back until she bumped against the cabinets. "How did you find me?"

"Through the owner of a sex club, believe it or not," Charlie muttered.

"What?"

Lisa gestured toward the couches at the back of the RV. "Let's sit and go over everything from the beginning. Our side and yours, okay?"

"All right." Addison slipped past Johnny and took a seat on one of the couches. As the partners joined her, she stared at Charlie until realization filled her features. "We have met."

"Huh?"

"You have an orange Harley."

He grinned and sat on the couch, squishing Johnny between him and Lisa. "Yeah, we tend to leave an impression. I'm—"

"Charlie." She nodded and leaned back slowly. "What the hell are you doing in my RV right now?"

"Um…" The shifter pointed at his cousin beside him before he scooted over to give Johnny more room. "I'm with them."

"And we've been handlin' one wild mess of a case we had no idea you were a part of," the bounty hunter added. "'Cause everyone thinks you're dead."

"I know." The woman clenched her eyes shut and shook her head. "I probably should be."

"Well, you can start there if you want," Lisa added. "With what happened that night on the docks."

"You guys were all inside the conference room tonight, weren't you?"

"Uh-huh."

Addison rubbed her palms down her thighs and shrugged. "Then you heard my story. Everything I said was completely true."

"You merely left out a few details about bein' pulled from the San Francisco Bay and hauled off across the country by a couple of strangers. And why you didn't think it was a good call to contact your fiancé and let him know you survived."

"Okay, look. By the time I recovered enough to even remember my name, everything had gotten way out of hand. Shifters were being killed in front of me and no one cared. No one else lifted a finger. And I...I got so swept up in what was happening that I didn't even stop to think about going back to my old life."

"It sounds like y'all weren't that close to begin with, then," Johnny pressed.

"You don't know what you're talking about."

"So explain it, then." Lisa nodded. "Help us understand why you chose to disappear and become Azure instead of going home again. Why did you want Bronson to think you were dead?"

"That's not what I wanted."

"It sure looks that way. Unless you're sayin' there's some other secret between y'all we oughtta know about."

"We didn't have any secrets but I'm the one who—" Addison clapped a hand over her mouth and stared with wide eyes at the floor. She took a deep breath through her nose, then tried again. "You saw what I can do. You know there are other transformed like me who can...use magic. I had no idea that was possible until I was shot three times in the chest and barely survived. Bronson would never—he wouldn't know how to handle it."

"And you didn't think he deserved to make that decision on his own?" Lisa asked.

"Of course I did. But I found out a few other things that made that impossible."

"Oh, yeah? Like what?"

The transformed woman fixed Johnny with a sharp gaze and bit her lip as she tried to decide whether it was worth telling her surprised visitors the truth. "Like the fact that Bronson's uncle Langley is Kaiser."

Luther lifted his head from where he'd rested it on his forepaws and uttered a low whine. "Hey, Johnny. Secret's out."

"Yeah, lady. We could have told you that."

"What?" Addison gaped at the hounds.

"Huh." The rough rustle of the bounty hunter scratching his bearded cheek filled the RV before he leaned back against the couch and settled his arm around Lisa's shoulders. "After all that work we did, we ain't even got extra information to share with Azure."

His partner glanced sharply at him. "You know that's not true."

"Maybe." He nodded at Addison. "Do you know anythin' about this Tyro rampagin' after Kaiser's leftovers? Oh, that's right. He's been ampin' up his game and hittin' transformed shifters first."

Addison shook her head and swallowed thickly. "No. I don't know anything about Tyro. But he's not the problem. Langley is. Without him, there's no reason for anyone to hunt transformed. If any of his copycats want to try, we'll be able to stop them."

"Oh, boy." Charlie dropped his head into his hands and sighed heavily. "This sucks."

"What?"

Lisa grimaced at the young shifter woman and opened her mouth, but it was way too hard to find the right phrasing for an information bomb like this. "Tyro is a very real problem, Addison. Especially for you."

"I don't understand." She looked quickly from Johnny to Lisa. "And how are you guys even involved in this anyway?"

"You know, it's the kinda case that gets dropped in your lap," the bounty hunter muttered. "A big one we thought would be simple to choose sides on. Transformed are gettin' killed, humans don't care, and magicals don't care. We thought someone had to stand up and get to the bottom of why Tyro sprang outta the ground not long after you were pronounced dead."

"Who's paying you?"

"No one." Johnny gestured at Charlie with his thumb. "My cousin brought this to us and lemme tell ya, it's been one hell of a case. I didn't even know he was one of y'all transformed until he showed up on my couch talkin' about all the secret shifter skirmishes I ain't heard a word about before. You wouldn't believe the things we've done to get this far or the things we found out along the way. And now we're sittin' here with Addison Taylor back from the dead and callin' herself Azure. Merely another mindfuck with so many shifters havin' multiple names and secret lives and—"

"Johnny." Lisa stared at him and shook her head. "That's not the right way to tell her."

"Tell me what?" Addison muttered as the color drained from her face.

"Hell, I was buildin' up to it." He shrugged. "But now that we've had us a little catch-up here, I don't rightly know what the best way is—"

"Oh, come on!" Charlie straightened abruptly and slapped his thighs with both hands. "It's Bronson, okay? And yeah, it sucks. You could have simply gone home to San Francisco and told him you didn't die and nothing would have gotten this bad."

"Bronson doesn't have anything to do with this."

Lisa pinched the bridge of her nose and grimaced.

"And how do you know him?" Azure demanded.

"All right, here's the abridged version." Johnny counted off on his fingers. "The first time we met him, he was workin' at Langley's weed farm and answerin' to the name Carp."

"What?"

"Johnny, don't," his partner warned.

"The second time, we went to a charity gala for the Harford Foundation. Only the real charitable folks get to go and we met Bronson there. He was all charm and responsibility and takin' over the whole damn organization from his dad. I have no idea if you saw that comin'."

Addison stared at him and didn't even blink.

"Then my cousin here was kidnapped by the same witch Langley AKA Kaiser's been siccin' on transformed everywhere. I wish I could say it was a fun little side trip but the truth is, shit only got more complicated from there."

"Come on, man." Charlie nudged his cousin in the side. "Maybe we should talk about a better way to—"

"Shut up," Addison snapped but didn't look away from Johnny's face. "Just say it."

"It turns out Tyro's been on a bloodthirsty hunt lookin' for the three transformed who split you and Bronson up the night you were shot 'cause he blames them and all the transformed for gettin' in the way. For takin' you away from him."

"No."

"It's true, lady," Luther said nonchalantly as he licked his forepaw. "It's a good thing you left, though, right?"

Rex snorted. "Yeah. Otherwise, you would have ended up marrying a murderer with three different names. No one wants that."

Addison's jaw clenched repeatedly and her hands balled slowly into fists in her lap.

"Aw, shit." Charlie lowered his head into his hands again.

Johnny and Lisa shared a wary glance but didn't dare say anything else.

Yeah, she's puttin' the pieces together, all right. Now we gotta see if she handles it like a righteous leader or a vengeful warlord rivalin' her fiancé. Any second now.

CHAPTER TWENTY

Waiting for Addison to give any form of response at all felt like an eternity. The only sound in the RV was Luther licking his forepaw until Johnny snapped his fingers irritably to get the hound to stop.

Finally, Addison inhaled deeply through her nose and looked him right in the eye again. "Get out."

"You're upset. I get that. But we ain't here to—"

"*Now.*" A blaze of red light crackled around her clenched fists.

"Now hold on a minute."

"Johnny." Lisa caught his wrist and gave it a warning squeeze. "I don't think we should push her."

"Hell, that's what we've been doing."

The transformed woman stood abruptly and her hands still sparked with angry red light as she pointed at the RV's side door. "I don't want to hear another word from any of you. And if I see you again—"

"You'll what? Kill the messenger?"

"I'm done." Charlie leapt to his feet. "This was a bad idea."

"Um…Johnny?" Luther stood and cocked his head. "I think—"

"Listen, Addison." Johnny pointed at the angry woman. "We're all for stoppin' a couple of shifters with a few screws loose, even if one of 'em happens to be the guy you were fixin' to get hitched to. But the real reason we're here is so you know how deep this rabbit hole goes."

"I don't need a lecture from a dwarf!"

"Johnny." Rex chuffed and stepped forward, his tail sticking straight up in the air. "There's something—"

"Y'all hush. We're gettin' down to the meat and potatoes now."

"Get out of my RV," Addison all but snarled, "or I'll—" She stopped and looked quickly at the vehicle's side door. "Is that why you're here?"

"What?"

"We've been trying to tell you, Johnny," Rex muttered. "But do you listen to us? No. We're only the—"

Charlie growled and threw himself at Johnny and Lisa on the couch. "Get down!"

He barreled into them and knocked them both sideways a second before the window above them shattered and a spray of bullets peppered the opposite wall of the RV.

"What the hell? Get off me." Johnny shoved his cousin onto the floor and helped Lisa crawl off the couch.

"Yeah, you're welcome," the biker dwarf muttered.

Addison snarled and pointed a magically glowing finger at the bounty hunter. "You brought them here, didn't you? You're not trying to help us at all."

"Aw, come on. Do you think we'd put ourselves in the line of fire simply to—"

Another burst of gunfire destroyed the cabinets above the other couch.

With a hiss, the woman stepped in front of the window and launched an attack into the dark parking lot—a red bolt of light instead of bullets.

The shouting grew louder from multiple voices and now

joined running footsteps, the crackle and snap of attack spells, and at least four more automatic weapons being fired.

"I can't believe I was so stupid." Addison stalked toward the front of the RV and blew the door off its hinges with a super-powered shove.

"Great." Johnny scrambled to his feet and helped his partner to her feet before he dusted the broken glass off his clothes. "She thinks we made the whole thing up."

"Johnny, I honestly don't care what she thinks right now. We're in the middle of—" Something large and heavy thumped against the side of the RV and rocked the vehicle violently. "An attack, in case you couldn't tell."

"Fine. Then let's show her whose side we're on." They raced out of the RV with the hounds and Charlie close on their heels and into a very different fight than they'd expected.

Two shifters were caught in red halos of light streaming from the fingers of Azure's closest transformed who'd demonstrated their abilities with hers onstage. They kicked and struggled within the grasp of the magic they hadn't expected, their guns on the asphalt.

Two more snarled and shifted in the parking lot before they launched themselves at the other magically-powered trans-formed. Red light blazed around both the defenders' hands, and they hissed before they swung their glowing fists and knocked two fully grown shifted wolves off all four paws.

The attackers yelped and skittered across the asphalt, but before they could recover to continue the assault, they were engulfed in the same red halos and returned to their human forms.

"Holy shit." Johnny stepped out of the RV, his hand poised over an explosive disk on his belt. "That's—"

"So badass," Charlie muttered as he hopped out. "There's gotta be a way to learn that, right? She's second-generation so I should be able to do that."

Lisa reached instinctively for her firearm and cursed herself for leaving the gun and the shoulder holster in their last-minute hotel suite. "That's it? Only four?"

"Five, it looks like." The bounty hunter pointed at a massive shifter who lay unconscious at the wheel of the RV.

A furious Azure stood over him and snarled as she glared at the attacker she'd apparently thrust into the side of the vehicle. "For now. They'll send more." She turned toward her team of transformed and nodded. "We need to leave. Now."

"Good idea." Johnny dusted his hands off. "Do you have a number or an email address? Some way we can get hold of you? We can regroup and decide how to move forward."

She laughed and shook her head. "You're insane."

"Hell, I wish I could say you're the first to tell me that."

"Veron's not here," Lisa said and scanned the unconscious bodies of their attackers. "They had guns, that's it. Agnes didn't show up."

"So maybe someone let word slip of a meetin' goin' down in Mandalay Bay." Johnny shrugged. "Kaiser probably doesn't even know yet."

"And he won't," Addison snapped.

"Well, yeah." Charlie gestured toward the bodies. "There's no one left to run back and tell him."

"Except for you."

"Now hold on a minute," Johnny protested. "We were shot at the same as y'all."

"Then you're lucky you didn't get hit." The leader of this new strain of transformed nodded at her team before she nudged the body of the shifter she'd thrown against the RV with the toe of her boot. "I hope that luck stays with all of us."

"Addi—" Lisa cleared her throat. "Azure. We came here to help you."

"You should have focused more on helping yourselves."

The transformed converged around Johnny and his team and their hands and arms blazed with red light.

It looks like Agnes' damn blood magic but these shifters ain't anywhere near as darkly involved. Probably.

"Whoa, whoa. Hey." Rex stepped slowly across the lot as a smiling transformed man stalked toward him. "Johnny? Why are they being creepy?"

Luther skittered away from another transformed, his tail between his legs and his eyes wide in terror. "Johnny! They're trying to touch me! I can't—ooh. Hey." The hound sniffed the air and turned to find his would-be attacker unwrapping a Slim-Jim in front of him. "Nice. Feel like sharing?"

"Don't you dare," Johnny ordered and lowered a hand to the utility knife at his belt.

Lisa summoned her golden Light Elf energy in both hands and glanced warningly at Addison before she took stock of the other three transformed who drew closer. She and the Walker dwarves backed together into a tight circle. "You're making a mistake."

"We'll see." The woman spread her arms and before Johnny and his team could react or try to fight to escape what should have been a friendly meeting—or at the very least a neutral get-together—the transformed attacked.

Darts of red light surged from every direction and struck the three investigators to freeze them instantly. Every muscle in Johnny's body seized, his jaw clenched, and Luther's voice sounded incredibly far away, even in his mind.

"Oh, man. That's delicious. Hey. Hey, what are you doing? We're all friends here. Johnny!"

The dwarf had barely enough time for a single thought before the entire world went dark.

Hell, not again.

CHAPTER TWENTY-ONE

The first thing Johnny noticed when he woke was how stiff his shoulders were. Then came the awareness that his eyes were open, he couldn't see a thing, and his cheek was squashed against a cold cement floor.

"Goddammit." He grunted and tried to push off the ground, but his wrists were bound behind his back with what felt like rope.

This ain't how solvin' a case and findin' a dead woman still alive is supposed to be.

With one hell of an effort given his pounding headache, he drew his legs beneath him and managed to haul himself into a seated position. He swiped his legs across the floor around him but didn't make contact with anything.

"Is anyone else in here with me or am I screwed all on my own?"

"Johnny?" Lisa's voice was raspy and sounded groggy in the dark.

He exhaled a sigh of relief. "Are you all right, darlin'?"

"We're tied up in the dark with no idea where we are." She cleared her throat several times and the sound of her struggle to rise off the floor made him wait. "I'm gonna have to say I've been better."

"Sure." He chuckled wryly. "We've seen worse too."

At least we ain't hurt as far as I know.

"Aw, shit…" Charlie's low growl came from somewhere on Johnny's right. "I don't remember getting wasted enough to feel this rough."

"Oh, good." The bounty hunter rolled his eyes. "We're all in one piece and stuck in here together. Boys?"

There was no reply from the hounds.

"They're not here," Charlie muttered. "I don't smell anything but the two of you."

"Okay, hold on," Lisa said.

Two orbs of golden light flared in front of Johnny and he blinked against the glare until his double-vision converged and he stared at Lisa's back. Her wrists were bound behind her as well and she faced away from him, but her summoned energy illuminated enough to see their immediate surroundings.

"This doesn't look good," Charlie muttered.

"Yeah, no shit."

Lisa kicked the floor to spin herself and face the dwarves. Johnny met her gaze in the low light and nodded. His cousin still lay on his side, his wrists bound as well, and raised his head to look at his companions before he lowered it gently to the cement again.

"I told you that was a bad idea, 'coz."

"This ain't the time for 'I told you so,'" Johnny snapped. "I need to find my damn hounds."

"Right. Yeah. Two friendly coonhounds who happened to be snatched with us." Charlie snorted. "That's the most important thing right now. Good thinking."

Lisa scooted back across the floor until her back met the plain cement wall, propped herself up against it, and pushed to her feet. "They came in more than a little handy the last time we were knocked out and tied up."

"Well, if we can't hear 'em, they ain't close by like the last time." The bounty hunter gazed around the dark room. Besides his partner and his cousin, their holding cell held nothing but concrete, dust on the floor, and a tin bucket lying on its side beside Charlie.

The shifter dwarf noticed that final detail as well and rolled his eyes. "Nice. They left us a crap bucket. It's kind of useless if we can't use our hands. Oh, wait. No… They wouldn't go that far."

"With what?" Lisa stretched out her neck from side to side.

"Make us beg them to help when nature calls. Right?" Charlie's eyes widened and his gaze darted from his cousin to the Light Elf. "Come on. That's inhumane treatment right there—"

"Charlie."

"Yeah."

Johnny stared expressionlessly at him. "Shut the hell up."

Lisa walked cautiously toward the opposite side of the room and turned now and then to bring her bound hands closer to the wall. The dwarves watched her light move away from them until she stopped ten feet from where they'd been unceremoniously dumped and turned toward them. "There's a door."

Johnny nodded at the steel door centered in the cement wall. "At least they didn't bury us alive."

"Well, that's a relief." Charlie kicked his legs out, didn't make contact with anything, and gave up trying to rise from the floor. "Man, for a minute there, I was worried this would turn out to be some kinda real-life *Saw*."

"What the hell are you goin' on about?"

"You know. The movie? Like, would we run out of oxygen down here before one of us decided to kill the others and maybe eat them to stay alive a little longer until help finally showed up and—"

"Dammit, Charlie. If you ain't got somethin' useful to say, keep your damn mouth shut."

"There's no handle," Lisa said. "And no way to open it from the inside that I can see."

"Fine. Come over here, darlin'." The bounty hunter scooted himself against the opposite wall and found his feet the same way she had. A wave of dizziness overwhelmed him but he shook it off with a grunt and leaned his back heavily against the wall. "I can't reach 'em myself but you can grab one of my disks and—" He froze when he looked at his belt and found it missing. "Damn."

She moved toward them and brought her elf-energy light with her. "A strip search and seizure isn't that much of a surprise."

"Strip search? While we were unconscious?" Charlie swallowed. "Damn. I haven't felt this violated since the summer after high school. Hey, Johnny? Remember that girl we were both into? Dorris something—"

"Shut up," the two partners snapped at the same time.

The mohawked dwarf stared at them, then shrugged against the floor and sighed.

"Might be they ain't searched everythin'," Johnny muttered and nodded for her to come closer. "I have those sticky beads in my pocket, darlin'. If Addison and her crew ain't searched every nook and cranny, at least. If you can get your fingers into my pocket and search…"

She looked at him and pressed her lips together. "It's worth a try."

With a brief frown at Charlie, she turned, pressed her back against Johnny's front, and fumbled for his pocket.

He grunted like he'd been socked in the stomach and shook his head. "That's front and center, darlin'."

"What?"

"It ain't my pocket."

"Oh. Sorry."

He tried to turn his hip toward her searching fingers. "A little more to the left. No, your other left."

"Johnny, your left is my left."

"Well, pick a damn side. Yeah, that's it."

"Okay, I think I got it." She hooked her fingers against the waistband of his jeans instead. "Crap. Hold on."

"Hey, guys."

"Not now, Charlie."

"Is anyone gonna ask the shifter if he can Hulk out and bust through the ropes around his wrists?"

Johnny and Lisa froze in their awkward grappling and turned slowly to look at the dwarf lying on the floor. She sighed. "Do you honestly need permission to try?"

"No. I'm merely thinking out loud. Hold on." Charlie clenched his eyes shut and puffed his cheeks out. Nothing happened. "Wait. I gotta try again." He scrunched his face up and grunted a few times as he rocked on his side.

The bounty hunter dropped his head back against the wall behind him. "I think he'll need that crap bucket sooner than we thought."

His cousin sighed and scowled at the floor in front of him. "Well shit. I never had a problem with breaking out of ropes before. Or chains. Or handcuffs. You know, this one time—"

"Back to the pocket, darlin'."

"Yep."

Lisa bent her knees a little to get her fingers to the edge of her partner's pocket. "Okay… A little higher."

"You mean lower."

"No, get your hip a little higher, Johnny."

"Unless you have a rope to hang me by, darlin', this is as high as I go."

"Fine. Okay—hold still!"

"Hey, wait." The biker dwarf raised his head from the floor. "Guys."

"We're a little busy here, Charlie." Lisa bent her knees a little more and jerked her hand around. Johnny grunted and almost staggered away from the wall. "Oh, come on. If you keep moving like that—"

"Then quit pullin' at me. Down and in. That's it."

"It's a little harder than it looks, okay?"

"Guys, I hear something," Charlie muttered.

"Unless it's the hounds or someone callin' our names, don't say another goddamn word!"

"Wait, wait." Lisa poked her tongue out between her lips and finally slid her hand inside his pocket. "Got it! Wait."

"Well, did you or not?"

"Johnny, it's empty."

"Damn. Try the other one."

"Are you serious right now?"

"I am." Charlie finally kicked against the floor hard enough to get his shoulders off the concrete and rocked into a sitting position. "I hear some—"

"This area's off-limits." The low male voice was muffled through the door. "Hey, you can't come in here—"

"Don't tell me what I can and can't do." The woman's low growl was filled with fury and somehow vaguely familiar. "I've been in this game longer than you've been alive, kid. I'll—hey! Touch me again. Try it."

"You're not authorized to—"

"Oh, give it a rest. You're not—this is ridiculous!"

There was a sharp gasp and a sputter of surprise from the man before a hollow thud knocked against the steel door at the far end of the room.

"That does not sound good," Charlie muttered.

"Pocket," Johnny said hurriedly. "Other pocket, darlin'. Come on."

"Yeah, yeah. Hold on." Lisa shuffled sideways against him and felt around at his other hip.

"Hurry."

"I'm working on it, Johnny! But—"

A loud metallic clang echoed through the concrete room and the heavy metal door swung outward and filled their prison with a blazing yellow light.

The partners froze.

Charlie squinted against the glare and leaned forward to get a better look.

A woman's dark silhouette filled the open doorway, her head and shoulders framed in a halo of wild curls that broke up the light. She snorted. "Huh. I knew you two were into each other but getting frisky in captivity takes it to a whole new level. And with an audience."

I know that damn voice. Who the hell is this?

Lisa tried to jerk her hand from his pocket and almost pulled them both to the floor in the process. She stepped away from him and turned sideways to look over her shoulder as the golden energy flared brighter in her hands. "We won't go down without a fight."

"I know you have good aim, Lisa, but with your hands tied behind your back? That's a long bluff."

"Who are you?" Charlie asked.

"Shut up." The woman stalked through the door and stormed toward them. "With all the other shit on my plate, I can't believe I'm doing this right now. You know how lucky you are, right?"

When she reached the glow of Lisa's magic, Johnny gaped at the redheaded shifter woman and grunted in disbelief. "Fiona."

"Johnny."

"What the hell are you—"

"You're in no position to be interrogating me right now. I think that's perfectly obvious." The delegate from the Coalition of Shifters caught a dumbstruck Lisa by the wrists and swiped one hand across her bonds. A flash of silver erupted from her finger like a knife and severed the ropes so they dropped to the floor.

The Light Elf rubbed her wrists and looked at the woman in astonishment. "How did you—"

"When, where, how, why. Yeah, we all have questions." Fiona tugged Johnny roughly away from the wall. "Hold still."

Charlie strained and grunted. The sharp tear and snap of the ropes around his wrists were followed by a sigh of relief as he pulled his arms apart and stared at his freed hands. "There it is."

"Were you fuckin' with us the whole time?"

"Hey. Do you think I like being tied up in a concrete box with you?"

The ropes dropped from around Johnny's wrists and he lurched away from Fiona toward his cousin. "You merely like jerkin' everyone around by the—"

"Hey!" Their rescuer spread her arms and gazed around the cell. "Magic-dampening reinforcements. The door's open so the seal's broken." She glanced at the door. "And I would like to get out of here before that twenty-something transformed with his head up his ass comes to and locks us all in here together. Jesus, I didn't think I'd have to try to convince someone to let themselves be rescued. Keep up."

Without waiting for anyone to reply, Fiona stormed out of the room and into the brilliantly lit hallway beyond.

The partners stared at each other. "What is she doing here?"

"Hell if I know." The bounty hunter slid his hand into his right pocket and pulled out a handful of the sticky gelled beads used as tiny explosives. With a snort, he showed them to Lisa before he shoved them into his pocket again and strode toward the door. "We didn't need a damn rescue. We need answers."

"Oh, trust me. We'll get them." She stormed after him.

Charlie leapt to his feet and spread his arms. "Yeah, I'm okay, guys. Thanks for—shit!" The door started to swing shut and he raced across the room to slam his hands against it before it could. "Which one of you tried to lock me in there?"

A young shifter man in all black lay propped up against the wall beside the door, his chin lowered almost to his chest. He groaned and started to stir.

Charlie shoved him in the shoulder and he toppled sideways to the floor. "And stay down. Johnny! Wait up!"

CHAPTER TWENTY-TWO

"What the hell are you doin' runnin' around with Azure?" Johnny asked as he stormed down the long hall after the swiftly moving Fiona.

"I'm not running around with anyone," she retorted. "And her name isn't Azure although I have to give her credit for such a badass-sounding alias. Her real name is—"

"Addison Taylor," Lisa added. "We know."

"You know?" The redheaded shifter stopped short and turned to look at them in disbelief. "Does she know you know?"

"Yep."

"And she still locked you up. Of all the—" With an angry snarl, Fiona spun and marched forward again. "It's merely another thing to add to the list of why this girl needs to open her eyes. Attacking the two of you? Locking you in a cage? If she thinks she's ready for the big leagues, she'd better start acting like it."

"You've been helping her?" Lisa asked.

"Help is a strong word."

"It's more than you pulled through for with Amanda, that's for damn sure."

"The kid has nothing to do with this, Johnny."

"Except for the fact that you promised a call. We ain't seen hide or hair of you all summer, then you show up here soundin' as crazy as Addison Taylor. Is this more important to you than the trainin' you promised her?"

"You know what? You'd still be in that cell rubbing up against each other if it weren't for me, so how about a little gratitude, huh? Trust me, it wouldn't be misplaced. And don't tell me training Amanda is more important to you than not being killed for your stupid decisions."

"Do you know how hard it is to deal with a moody thirteen-year-old girl all summer?"

Fiona turned left down another corridor and shook her head. "That's part of the package when you have a kid, Johnny. You know that."

"It ain't when you're the reason she said her entire summer was ruined. Do you think she'll simply play along when she finds out you were gettin' twisted up in a shifter war instead—"

"I'm not interested in a war." She whirled on him and thrust a finger in his face. "I'm not interested in these skirmishes or the natural-borns versus transformed. The Coalition has no part to play in this beyond our work with divergents."

He glared at her and sniffed. "Get that finger outta my face."

"You haven't lightened up at all in the last few decades, have you?"

"Not when you can't keep your hands to yourself."

Fiona lowered her hand and glanced behind him at Charlie who huffed and puffed to keep up. "Amanda won't hear about this. I'll visit her at the school when I can. After I deal with the most important problem first. Is that clear?"

"It will be when you tell us what's going on," Lisa said.

"Yeah. We'll get to that part later." The redhead spun away again and continued down the hall with renewed determination. "After I give an emerging leader a piece of my mind."

Johnny clenched his fists and glowered after her before Charlie finally reached them, breathing heavily.

"Seriously, guys. Who's the redhead—"

"Don't." With a growl, the bounty hunter strode forward after Fiona.

"Do you have any idea what she's talking about?" Lisa asked. "Divergents?"

"Not a damn clue. I expect we're fixin' to find out when Addison Taylor gets an earful from an angry shifter too big for her boots."

The shifter in question glanced at her watch and rolled her eyes before she jerked open a door in the hallway. She stormed inside and her shouts rose above the scrabble of chairs against the floor and warning growls. "I thought we had an understanding but it looks like you're trying to branch out on your own in all the wrong directions."

"We're in the middle of a meeting—"

"A meeting you wouldn't even be having if it weren't for me!"

The partners hurried into the room with Charlie close on their heels and stopped.

Addison and the higher-ranking followers of her transformed army stood around a circular table in the center of the room. She'd reapplied the heavy eye makeup and pulled her hair into the severe bun, and she now glared at Fiona in warning. Her scowl deepened when she saw her prisoners standing free and completely clueless behind the Coalition delegate. "I know I didn't authorize their release."

Fiona snorted. "No. I did."

Johnny stepped forward. "And now you're gonna tell us why you locked us up in the first place and what you did with my coonhounds."

"I'm not telling you anything."

"Fine. So we'll do this the hard way—"

"Shut up, Johnny," Fiona yelled. "I'm this close to locking you up again myself. Everyone out."

Addison's followers looked at her for permission and she pressed her lips together but nodded in assent. The transformed left their places around the table and filed out of the room. Lisa stepped aside to let them pass. Johnny and Charlie glared at them with matching sneers and didn't bother to get out of the way.

"Take the dwarves and the Light Elf with you," Addison muttered.

"No." Fiona shoved her hand against the chest of a transformed who reached for Johnny but held Addison's gaze. "They're with me."

"They brought an attack down on my RV behind Mandalay Bay. You can't—"

The redheaded shifter shoved the transformed aside and finally turned her glare onto him and pointed in warning. "Out."

He hurried into the hall and she slammed the door shut behind him. She reached for a lock on the doorknob, found none, and shook her head. "We seriously need to get you a few upgrades here."

"You broke my meeting up and freed my prisoners to talk about upgrades?" Addison folded her arms. "What is this?"

"Don't be stupid. They aren't your prisoners. Sit."

"If you'd heard what they told me, you would have locked them up too."

Fiona snarled and stormed around the table to clamp a hand forcefully on the younger woman's shoulder. With the other hand, she gestured to the open chair. "I don't care what they told you. Johnny Walker and Lisa Breyer don't screw around and they sure as hell wouldn't bring Kaiser's flunkies with them to try and fail to take you down. Sit."

Her eyes wide with confusion, Addison lowered herself stiffly into the chair.

Charlie looked dejected. "Nothing about me, huh?"

Fiona looked blankly at him and shook her head. "I don't know you. So no."

"You know them?" Addison's frown deepened. "How well?"

"Well enough to tell you with complete certainty that you're making some epically giant screwups before you've even started." The redhead sat abruptly and nodded at the two partners. "Jesus, is everyone in this place stoned or something? I said sit."

The biker dwarf scrambled toward a chair, dropped into it, and rested his hands in his lap.

Johnny pulled another chair out for Lisa and scooted it in beneath her before he sat, glaring the whole time at Addison Taylor playing her Azure warlord persona. "Where are my hounds?"

Fiona snapped her fingers. "Drop the dogs, Johnny. They're fine."

He folded his arms and leaned back against the chair.

If she's lyin', I don't give a flyin' shit how high up she is with the Coalition. I'll bring her all the way down.

Lisa's foot nudged up against his under the table and helped him calm his anger a little.

"Now." Fiona folded her hands on the table and leaned toward Addison. "I want you to tell me exactly what you were smoking when you decided attacking these magicals and imprisoning them in this facility was a good idea."

The younger woman grimaced and turned slowly to look at the redhead. "I told you. They found me in my RV and sat down to offer a bullshit story about Bronson, and the second I told them to leave, Kaiser's shifters opened fire."

"Bronson." Fiona's eyes widened at the investigators. "Harford, I'm assuming."

"He sure as shit had better be the only one," Johnny grumbled. "Multiple names? Fine. I can't handle more than one transformed runnin' around with the same name."

She frowned quickly at him before she shook her head. "What about him?"

Lisa nodded at Addison. "Ask her. She knows it's true or we wouldn't be here right now."

"It's not true." The young shifter shook her head. "It's impossible. You're trying to break me down—"

"Well, you came back from the dead to raise an army," Fiona interjected. "Don't talk to me about impossible. Talk to me about your damn fiancé."

"They—" Addison gritted her teeth, sighed heavily through her nose, and met the redhead's gaze head-on. "They think he's Tyro."

The room fell incredibly silent until Charlie sniffed and rubbed under his nose before he folded his arms.

"Huh." Fiona cocked her head. "And that surprised you enough to make you throw all common sense out the window."

"It doesn't make sense." The younger shifter shook her head and tried to hold herself together despite her intense scowl, and her lower lip started to tremble. "At all. Before I was shot, we were... I knew he was going to propose to me. Bronson never had an issue with transformed. He wouldn't be jumping on Kaiser's train to start killing my kind all on his own. That's not who he is."

"Grief changes a fella," Johnny said. "I can tell you that from personal experience."

Fiona jerked her thumb toward him. "Take it from a dwarf who lost his only kid and didn't go on a killing rampage."

He shook his head and glared at the shifter woman's profile.

"That proves my point," Addison started. "Bronson isn't the—"

"Your point doesn't matter right now!" The other woman slammed a fist on the table. "The guy's uncle is the one who started all this nonsense in the first place. Even without proof, Bronson as Tyro makes more sense than any of the other crap theories I've heard floating around the last few months."

"We have proof," Lisa said. "Or we did, at least."

Charlie cleared his throat. "He attacked me."

"Who?"

"Tyro. Then Johnny thought the wolf was me and punched him in the face. The blood witch took a bullet in the leg. Ha. Who knew that was what it took to bring her down? We tied Bronson up and a couple of buddies of mine threw them into a van before we—"

"Stop. Please stop talking." Fiona stared at him in confusion. "Who are you?"

"Charlie Walker."

She raised an eyebrow at Johnny.

The bounty hunter took a deep breath and gritted his teeth. "My cousin."

"You have actual living, breathing, blood-related family. Huh." She looked at him with what might have been a smirk. "That's a surprise. And he's a part of this because…"

"He brought us the case," Lisa said.

"What case?"

"The goddamn case we were workin' to get to the bottom of the faction skirmishes and the shifter war," Johnny snapped. "Langley Appleman is Kaiser. Bronson Harford is Tyro. And Addison Taylor came back from the dead as Azure the damn transformed warlord with magic and her head up her—"

"Johnny." His partner placed her hand on his thigh and shook her head. "Not now."

"Naw, I'm done holdin' back. We've been nothin' but honest and straightforward this whole damn time and whoever said the truth will set you free ain't been turned on by a heartbroken transformed and tied up in a goddamn cement box!"

Fiona fixed him with a glare. "Are you finished?"

He cleared his throat and nodded. "For now."

"So let me get this straight." The redhead pointed at Charlie. "You saw Bronson Harford with your own eyes."

"Uh…yeah."

"And he was acting as Tyro."

"Uh-huh…" Charlie glanced at his cousin. "Why is she asking me?"

"Well, you're a damn transformed too, aren't you?" she snapped. "I can smell it all over you. It's weird on a dwarf but we all know the Dark Families didn't discriminate. At least not like that."

"We had 'em locked up," Johnny said. "Bronson and his uncle's shifter-huntin' blood witch on a long-ass leash."

"Who?"

"Her name's Agnes," Lisa added. "And she's…the most dangerous magical I've come across in a long time. On her own."

Charlie snorted. "She's almost as invincible as Addison. We hit her with a freaking SUV and she still didn't die."

"Okay, no more out of you, Chuck." Fiona pointed at him. "You stopped making sense before you opened your mouth."

Addison sat perfectly still with her fists clenched tightly in her lap and stared at the tabletop before she muttered, "Blood witch. She's the first one."

"First one what?"

"Hold your horses, Johnny." The redhead raised a hand to silence him and leaned toward Addison. "You're talking about the divergents, yeah?"

Nodding slowly, the younger woman lowered her gaze to her white-knuckled fists. "Like us."

"Well, shit." Fiona ran a hand through her hair and sighed. "I thought we were lucky when we got the witch's signal out in the middle of nowhere California before finding the rest of you halfway across the country. I should have known you'd all be in the same boat. And no, there's nothing lucky about finding divergent magicals instead of Oriceran creatures with a penchant for Earthly evolution—"

"Now you're losin' the mark," Johnny muttered. "I ain't followin' a word you said."

"That's probably because I wasn't talking to you." She glared at him. "But now it's all playing too close to home. Fine. Listen up because I'll only say this once. Then we're making some serious adjustments to our plan, which Addison will follow to the letter this time. Because she has too much riding on the line at this point, isn't that right?"

The younger woman nodded curtly and continued to stare at her hands.

"Good." Fiona nodded. "The Coalition's been tracking divergent magic for a while now but only little blips in signatures here and there. Until we noticed one particularly virulent strain we hadn't seen before because we hadn't been looking in the right places."

The bounty hunter narrowed his eyes. "Agnes."

"If that's her name, sure. That witch has something different about her and we spent way more resources than we should have finding out that her magic was the first to move into an entirely different category of 'does not exist.' As far as we can tell, she's been that way for the last thirty years."

"Since the transformed," Lisa added.

"Bingo. And given that the Dark Family assholes didn't know what they were doing when they tried to magic their way into a DIY army of shifters, they had no idea that it backfired or what the consequences would be."

"You're tellin' me Agnes is a transformed?"

"Well, she sure as shit isn't a regular witch." Fiona shrugged. "And she's maintained her disguise well enough if she's lasted this long with Langley Appleman. But it doesn't change the rest of the facts. Addison and a select few of her loyal devotees have developed the same mutation."

The younger shifter woman sucked her teeth in frustration. "I told you not to call it that."

"Well, when you're speaking scientifically—and trust me, I've spent way more time around hardcore science nerds than I ever expected—that's what it's called."

"So let me get this straight." Lisa placed her palms flat on the table and leaned forward. "The natural-borns and the transformed are at war, it's about to get much worse, and the Coalition's getting involved because…"

"We don't give a rat's ass about the war." Fiona shrugged. "Sorry, but we don't. We don't take sides, either. The bigger threat at this point is to the entire magical community and most likely humanity too. Because let's be real. We all share the same planet and unfortunately, they have no way to get themselves out —divergent species, new magic, and magicals who can do what no one should ever be able to do."

"Shifter magic ain't new." Johnny pointed at her. "Unless you been feedin' my kid a buncha damn lies since the spring."

"Don't be an idiot, Johnny. Of course it's not new. But like this?" She gestured toward Addison. "Like what this Agnes witch or whatever she is can do? That's certainly new. We're seeing the changes in dozens of Oriceran creature species who came through the gates to Earth and the Coalition is seizing this little shitshow with both hands. I'm very sure we all know what would happen if the rest of the world found out the original source of divergent magic comes from shifters of whatever shape and size. Especially transformed."

He rubbed his mouth in agitation. "I gotta admit I did not see that comin'."

"Yeah, you rarely do." The redhead ignored his scowl and turned to Addison. "Is there anything I left out?"

The younger shifter ignored the sarcasm and didn't say a word.

"So how does the Coalition play into this if you aren't…you know." Lisa spread her arms. "Stepping in to stop the war?"

"The Coalition's top priority is to make sure shifters have

what they need. Period." Fiona shrugged. "Again, we can't choose sides because there are shifters all across the board. But Addison and her army have more divergent magic at their fingertips as opposed to Kaiser's one insane shifter hunter, as you put it. It's a bigger threat of the annihilation of all our work, not to mention millions of dollars down the drain if Azure here and her fun-loving generals—is that what you're calling them?"

Addison closed her eyes and sighed in exasperation.

"Whatever." The redhead waved her off. "We train shifters to use what they have in the best way possible and according to their capabilities. Our deal with Addison was that we'd train her and her magic-wielding followers to use their new abilities in a way that ensures they don't blow themselves up while they wage this war and most importantly, that they don't blow the lid off everything the Coalition has been working to create. And in return for skilled guidance, Addison agreed to not do anything stupid that could jeopardize all of it. Look how well that turned out."

"We?" Charlie's eyes widened. "You mean there's more than one of you?"

"Ha. Please. The world can't handle more than one Fiona." She smirked. "But no. Technically, I'm the lucky sap who drew the short stick. Woohoo. I've been training them. And yes, Johnny, instead of the girl, and there's no way you can tell me right now that I mixed my priorities up."

He raised an eyebrow and said nothing.

I can't argue with that, much as I wanna.

"You can't believe letting them wage this war without Coalition interference is the best way to go about this," Lisa said. "She has an army. There's already been enough bloodshed."

"Very true. Honestly, though, I'd given up trying to reason with this stubborn little shifter gunned down in the San Francisco Bay and brought back to life with a hell of a purpose. But now that we know her fiancé is the asshole killing transformed like a damn exterminator, I think we have a few more options."

"It's not Bronson." When Addison looked up from her lap, her eyes brimmed with tears that didn't quite spill over. "I can't believe that."

"Listen, kid." Fiona placed a hand on the younger shifter's shoulder. "I get it. It's hard to find out someone you loved turned into a monster because they thought you were gone. But if Johnny Walker says your man's our guy, he's our guy." She frowned and darted Johnny a hard glance. "You are sure about that, right?"

"That ain't a serious question."

"I merely thought I'd check." She clapped and nodded. "So. Time for a strategy meeting. I'm thinking something like a nice back-from-the-dead reunion. Addison, you might be the only way to get Bronson off his murdering high horse so we can wrangle this under control without anyone else dropping dead because of it. And none of us will leave this table or this room until we have a solid plan for how to move forward."

Charlie shook his head, his eyes wide and slightly glazed over. "I can't believe this."

"Except for you." The redhead pointed at him. "If you wanna leave, feel free. I don't think I like you."

"What?"

Johnny sniffed. "I don't much care for him either most days, but Charlie stays."

"What?"

He ignored his cousin and stared at her. "We wouldn't be here without him. He's been on this case with us the whole damn time and he ain't gettin' off easy by slippin' out now when things get a little hairy."

Lisa pressed her lips together and lowered her head to hide a smile.

The biker dwarf gaped at his cousin and whispered, "What?"

"Fine." Fiona shrugged. "Honestly, I couldn't care less about who's involved as long as we pull something solid out of thin air so we can all get off our asses as soon as possible. Ideas."

No one said a word.

With an exasperated sigh, She slumped her shoulders and lowered her hands at her sides. "Come on, people. We have some of the most brilliant non-shifter minds in the country seated right here at the same table and no one has anything to say. Think!"

"It's a little hard when you sit there yelling at us," Charlie muttered.

"You mean Johnny doesn't already yell at you enough?"

The bounty hunter shifted in his chair, scratched the side of his face, tugged on his beard, and went to the moment that had confused him most while interrogating Bronson Harford.

I mentioned family secrets and he almost lost his shit until I spilled the beans about his adopted mama. Those had already been spilled.

"I think I have somethin'."

"Yes, please, Johnny." Fiona gestured flippantly toward the table. "By all means. The floor's yours."

He nodded at Addison. "What do you know about Bronson's mama?"

"I… What?"

"Exactly what I said, darlin'. We're goin' over everythin' Bronson told you about his family."

"Well, okay then." Fiona nudged the younger shifter with her elbow. "So buckle up, buttercup. There's nothing like walking through all the painful memories of a relationship you'll probably never have to get your soul toughened up and ready for battle. Take it from Johnny. He knows."

He shook his head slowly and forced himself to not mouth off at her again. "Don't listen to her. It ain't that bad."

All right, fine. If I gotta tell a lie in this case, I think that's one worth tellin'.

CHAPTER TWENTY-THREE

They spent another three hours around the table, asking Addison Taylor prying and personal questions about her relationship with Bronson Harford, his father, and whatever stories and secrets about the well-to-do family might be useful for their plan.

There wasn't much to glean from the grueling examination of the young woman's memories other than the fact that Bronson hardly ever spoke about his mother at all. Neither did Jasper Harford. And Addison knew absolutely nothing about who Helice Harford had been before she died thirteen years earlier.

But Johnny, Lisa, and Fiona—with an occasional comment thrown in by Charlie for whatever it was worth—managed to put their heads together and find the next piece of the puzzle.

"It ain't an actual piece if you ask me."

"You're such a Debbie Downer, Johnny." Fiona chuckled. "We're building a masterpiece. I'm surprised you'd turn your nose up at a little extra investigative work. That is what you do now, isn't it?"

He licked his lips slowly in agitation. "We'll find 'em."

"Good. If anyone can, it's you." The redhead slapped her hands on the table and stood. "And I assume you won't go off script this time with a half-cocked plan that hasn't been approved. Right?"

Addison looked at her and nodded. "I can handle this."

"It's gonna be rough."

"It can't be worse than three bullets in the chest and almost drowning."

"Ha. Good girl." The Coalition delegate rounded the table and moved to the door. "Nice chat, people. See you on the other side."

"Hey." Johnny stood and spread his arms. "My hounds."

"You're way too attached to those chatty canines, you know that?" She smirked and opened the door. "I'll have someone bring them in. Let me know how it all works out, huh? I'll be busy for a while. You know, training a fourteen-year-old shifter girl who has no idea yet how special she is."

"Trust me," Lisa said. "She knows."

"Yeah. She's one tough cookie. No fooling her. I guess she truly is your kid, Johnny. Later." Fiona strode out the door and into the hall. She snapped her fingers and barked, "Release the hounds!"

Her laughter echoed into the room before it cut out abruptly, and Charlie shoved himself away from the table before he hurried into the hall. "Wait a minute. Hey. I have questions about training…"

He stopped in the middle of the hall, which was completely empty now. When he turned in a quick circle, he found only more empty hallways and scratched his head. "Where did she go?"

"You don't wanna know." Johnny clapped a hand on his cousin's shoulder. "She does that. Come on."

Lisa stayed where she was across the table from Addison and watched the young woman carefully. "Are you okay?"

"I'm fine."

"And you're ready to do this? It's a huge responsibility on your shoulders, not to mention a little more...personal than the rest of this faction war."

The young transformed looked sharply at her and her blue eyes flashed as she grimaced in determination and stood. "We all do what we have to do if we want what's right. Don't worry. I'm not getting cold feet."

Lisa flashed her a small, brief smile. "I'm not worried about you in the slightest. We'll call you when everything's ready."

"Yeah. And I'll hold back until you do."

"Good." The Light Elf moved to the open door but paused and looked over her shoulder. "You know, despite being attacked and held prisoner, I'm glad you're not dead. It was nice to meet you."

Addison pursed her lips and laughed wryly. "Thanks."

"Hey, hey. What's going on?" Luther's voice finally filled her mind and she hurried into the hall to join the Walker dwarves.

"Johnny."

"Yeah, I hear 'em, darlin'." They both turned in the hall to scan for signs of the hounds.

"Yeah, seriously," Rex added. "We like long walks and everything, but it's not as awesome when you won't tell us anything."

"Where's Johnny? And Lisa?"

"And the pirate dwarf?"

"Come on, shifters. The whole silent-and-broody attitude is starting to lose its—hey!"

"They're here!"

Wild baying echoed from another branching corridor down the hall, followed by a shout of surprise and a snarl barely audible over the scrabbling of claws across the linoleum and the wild barking of two coonhounds on their master's scent.

"Johnny! Johnny, Johnny, Johnny!" The hounds barreled around the corner, their tongues lolling from the sides of their mouths and ears flapping against their heads as they skittered across the floor. "You're alive!"

"We're alive!"

"No thanks to you. What the hell happened back there, Johnny?"

"Oh, sure." He spread his arms. "Blame me for the—"

"No one cares!" Luther threw himself at his master first, quickly followed by Rex.

"Yeah, shut up and get licked, Johnny."

He stumbled back under the weight as both hounds leapt onto him and covered his bearded face with canine kisses. A sharp laugh escaped him before he cleared his throat and forced a serious tone. "All right. That's enough."

"We thought we were gonna have to deal with shifters forever, Johnny."

"Yeah, and they're so grumpy. Wouldn't even tell us their names."

He snapped his fingers. "Off."

"But they fed us. Lots of beef jerky."

"Luther puked half of it up again."

"Bro, it wasn't half—"

The bounty hunter's sharp whistle cut them both off and he shoved the hounds down to all fours. "I said down."

"Yeah, sure. Johnny."

"Anything you say."

Their tails whipped furiously and thumped against Lisa's thighs. She laughed when they lowered their heads under their master's hands for more scratches.

Addison closed the door to their strategy room behind her as the shifter who'd been leading Rex and Luther rounded the corner. In his hands were two thin nylon leashes, both of them snapped clean through.

"You should train your dogs to heel," he grumbled.

"They already do." Johnny sniffed and fixed him with a blank expression. "To me."

Shaking his head, the shifter continued down the corridor that intersected with the hallway and disappeared.

"Great." Charlie clapped briskly. "Now that we're all saved, we have a ton of Internet scouring and phone calls to make. Right?"

His cousin clicked his tongue. "Speak for yourself. I only have one call to make." He frowned at Addison. "As soon as y'all give back what ain't yours."

She rolled her eyes. "I'll have someone bring you your things."

"Damn right. Now…" He turned to glance up and down the hall. "How the hell do we get out?"

"Follow me."

"Hey, Johnny." Luther licked his master's hand as they followed their transformed leader guide. "Did you tell these shifters what we know?"

"Yeah, 'cause you wouldn't believe how dumb they are," Rex added. "We told them everything and no one believed us!"

"That sounds about right," Lisa muttered.

"Oh, hey, Lisa." The larger hound sniffed her ankles before he tried a friendly lick on her calf. "Good to see you too."

"We're all on the same page now, boys," Johnny muttered. "As long as everyone sticks to the plan."

Addison stiffened but didn't turn to look at him.

It looks like she's learned a few rules of leadin' an army. Don't let the dwarf get under your skin where everyone can see.

After leading them through an incredibly long series of complicated twists and turns in her army complex, the transformed leader finally stopped at a door that looked like an exit and shoved it open. "After you."

The blindingly bright sunlight that spilled through made Johnny and his crew flinch. The dwarf's eyes watered when he squinted against the glare. "Where the hell are my sunglasses? And all our other effects?"

"Waiting for you in the car." She gestured toward a slate-gray Humvee idling yards away, not on a parking lot or even near a road but in the middle of hot, dazzling brown-yellow sand. "He'll take you wherever you want to go and I don't want to hear from you again until we're ready to move."

"We'll call you," Lisa said.

"On a cell phone?" Charlie turned. "You blocked all the magic out of that cell. Do you even have service in that—" The door slammed shut with Addison Taylor on the other side of it, and the mohawked dwarf sighed in indignation. "Sure. Stop talking. I get it."

"It's about time." Johnny raised a hand to shield his eyes from the glare of the sun and turned to study the building they'd exited. "The middle of the desert and no roads. Does this look like Area 51 to you, darlin'?"

Lisa raised an eyebrow. "If it did, I'm very sure I wouldn't be able to tell you anyway. Without killing you afterward, of course."

"Yeah. Me neither."

"Wait, seriously?" Charlie looked from one to the other. "You guys have been to Area 51?"

The bounty hunter trudged across the sand toward the car.

"Oh, come on. You can't drop a bomb like that and expect me to go along with all that 'can't confirm or deny' bullshit. Johnny."

The hounds skittered toward the car as well and pranced uncomfortably on the hot sand before they bounded into the back seat once Johnny opened the door.

"Holy crap, it's hot out here."

"Tell me about it. Hey, Johnny. How about inventing us some hound boots, huh?"

"Or at least give us something to not feel it."

"Bro, then we'd melt our paws off."

"Yeah, but we wouldn't feel it."

He nodded for Lisa to take the front passenger seat, climbed in beside the hounds, and shoved them together against the far window. "I ain't puttin' boots on two hounds. Next thing you'll be askin' me to knit y'all a couple of sweaters."

"Johnny, I didn't know you could knit." Luther's hindquarters wiggled despite his tail being crushed against the back of the seat. "Now that you mention it, though—"

"No."

Rex snorted. "Stingy."

Charlie took the last seat in the back and stared at his cousin as he closed the door. "You have to tell me, Johnny. I'm family."

"Tell you what?"

"If you've been to Area 51. Are we there right now? Or close? Or hey, did you get a chance to walk inside and see all the…top-secret stuff? Hell, the whole world knows aliens exist. Technically, that's us. But there's gotta be something—"

"Listen up." The transformed in the driver's seat growled as he adjusted the rearview mirror. He hooked his fingers over his sunglasses and pulled them slightly down the bridge of his nose to fix Charlie with a warning gaze. "If he tells you, I'd have to kill you both. I might still kill you anyway if you don't shut up."

Johnny smirked and nodded at the driver, who slipped his sunglasses up and shifted into drive.

Lisa turned to hand her partner a clear plastic bag with his belongings. "Is that everything?"

"It had better be." He put his sunglasses on first, then slid his wallet into his back pocket—pushing Charlie against the rear door in the process—and finally drew out his keys and the utility belt before he tossed the empty plastic bag into the back.

"Come on, man." The biker dwarf grimaced as his cousin squashed him again to get the utility belt strapped around his hips. "I'm sitting right here."

"Yep." The bounty hunter checked his belt and grunted. "Dammit. I'm missin' a disk."

"Not including the one you tried to use on the bar the other night?" Lisa asked.

"I know how many I have on me at any given time, darlin'. I'm tellin' ya, one's missin' and it ain't lost or used. Hey." He slapped the back of the driver's seat. "Turn around."

"I can't do that."

"Why the hell not?"

"Orders." To accentuate his point, the shifter accelerated and the Humvee lurched forward across the sand and threw up a thick plume of yellow-brown dust behind them as they bounced along.

"Well then, tell me who the hell took my disk."

"I can't do that either."

"Yeah, you're only the damn driver, ain'tcha?"

"Hey, Johnny." Luther licked his master's face again. "I missed you."

"Aw, come on." He wiped the slobber off his beard and flicked his hand in the other direction.

Charlie hissed and moved his hands from the splatter in his lap. "What the—"

"Yeah, you missed us too." Rex sniggered. "Duh."

"Yeah, but that's not what I was gonna say."

The bounty hunter leaned against the back of the seat. "Save it for when we ain't sardined in a Humvee in the desert, huh?"

"Yeah, yeah. Sure. I'll wait." Luther stared ahead and panted for a full ten seconds before he whipped his head toward his master again. "But then you won't know the shifters took your boom-frisbee."

"It ain't a frisbee—" Johnny looked slowly at the driver in the rearview mirror, who remained completely expressionless. "The transformed army stole my shit?"

"Yeah, that's what he said." Rex chuffed. "Unless you're talking about actual shit, Johnny. Then that would be weird and—"

"Pull over."

Lisa lowered her head to rub between her eyes. "Johnny, it's one disk."

"It ain't the number, Lisa. It's the damn principal. Hey. Shifter. I said pull over."

"I can't do that—"

"Yeah, well that's an order from me. Do it."

The shifter kept driving and Johnny snapped his fingers. "Boys. You know what happens to folks who steal from me."

"Aw, right now, Johnny?"

"Yeah, we're tired."

"Last chance, pal." He pointed at the rearview mirror. "You pull this hulk of metal over right the hell now or I'll do it myself."

The driver snorted and shook his head.

"Yeah, boys. Right now."

"Ugh. Fine," Luther muttered.

"But next time, Johnny, you do your own dirty work. You're not paying us nearly enough for this."

"I feed y'all and put up with y'all's constant backtalk when you should be doin' what I say."

"Okay, okay. Jeez. Keep your pants on. You ready, bro?"

The shifter in the driver's seat started to look over his shoulder but caught himself and snapped his head forward again instead.

"Am I ready?" Rex scoffed. "Please. You want the first shot?"

"Nah, go ahead. After you."

"Aw, that's real sweet, bro. Thanks."

CHAPTER TWENTY-FOUR

Charlie stared with wide eyes through the rear window of the Humvee as they raced across the Nevada desert. "I can't believe you did that. I can't believe… Holy shit, Johnny. You left him out there to die. What's wrong with you?"

The bounty hunter smirked in the driver's seat and tightened his hold on the steering wheel. "Nothin'."

"You made your point," Lisa said, "but I think we should go back for him."

"We ain't three miles out from the front door of that compound, darlin'. If that shifter can't walk three miles, he shouldn't be part of that army in the first place."

"You're crazy." His cousin shook his head. "Completely nuts. I bet it's all the drinking. You should pull back on that, 'coz. It's making you—" He paused and turned his head slowly to where the end of Luther's snout and the hound's lolling tongue were an inch away from his face. "What?"

"Waiting for you to give us compliments too," Luther added.

"Yeah, we're waiting." Rex turned on the seat and pushed Luther and his tongue into Charlie. "Because let's be real, here. That was all us. Johnny's good and everything…"

Luther licked his muzzle and righted himself on the seat again. "But we're good at throwing two-legs out of cars."

"Any two-legs."

"Magical two-legs."

"Especially magical shifter two-legs."

"Yeah, but not all of them." Charlie wiped the dog drool off his cheek and grimaced. "You can't catch me off guard that easily."

"Wanna bet?"

"Ooh, ooh! Rex. I'll take that bet."

The hounds sniggered.

"That's enough," Johnny muttered but his smirk lingered. "Besides, Charlie ain't got a soul in the desert to go runnin' back to sayin' it was a bad idea to steal from me."

The biker dwarf scoffed. "I haven't?"

His cousin lowered his head to glance in the rearview mirror over his sunglasses.

"Okay, I haven't in a very long time. Why is it such a big deal to you anyway? I've seen the weird lab in your house. Go home and make another one."

"Workshop. It ain't a lab." The bounty hunter sniffed. "And it's a big deal 'cause Azure didn't wanna let us go Scot free. If she's usin' that complex and has a magic-dampenin' hole for lockin' magical prisoners up, she's keepin' that disk of mine to pick it apart and find out what I built."

Lisa hummed in disagreement. "No, she seems more like the 'knock them out with transformed magic' type. I wouldn't peg her as a tinkerer."

"Tinkerer?" He grunted. "It ain't tinkerin'. And Addison Taylor's only the messenger."

"Okay, now I'm confused."

"She's funded by the Coalition, darlin'. You heard it straight from Fiona's mouth."

She wrinkled her nose. "She didn't exactly come right out and say that."

"That's what it is. Now the shifters callin' themselves neutral have their hands on one of my weapons 'cause they know I'm the one who made it. It means I gotta redo my whole damn arsenal of disks and make 'em different enough."

"Different enough to do what?" Charlie asked.

"To be mine. Hell, I can't go runnin' around with the same weapons the Coalition knocked off."

The Humvee raced through an open chain-link fence and finally turned onto the road.

Lisa cleared her throat. "It's not like going to a gala and wearing the same white suit as a movie star, Johnny."

"No, it's worse."

Charlie snorted and shook his head.

"Speaking of Fiona, though." The Light Elf turned to study her partner's profile. "You never told me how you and Fiona know each other."

"What's that got to do with anythin'?"

"Well, you two obviously have a history. She knows you enough to bust your chops the way she did."

"Naw, she does that to everyone."

"See, that's what I'm talking about."

Johnny growled and rolled his eyes, which no one could see behind his dark sunglasses. "Fine. I might have put together a few pieces of tech for the Coalition back in the day."

"A few pieces of tech." She folded her arms. "Go on."

"All right, more than a few. Big ones." He flexed his hands on the steering wheel before he grasped it tightly again. "Maybe even the same tech they're usin' now to find this so-called divergent magic crap."

"You built the Coalition of Shifters a massive magic tracker they're using to find transformed shifters and…what? Mutated Oriceran creatures?"

"Well, it wasn't meant for that, but sure."

"Ha." Lisa swiped her hair away from her face and grinned

broadly. "How in the world did you end up doing something like that?"

"Fiona helped me with a case. Back before I was technically takin' cases at all."

"She beat someone up for you, didn't she?" Charlie chuckled. "Yeah, that makes sense."

"Yeah, I brought in an angry redheaded shifter to fight dirty for me." Johnny scoffed. "It sounds exactly like me."

"Okay. You don't have to go into specifics," Lisa told him.

"Good, 'cause I ain't."

"You trust her enough to train Amanda and I guess that's all that matters."

"Damn right. I trust her enough to—" Johnny glanced at his partner, did a double-take, then nodded at the road on their way south to Vegas. "Yeah. Uh-huh. I trust her completely."

They reached Mandalay Bay a little after noon, which also happened to be slightly before the twenty-four-hour grace period on their illegally rented hotel suite had passed. It took trying to open the door with his key card three times to no avail for Johnny to finally accept that they'd been locked out. And that his friends running a Vegas pawn shop and then some had screwed him over.

They asked at the front desk if anyone had turned their things in, but the concierge was less than helpful. When they returned to the parking lot in front of Henderson & Hawk, Johnny was ready to pound a few pawnbrokers' heads together.

"Silas!" he roared as he stormed through the front door. "Get out here! I swear to high heaven, if you ain't bein' straight with me, I'll—"

The door behind the counter burst open and Silas stepped out wearing a pastel-yellow suit this time with the same tan fedora partially covering his hair snakes. "Johnny!"

"You told us twenty-four hours."

"Oh, yeah." The Atlantean glanced at his watch. "Which was up about half an hour ago. How was the room?"

"A scam." Johnny slammed both hands on the counter and leaned over it with a snarl. "Where are our bags?"

With a chuckle, Silas bent at the knees and rose again to swing both Johnny's duffel bag and Lisa's overnight suitcase onto the counter. "Someone's in a mood."

"Funny." The dwarf grabbed the bags but the proprietor clamped his hands around his wrists to stop him.

"I tell you what. I'll sell all of it back to you at a hell of a good price."

Johnny jerked the bags off the counter and dropped them on the floor. "You're a piece of work."

"Thank you." The Atlantean's gold tooth winked in the light when he grinned. "It's a good thing I was paying attention, right? You have some real great pieces of work in that bag."

"Keep your slimy hands outta my things, Silas. I mean it."

"You didn't take anything, did you?" With wide eyes, Charlie approached the counter and leaned conspiratorially toward Silas. "Johnny killed a guy in the desert for knowing who stole from him."

The Atlantean chuckled. "Nice try. Is there anything else I can get for you, Johnny? Maybe put out some feelers and find who did steal from you?"

"Naw, keep your snakes on." He hauled the strap of his duffel bag over his head. "I gotta call a wizard about diggin' up old relatives."

"Ooh." Silas rubbed his hands together. "Morbid. I like it. Hey, I can sell you a couple of shovels. One of 'em's for show. It's covered in fake diamonds. Don't ask me why but I bet it'll do the trick just the same."

"It ain't that kinda diggin'. Tell Mitch thanks for me."

"Don't I get one?" Silas gestured expansively.

"Y'all can share it. Come on, darlin'."

Lisa grabbed her suitcase and rolled it with her toward the door. She paused to look over her shoulder and whispered, "The room was very nice, thanks."

"I know." Grinning, Silas pressed the tips of his fingers on the top of the counter and watched a wary Charlie as the mohawked dwarf hurried in quick bursts across the pawn shop. "Don't be a stranger, Johnny!"

The bounty hunter didn't reply.

"Okay." Lisa hauled her suitcase into the back of their rental. The hounds panted happily in the back seat with the air conditioning on full blast and she chuckled before she shut the hatch. "Remind me never to take a room again from that friend of yours."

"A couple of fellas I know, darlin'. Not friends. There's a difference. And I already know you have an issue with rentin' rooms off the books. That'll be the last time."

"Sure, that was the issue." She moved to the front passenger seat and shivered. "But now it's the mental image of Silas' hair snakes creeping into our room to snatch our luggage. What's stopping him from doing that when magicals are in their seemingly private rooms sleeping? Or taking a shower?"

"Well now, it's…" Johnny drummed his fingers on the driver-side door. "Hell. I ain't thought of it like that before."

"My point exactly."

They both climbed into the rental as Charlie headed to his Harley still parked outside the building. "It's a damn shame Silas didn't try to pawn that ugly thing while we were gone." He rolled his window down and draped his forearm over the edge. "Hey."

"What's up?" His cousin looked at him with wide eyes.

"Do you know where we're goin'?"

"You sent me the address, 'coz. I have nowhere else to be."

"All right. You wait for us there—"

"And don't do anything else. I get it." Charlie waved him off and straddled his bike before the engine roared to life beneath him. He gave the SUV two thumbs-up and shouted, "I'm merely glad we're not dead."

"Yeah, so far," Johnny muttered. The orange Harley growled out of the parking lot and he rolled the window up and got them back on the road.

"He's doing better," Lisa mused.

"Than what?"

"Okay, you can pretend you haven't noticed if you want. But I think he's come a long way in the last two weeks. Okay, yeah, he's… Well, he's Charlie."

"Uh-huh."

"But telling Fiona we need him was a big step. For him, at the very least."

"Trust me, darlin'. I ain't fixin' to take bigger steps than I have to." Johnny snorted. "But yeah. He ain't nearly as useless as he's always been."

She grinned and looked out her window. "Yeah, okay."

They stopped at a motel in Bakersfield, California, the quality of which fell somewhere between the worst motel ever that happened to be on this case and their brief stay at Mandalay Bay. Charlie was waiting for them in the parking lot with a grin and plastic bags dangling from his arms.

"What's all this?" Johnny asked.

"Dinner. I thought I'd kill some time."

"Hey, guy." Luther padded toward him. "You get any for us?"

"Yeah, we're hungry too, you know," Rex added. "Everyone seems to forget that."

"Of course I got you something." Charlie laughed, then froze and looked at his cousin. "If that's…okay."

"As long as it ain't chocolate, grapes, or onions. Or fish." Johnny pointed at the hounds. "You let Luther eat fish, he's sleepin' in your room."

"Right. No fish. Got it."

They checked into two adjacent rooms, this time without the

necessity of an intersecting door between them. Charlie retired to his room after they ate to relax and watch whatever he wanted on TV without two transformed shifters nagging him to share.

Johnny crumpled the wrapper of his deli sandwich and shoved it into the plastic bag. "It ain't a bad meal."

"Again, he's trying."

"He forgot to put mustard on it."

"Johnny."

He shrugged and took his phone from his pocket. "Do you think he's goin' deaf with the damn TV turned up that loud?"

"Um… You know, I wouldn't be surprised if he was trying to drown everything else out instead. Shifter hearing."

"Huh. No wonder he's goin' deaf." He pulled up the number he wanted and made the call, scowling at the wall their room shared with Charlie's and the muffled noises from some car-chase scene on the TV.

"Johnny."

"Hey, Davie."

"Man, you're calling in favors these days, aren't you?"

"Listen, if the IOUs have run outta steam—"

"No way. Dad never took your money and I'm not gonna start now."

"How's the old man doin' anyway?"

"He's, um… Well, not anywhere near where he was the last time you called. Yeah, when you had me look into that girl Lucy Hamilton and her parents for you. That was months ago. And he's… Honestly, Johnny, we're all surprised he's lasted this long."

"Huh. I'm sorry to hear it. Do you think he'd be up for a visit? It might make the old geezer laugh one more time at the very least."

"Sure, Johnny." Davie sighed. "He'd like that but I can't promise he'll be around when you can make it."

"I'll make it a point." The bounty hunter cleared his throat. "Is this a bad time to ask for a little of your family magic at work?"

The wizard clicked his tongue. "I wouldn't have answered if it was."

"All right. Listen, it's a diamond-in-the-rough kinda thing. Diamond ain't around anymore, and there's a hell of a lotta rough."

"What's the name?"

"Helice Appleman. I'm lookin' for who she was before Appleman."

Davie hummed. "Okay, sure. So you want a maiden name."

"Naw, that was her maiden name—adopted. I'm lookin' for farther back."

"Whoa. Yeah, if you can spare a day or two, it shouldn't be a problem."

Johnny nodded. "If a day or two is what you need for this one, it's better than what we can do on our own. Thanks."

"You bet. Hey, I meant it about stopping by to visit Dad. He's still lucid most of the time and I'd love to see him joking again the way he did whenever you passed through. It's weird to think about it now before any of us thought we'd have to. You never know when family won't be around anymore, you know?"

"Sure. I know. I ain't rightly family to y'all, though."

The young wizard laughed wryly. "No. You're merely guilty by association. Talk to you soon, Johnny."

"Yep." He closed his flip phone and stared at it before he tossed it onto the bed.

"That sounded like much more than asking a guy about a name." Lisa looked up from her tablet. "Is everything okay?"

"His old man's on the way out. We might have to stop by their place when all this is over. There's no tellin' when family won't be around anymore, right?"

"Very true. I'm sorry to hear about your friend."

"Yeah. Me too. Hell, he'd love you." The bounty hunter chewed his bottom lip, then stood and headed to the door.

"What's going on?"

"It's only a little conversation needs havin'. It won't take me a minute." He stormed out of the room, closed the door behind him, and stopped at the next door before he pounded sharply on it with a fist. "Charlie."

There was no answer.

"Dammit, Charlie." He pounded harder. "Turn off the damn TV and open the door."

The TV finally clicked off and there was a quick, hurried scuffle inside before his cousin opened the door to his room and stared at him with wide eyes. "What's wrong?"

"We need to talk." Johnny brushed past the other dwarf into the room and stood there in the center of what little space there was as he clenched and unclenched his fists.

"Okay… Come right on in." Charlie shut the door and spread his arms. "What?"

"Listen, I been thinkin'."

"Uh-huh. That happens." The mohawked dwarf gazed around the room in confusion. "Well, if that's all you wanted to say—"

"Naw, I been thinkin' about this whole…" Johnny gestured between them. "Bein' related thing."

"I get it. You think you were adopted too, huh? Trust me, it's gone through my mind a few times but we look so much alike, you know? Hey, I'm going to get a blood test done. You know, find out if we're related or—"

"Dammit, Charlie. Zip it for a goddamn minute and let me say my piece."

His cousin shut his mouth instantly and frowned.

"You've been a real pain in my ass. Yeah. And I ain't been too keen on stayin' in touch over the years. Hell, I thought I'd never see you again and that was fine by me."

"Johnny, that's not—"

"Shut up." He pointed at him and his scowl deepened. "For fifty years, you were bustin' my balls when you could and overall tearin' your life apart. Maybe you tried to suck me in with you, maybe not. It doesn't matter. We went our separate ways and that's that." He drew a deep breath, scratched his chin, and met his cousin's gaze briefly. "But I can't help feelin' like the last thirty years might have turned out different if you didn't have to go through 'em on your lonesome. I ain't takin' responsibility for your messes. What you've done is on you. You gotta fix it. I'm only sayin'… Well, what I mean is…"

"Hey."

"I told you to shut up."

"I get it." Charlie scratched the shaved side of his head and stepped slowly toward his cousin, his mouth quirked into a crooked, self-conscious smile. "And we both know how hard it is for you to say something that doesn't suck a guy's soul right out of him. So don't worry about it."

"Hell. I ain't tryin' to suck your soul—"

"Yeah, I know. I've done enough of that myself already." The biker dwarf stuck his hand out and nodded. "Thanks for saying it. Or…trying to. I guess."

"You ain't even heard what it is."

"Nope. But I heard your conversation with Davie on the phone and you saying the same thing before you showed up to bust my door down." He grinned. "I can put two and two together."

"Well, all right." Johnny took his cousin's hand with a firm grip. When the appropriate amount of time had passed and Charlie wouldn't let go, the bounty hunter cleared his throat. "I think we're done here now."

"Yeah. Yeah, sure." The shifter dwarf clapped him on the shoulder and finally released him. "And listen, if I'm ever crossing a line in your personal space, stepping out of bounds or whatever, you let me know. Say it like it is, 'coz. I can handle it."

"That's what I been doin' since you showed up on my couch."

"Well, yeah. But I mean now that we… You know. Handshake. Touching moment or whatever. And me coming on as the official consultant for Johnny Walker Investigations. It's kind of a new start, don't you think? So I think it's important to step out on the right foot and lay out new ground rules. Even if they're the same."

"I ain't said nothin' about—"

"Good talk, Johnny." Charlie patted his cousin on the back as he walked past him, flopped on the bed, and snatched the remote. "Lemme know when you're ready to get going and kick some ass Walker-style."

He turned the TV on and the startlingly loud blare of more car chase filled the room.

With a snort, the bounty hunter strode out of the room and slammed the door shut behind him. He paused in the hallway and the smile that crept up on him didn't piss him off nearly as much as he thought it would.

That damn dwarf's weaselin' his way in again. 'Cause that's Charlie. It's a hell of a skill. Shit, maybe we oughtta bring him on full-time after all.

Chuckling, he returned to his room and flashed the key card in front of the door.

Naw. He can be a contractor. I ain't payin' him full-time to sit around in a hotel room and veg out on bad movies.

CHAPTER TWENTY-FIVE

Davie followed through in true form less than forty-eight hours later with all the information he could gather on Helice Harford before she was adopted by the Applemans. Johnny scribbled notes as fast as he could, thanked his contact who could find anyone anywhere—living or dead—and shared the details with Lisa.

They spent the rest of the day holed up in their motel room making phone call after phone call. Most of them were dead ends. Three of them might have gone somewhere if the strangers on the other end of the line weren't terrified enough as it was merely to be called by someone asking about Helice and her shifter roots.

But they did get through to two different people who took the time to speak to them, and they found out more about the woman, her life before becoming an Appleman, and the magnitude of the last family secret the Harfords had kept for thirty years.

A few arrangements were made, times, dates, and locations confirmed, and Lisa made the call to Addison to let them know where and when.

When they were finished, she placed her phone on the table beside the armchair and dropped her head back against the upholstery with a sigh. "That was rough."

"Tell me about it." Johnny sighed and retrieved the plastic cups they'd used for three days to pour them both a stiff drink. "But this might put an end to all of it. If Bronson starts actin' the way we expect, anyhow."

"It's a long shot but at least we're prepared."

"Uh-huh. As long as Azure can keep her end of the deal. It's hard to tell exactly what that'll be."

"True." She accepted the cup from him and sipped the whiskey. "I know we can handle it. Addison can deal with whatever happens. She has her army. Bronson's the wild card here."

"Yep. He always has been 'cause he's the only one left livin' in this world who knows his mama's little secret."

"Well, it explains a lot about how he's reacted to the transformed. To Addison. I only hope it doesn't push him too far over the edge."

"If it does, he has more than enough of us standin' around to haul him up. Or kiss his ass, either way."

Lisa snorted into her cup and he chuckled before he swallowed his in one gulp.

Three days later, they stood in front of the Summer Dayz salon in Chico, where they'd planned their next meeting with those from Bronson's past. All of them were strangers to Johnny and his team, not to mention the Harford heir.

Charlie stepped outside and nodded at his cousin. "They're getting a little antsy in here, Johnny. I already laid out all the cookies and pop. I don't know what else to do."

"All right. Give it another minute."

"Okay…" The mohawked dwarf darted inside to take care of

the small crowd who sat and munched hesitantly on store-bought cookies.

"You remembered to tell Jasper how important this was, right?" Lisa asked.

"'Course I remembered."

"And you think he meant it when he said he'd keep our names out of it?"

"Hundred percent. Jasper's a shifter of his word, darlin'. He didn't even ask for an explanation. He ain't the type to back out and cave."

"I hope so. He's probably the only magical Bronson thinks he can trust these days."

"Yep. If this goes the right way, he'll have a whole room of family he never knew he had sittin' right inside this salon and waitin' with open arms."

"Johnny." Charlie poked his head out again. "They want to talk to you."

"Fine. Fine. When Bronson arrives, we'll be ready for him."

Lisa nodded and when they turned together to step into the salon, everyone gathered in the room for the big reveal that wasn't quite a reveal looked at the bounty hunter with wide, hopeful eyes.

Johnny managed a smile. "Well. This ain't exactly the party I was hopin' for but I reckon it'll get the job done."

Get sneak peeks, exclusive giveaways, behind the scenes content, and more. PLUS you'll be notified of special **one day only fan pricing** on new releases.

Sign up today to get free stories.

Visit: https://marthacarr.com/read-free-stories/

I spent last weekend in my old hometown of Chicago at a small wedding of about forty people. It was the sweetest, happiest wedding I have ever attended. The mood started with the happy couple. They had already worked out all the kinks with each other about money, children, work. The usual. An understanding was in place of compromise and a consideration of kindness.

That's the thing we sometimes forget to offer each other. A consideration of kindness.

Sometimes we're too tired, or overwhelmed or distracted and fearful and we want to know when things will work out for us?

That has always translated for me to more tension, sense of loneliness and frustration. The opposite of what I had hoped for.

But not at this wedding. The mood was that everyone was okay just as they are and with whatever happens.

They forgot to do the traditional 'cut the cake' and one of the brides (there were two brides at this wedding), said, "Everyone has seen me hold a knife before. It's okay, let's just slice it up and hand it out." And she went back to dancing. No one missed a beat.

One particular guest stood off to the side, looking awkward

and out of place. Other guests swooped in and started a conversation, got them on the dance floor and kept the party going. In the end, they were all smiles, staying till the end of the party.

No one was thinking, 'what about me?'

Everyone felt a part of a group, connected one to the other and confident that all was well.

You know, it's actually possible to have that feeling all the time. Sometimes easier than others, but still possible.

It starts with an optimism that most things will work out to our benefit and the rest we will deal with together – not alone. Instead of looking for problems and feeling overwhelmed, we trust there are solutions and look for those. We're more likely to speak up and ask for what we need because we believe someone will listen, and there's something to offer that will help.

I'm a better listener when I'm in that mode because I'm not thinking about what could go wrong, or what I see as wrong, and instead I'm actually here with you – listening. Not with the idea that I can fix everything, but with the idea that the two of us sharing a connection can actually help, and it does. It really does.

Then, when we get to those big celebrations in life, like a wedding, we can all come together and rejoice in whatever happens on that day with no expectations and see everything there is to be grateful for – and let the rest go. More adventures to follow.

AUTHOR NOTES - MICHAEL ANDERLE

JULY 30, 2021

Thank you for not only reading this story but our author notes here in the back.

I'm blaming the travel I'm doing for the train of thought which prompted the op-ed piece below.

<< I am imagining a situation where someone is railing against monster hunters for their murderous efforts to eradicate creatures who have a penchant for killing humans. Therefore, we have an opposing op-ed piece related to someone else's opinion. >>

Today's discussion is about monsters and their proclivity to be hardheaded about their way of life. It's not like monster hunters aren't willing to call off the tit-for-tat efforts to kill them if they would consider coming to a negotiation table.

I mean, they refuse (for example) even to have a discussion regarding their desire to eat other creatures. No one who might be attacked should be willing to put down their weapons if they are on the night's dinner menu.

Right?

I don't think I'm being too hardheaded about this. Just because all their teeth are built by Mother Nature to rip and tear meat, I'm sure we still have the chance to have a civil discussion where they should be willing to start eating vegetables.

I understand a Mrs. Periwinkle went into the Florida Everglades just last week to use the newfangled Magitech product to allow her to communicate with eons-old alligators. My understanding was she intended to become the alligators' negotiator.

Unfortunately, we lost contact with Mrs. Periwinkle about eighteen hours into her effort to reach a consensus with the first group of the reptiles. The last words we have from her radio communications device was, "What big teeth you have!"

It's all static after that.

If the alligators are willing to eat their first diplomat, I'm not sure any monster hunter is going to feel comfortable with just setting down their arms to chum it up with creatures who have murderous intent.

Now, I know that some say the Ergenlartick quadrupeds with the stinging tails just have a bad rap, but I'd like to point out they eat their young, too. Not a big fan of putting down my weapons if little Johnny or little Susie has to wonder if Mom or Dad are going to eat them at bedtime tonight.

I agree that could cause its own form of PTSD, which is now the acronym for "Parents Trapped Sis for Dinner."

Unfortunately, I suspect those who disagree with me will fail to understand my logic, no matter how I explain my opinion. Or, if you believe those who have already accused me of spinning the facts, I am not willing to have any conversation.

So, I'm prepared to use my personal funds to provide the first one hundred, that's right, one hundred magitech communication devices to the opposite side. This is a generous show of solidarity to allow those who feel the strongest to engage with monsters… I'm sorry, "maladjusted and misunderstood contingent of God's creatures."

May God have mercy on your souls.

<< End Op-Ed piece from one of the monster hunters. The

book's producers understand that of the eighteen times individuals who took this hunter up on his offer, thirteen were never heard from again, three are still in ICU, and two gave them to their spouses, who were never heard from again. Those two individuals are presently up on murder charges. >>

I'll be back home in a day or so. Perhaps my author notes will go back to normal.

Ad Aeternitatem,

Michael Anderle

Solve a murder, save her mother, and stop the apocalypse?

What would you do when elves ask you to investigate a prince's murder and you didn't even know elves, or magic, was real?

Meet Leira Berens, Austin homicide detective who's good at what she does – track down the bad guys and lock them away.

Which is why the elves want her to solve this murder – fast. It's not just about tracking down the killer and bringing them to justice. It's about saving the world!

If you're looking for a heroine who prefers fighting to flirting, check out The Leira Chronicles today!

AVAILABLE ON AMAZON AND IN KINDLE UNLIMITED!

CONNECT WITH THE AUTHORS

Martha Carr Social
Website:
http://www.marthacarr.com
Facebook:
https://www.facebook.com/groups/MarthaCarrFans/

Michael Anderle

Website: http://lmbpn.com

Email List: http://lmbpn.com/email/

Social Media:

https://www.facebook.com/LMBPNPublishing

https://twitter.com/MichaelAnderle

https://www.instagram.com/lmbpn_publishing/

https://www.bookbub.com/authors/michael-anderle

ALSO BY MARTHA CARR

Other series in the Oriceran Universe:

THE LEIRA CHRONICLES

THE FAIRHAVEN CHRONICLES

MIDWEST MAGIC CHRONICLES

SOUL STONE MAGE

THE KACY CHRONICLES

THE DANIEL CODEX SERIES

I FEAR NO EVIL

SCHOOL OF NECESSARY MAGIC

THE UNBELIEVABLE MR. BROWNSTONE

SCHOOL OF NECESSARY MAGIC: RAINE CAMPBELL

ALISON BROWNSTONE

FEDERAL AGENTS OF MAGIC

SCIONS OF MAGIC

MAGIC CITY CHRONICLES

Series in The Terranavis Universe:

The Adventures of Maggie Parker Series

The Witches of Pressler Street

The Adventures of Finnegan Dragonbender

OTHER BOOKS BY JUDITH BERENS

OTHER BOOKS BY MARTHA CARR